Someone to Love

A **SOMEONE TO LOVE** BOOK

Someone to Love

ADDISON MOORE

SKYSCAPE

SKYSCAPE

The characters and events portrayed in this book are fictitious. Any similarity to real persons, living or dead, is coincidental and not intended by the author.

Published by Skyscape, New York

www.apub.com

ISBN-13: 9781477847107
ISBN-10: 1477847103

Book design by Kerrie Robertson

Library of Congress Cataloging-in-Publication Data available upon request.

Printed in the United States of America
First edition

Books by Addison Moore

Ethereal (Celestra Series Book 1)
Tremble (Celestra Series Book 2)
Burn (Celestra Series Book 3)
Wicked (Celestra Series Book 4)
Vex (Celestra Series Book 5)
Expel (Celestra Series Book 6)
Toxic Part 1 (Celestra Series Book 7)
Toxic Part 2 (Celestra Series Book 7.5)
Elysian (Celestra Series Book 8)

Ephemeral (The Countenance Trilogy 1)
Evanescent (The Countenance Trilogy 2)

Ethereal Knights (Celestra Knights)

Someone to Love (Someone to Love)

*To my husband,
who taught me all the best parts about love.*

PREFACE

It was that season in my life, the coming of age of the woman inside me who longed to know the secrets of the universe—those potent with lust and desire—the very things that harnessed a sexual frenzy and drove humanity along on its erotic trembling wings.

I've always thought of love as a very sharp knife that held the promise of exquisite pain, never one that satisfied, never a theory you could nestle in, warm and safe, forever. Love was dangerous terrain. It was where you met your enemies and gutted them before you sacked their belongings, hitting the road long before the ink dried on the divorce papers—that's what my mother taught me.

I was my own universe. I guarded my heart, froze and buried it in the tundra of my own misgivings. But now that I was clear across the country at Garrison University, desire and passion reared their ugly heads. My body ached to know things, and those kinds of lessons could only come from a heated body pressed against mine.

Sex manifested itself in all things. It was all around me—the hibiscus with its sticky pistil, its stamen hungry to release; the perfect round bottom of the peach; the fig tree heavy with its sacks of seeded fruit; the stray cat locked in heat as she begs for a companion. It was everywhere, viral and prolific. All of nature was making love, encouraging humanity with its undeniable whispers. Every day it resonated like an erotic echo. I was envious, greedy to experience the gnashing of hips, the interlacing of hands, knees tucked against mine. I wanted to glean all of the sensual knowledge firsthand.

I had held onto virginity and reason long enough—staved off the enemy far too long. And now here I am, standing in front of the god of Garrison in the exact amount of clothing I was born in. Every intimate part of me is quivering, cheering on my newfound carnal revolution.

"Down," he instructs.

I get on my knees and he pulls my head back. Instinctively, I know this is going to hurt and I want it to. I want to feel everything Cruise has to offer—all that he's willing to thrust my way.

He steps toward me and unbuttons his jeans. He flicks at his zipper and gives the impression of a wicked grin.

"With your teeth," he commands.

And I do.

1

PLEASED TO MEET YOU

Kendall

"Coke or Pepsi?" the Adonis before me asks, as if the only thing he intends on quenching is my thirst. I think inaugurating me as his love slave for the evening is more to the point.

He's tall with broad shoulders and light-blue eyes the color that rain wishes it could be. He sports a five-o'clock shadow; the stubble is a little darker than the caramel hair protruding from his ball cap. His cheeks are cut high and chiseled. He's one of *those* guys—the ones that make your stomach squeeze tight with just one wayward look. We've been stealing glances for the better part of an hour even though he was seven deep in girls, two of them gnawing on his ear and neck.

The Christmas lights on the anemic tree behind him blink on and off spastically in a rainbow of holiday hues with a pink bulb winking out of sync.

"I haven't played Questions since ninth grade," I say, turning to the burgeoning crowd, pretending like I'm not interested. Not that I didn't get that he was offering me a drink. Honestly, if a guy of his loose moral caliber wants to sleep with me, the first thing I'm going to do is make his brain cells strain a little—that is, if he has any.

All I really want to do is find Pennington and convince him to stop guzzling his high-octane beverages long enough to show me to my dorm. That was my first stupid move in what's panning out to be a bona fide fiasco—trusting a moron with my housing arrangements.

"Questions?" The Adonis dips in with a lewd smile budding on his lips. He's wearing a white cotton T-shirt and dark inky jeans—my all-time favorite combo on a guy. His tennis shoes look as though they've seen their fair share of the great outdoors. He's probably the type who overindulges in half a dozen sex sports before breakfast. I bet he's some kind of perverted adrenaline junky. God knows he's pumping up mine.

He drinks me in with a fondling gaze, undressing me with those blue-cellophane eyes. He's rounding out all the bases mentally—he's already bent me over home plate, I can tell.

"You know, Questions," I say, "Coke or Pepsi, male or female, in or out." I'm not sure if peppering the conversation with innuendo is the best idea, although it's most likely his native language. I look past him at the crowd, trying to distract myself from the fact that he's even more alarmingly handsome up close than he was clear across the room.

"*In* or *out?*" he says seductively. "Definitely in, and for sure, female." His heated whisper just over my ear rips a fire through my insides and awakens something primal in me. His voice resonates above the raucous music, and my eyes close involuntarily at the quasi proposition.

Shit. I startle to my senses and scan the room for the simpleton I might be moved to strangle once I locate. It's my first day here at Garrison, and I've landed at some frat party hosted by my mom's best friend's son, Pennington, at Alpha Sigma Phi, with my luggage sitting in the corner still fresh from the airport.

The Adonis pushes out a smile, and a pair of deep-set dimples goes off, rendering me defenseless.

Honest to God, I'm about five minutes from pulling Mr. Coke or Pepsi into the corner and raking my body against his. Not that I've ever done that before, and I've never been motivated to do so. But after a long travel day and a four-hour layover in five-inch heels, spontaneous sex doesn't sound so bad.

"Cruise Elton." He shoves his hand at me as if we were about to conduct business, and something in me softens to him. His glacial eyes burn into mine. He's watching me, drilling his watery pools through all of the formidable layers I hide beneath. He's inspecting me for the truth, for the underpinnings of who I really am. I bet he's embroiled in deep philosophical questions like do I know how to properly utilize my tongue and whether I have a piercing that could pleasure him into an erotic nirvana.

"Kendall Jordan," I yell over the music, taking up his warm, thick fingers. He feels safe, reliable, and something stirs in me when we touch.

"Nice to meet you, Kenny." He gives a wicked grin and swivels his hips into mine. He's still acting like the playboy he's been for the last hour, but something in his eyes tempers when he says my name, albeit incorrectly.

"It's *Kendall*," I repeat, rubbing my thumb over his knuckles, memorizing how he feels before letting go. I wish I were one of "those" girls. If I were ever going to be one, tonight would be the night.

"You look more like a Kenny to me. Cute and sporty." He plucks off his baseball cap revealing dark-blond waves before settling it over his head again. His shirt rises over his tan stomach, offering me a glimpse of rippling muscles, solid as granite, and I resist the urge to run my fingers over him like some erotic form of Braille.

I don't know what he wants from me. At least six girls stand ready to commit an entire slew of indecent acts with him right here in the commons room with total disregard to the bodies crammed into this place. I'm still in the awkward-glances phase when it comes to guys. For sure, I haven't graduated to one-night stands at frat parties.

I grind my heel into the floor. Perhaps it was my sexy stilettos that inspired him to slither on over.

"You go to Garrison?" He takes a swig from his soda. Odd that it's not a beer, but a refreshing change of pace. On second thought, he's probably got it locked and loaded with an eighty-proof fuel enhancer.

"Just transferred in." I turn in an effort to shut down the prospect of evoking an erection out of him, but he's quick to jump back in my line of vision. "Look…" I sigh. "I'm actually engaged to Pennington." Sadly, I've resorted to playing fast and loose with the truth in hopes he'll find someone else to sexually assault for the evening.

He nearly chokes on his drink. "Really?" His face ignites in an ear-to-ear grin like he knows I'm lying.

"Really. Our mothers arranged the whole thing when we were like twelve." I leave out the part about meeting Pen for the first time last week in cyberspace. "He's pretty nice." Nice as a donkey's ass, but that's none of Cruise Elton's freaking business. Besides, I don't like the smug look on his face, like I'm fresh meat ready for the sexual slaughter.

"That's too bad about the betrothal," he says, moving in close as an entire stream of bodies push in behind him. His soft cologne wraps around me like a pair of strong arms, and I feel the heat radiating from his body, covering me like a coat.

A linebacker carrying a keg in his arms barrels through the center of the room, parting the crowd like a Red Sea miracle. The swell of humanity forces Cruise into me and we land flattened against the wall, with his iron abs pressed against me so tight you couldn't squeeze a quarter between us. His hips adhere to mine with a noticeable protrusion pressed against my thigh.

Cruise runs his heavy gaze over my features. His lips part involuntarily. We lock eyes, and neither of us moves from this compromising position.

The music dies down and a familiar Christmas carol belts over the speakers, inspiring a bunch of girls in the corner to sing along.

He grazes his bottom lip with his perfectly straight teeth, so unearthly white they glow. "Do you believe in love at first sight, Kenny?"

Everything in me freezes. If I did believe in love at first sight, I would hope it would be with someone as godlike as Cruise Elton who saw fit to back me into a corner and bless me with his rock-hard body—but, alas, the answer is no.

"After my mom's fifth marriage ended, I stopped believing in love—and Santa." It comes out much cheerier than the sad news it really is.

He gives a sexy smile that sears me with heat in places I've never felt before.

"I don't believe in it, either. But you can't tell me Santa isn't real." His grin widens. "I knew I liked you." He cups the side of my face and swallows hard. Gone is the playful flirt as his features take a turn for the serious. His eyes close as he comes in for the kill. My heart gives a few wild thumps, alerting me to the fact that Cruise Cock-on-Fire Elton has the power to induce a cardiac episode in me if he wanted.

"Whoa." I slap my hands over his chest and give a good shove. "Sorry, cowboy, I'm not into one-night stands either. I get it. I really do," I say, trying to maneuver my way from under him. "You're on a road show with your penis, and trust me, I'm the last person who wants to get in your way. But I'm telling you, Operation Occupy My Vagina is a no-go for the evening."

"Road show?" He mouths the words, perplexed by my penile analogy just long enough for me to twist myself free and speed over to a couple of girls as if I knew them. They're standing in front of a vast display of beverages, all of which guarantee a hangover, with the exception of Coke or Pepsi.

I dart a glance back to Cruise only to find he's once again surrounded by his hormone-happy harem.

A brunette digs her hand into the back of his jeans while a gorgeous blonde whispers in his ear, inspiring a laugh out of him. My stomach cinches at the sight of all those bimbos pawing at him. An unexpected pang of jealousy spreads through my chest, and I force myself to look away.

"Nice," I whisper.

"Ally Monroe." A chipper blonde with bright-red lipstick takes up my hand. She's wrapped in a black-and-white-checkered coat, paired with patent leather boots that inch past her knees. I have on my less-than-warm jean jacket and spiked, knockoff Manolos. Having lived in LA all my life, I'm pretty sure I'm ill-prepared for a brutal Massachusetts winter.

"Kendall," I say to the two of them.

"Lauren Ashby." The brunette gives a brief nod. Her hair cascades around her shoulders in waves, and I admire it for a moment. My own hair hangs long and, for the most part, straight—dark as soot. Most of the time it just looks like a bad Halloween wig. "We see you've met Cruise." She tips her head back and laughs, revealing a pair of light-up Christmas tree earrings hidden beneath her dark tresses.

"Is he a graduation requirement?" I ask. Not that I'm anywhere near graduation. I'm a sophomore who recently upgraded her undeclared status to liberal arts with no real intention of doing anything productive with it.

Lauren laughs so hard she spills her drink over her bright-red heels. "No, but *God*, wouldn't that be great? Actually, he's a mess. Stay away from him. He had a rough time last summer, and now he's nothing but a ball of testosterone on fire."

"He was shit on." Ally nods as if to testify to this.

"He was *shat* on." Lauren spears her with a look. "Get your grammar straight."

Pennington struts by with his collar turned up like a preppy and a pair of sunglasses firmly planted over his face, which cements any pending douchebag status I may have afforded him. I've seen enough pictures to know it's him, plus we Skyped twice last week to finalize my arrangements. He was supposed to pick me up from the airport, but he said he had a last minute "emergency," so I blew through half the twenties in my wallet just transporting myself to this hotbed of immorality. Something tells me the crisis had to do with malt liquor.

"There's my future husband," I say sarcastically, mostly to myself since Lauren and Ally are locked in a heated argument over semantics.

"Pennington?" Ally gasps, and the two of them break out in cackles.

I rush over and yank him aside.

"Hey! How's it going? It's me, Kendall!" I pony up all the mock enthusiasm I can muster. "The party was fun and all, but I sort of just want to get settled in my room. Can I have the key?"

Pennington secured me a dorm room on campus, which is really hard to do since they're usually booked by August, and here it is December, so I guess it's sort of my Christmas miracle.

His lips crimp. "About that..."

Or not.

"What happened?" I don't need to be Nancy Drew to know this isn't going to end well.

"Nothing happened." He sloshes his drink over the floor, as if trying to wave off the absurdity. Pennington is tall and decent in the looks department, not in the caustic jump-in-my-bed sort of way that Cruise is—Pen is more your stoner boy next door. I'm sure every female within a twenty-mile radius would love nothing more than to drag Cruise off to the nearest bushes, but Pennington—well, he's the reason girls carry Mace in their purse.

He nods into me. "You're going to have to crash here a few nights, just until I get everything squared away with the Housing Department. Turns out, I didn't get your name in on time." He rolls his eyes, as if little details like that are annoyingly unimportant. "But you're on a waiting list—put you there myself."

"What?" A thread of panic spikes through me. "I'm homeless?" It comes out more of a whimper than a question.

"No." He begins to sway because, clearly, he's wasted out of his irresponsible mind. "When school opens up again, we'll get this whole stupid thing straightened out."

"This whole stupid thing?" I'm so ticked I'm ready to douse him with the contents of his bright-red Solo cup. "School doesn't open for another three weeks," I squawk. "I was supposed to get settled, not arrested for trespassing. I can't stay here." I fan my arms out at the debauchery just as a dark-haired boy pukes in the center of the room.

"Suit yourself." He starts walking away. "Hey, my mom invited you to dinner Christmas Eve." He gives a thumbs-up before melting into the crowd. Pennington Andrew Alexander the Third is an ass of the highest order. And with a name like that, who could really blame him?

What to do?

What to freaking *do!*

I guess there's always Aunt Jackie. She's not my real aunt, and I've yet to see or speak to her. All I know is that she and my mother were besties growing up and kept in touch over the years. They both went to Garrison and now her unreliable spawn and I are following in their footsteps. I guess I could shake Pennington down for her number. I'm sure she wouldn't want me seeking shelter on park benches or in vomit-riddled frat rooms. Although, I'm not too enthused with the idea of shacking up with the elders either. I've been dreaming of having the full collegiate experience ever since I received my acceptance letter back in May. Having to wait until winter seemed bad enough already.

I scan the room for Lauren and Ally. Surely, they have a couch I can crash on tonight and maybe the next three weeks—at this point, I'd take the next three days. I pick up my pace and begin circling the room. Lauren cackles from the entry, and I catch them heading outside.

"Wait!" I bolt for my suitcase before maneuvering toward the door, but navigating my way out of this human maze is like moving boulders.

I make it to the porch, and the cold dew baptizes me with the perfumed scent of the evergreens. My suitcase bounces out of the house from behind and slices a nice clean gash into my ankle.

"*Pennington!*" Somehow shouting his name as an expletive makes the situation a little more bearable.

I look up in time to see a black Jeep pull away with Ally in the passenger's seat.

"Great." I let out a hard sigh and clop down the rest of the stairs like I actually have someplace to go. In the distance, an owl gives an eerie cry. The wind licks the wound at my ankle with its iced tongue, and I shiver. I've never been alone like this before, in a strange town with nowhere to go. It's as though I'd laid myself in a steel-jaw trap and the cruel world were closing in on me with its nefarious arms.

A couple to my left laughs while locked in an embrace. It's not until they pull away that I see it's Cruise and a tall redhead wearing thigh-high boots and a miniskirt that's violating more than its fair share of public indecency laws.

He catches my eye and holds it a second before glancing down at my suitcase. My stomach explodes with heat at the sight of him. Cruise whispers something in her ear, inspiring me to turn away as if I were at a bus stop waiting for my invisible ride. Only I'm not. I'm stuck at Garrison, at Alpha Sigma Phi no less. Tomorrow is Christmas Eve, I'm homeless and hungry, and my feet are pissed off and bleeding.

"Hey, Kenny." Cruise swoops in with a boastful smile.

I glance over in time to catch the girl in the thigh-highs making her way back to the party.

I give a private smile at the thought of Cruise striking out so close to midnight.

"I would have pegged her for a home run," I say.

"She was." He offers a lopsided grin and takes hold of my suitcase. "But I'd rather grab a bite with you."

Cruise

The moon glows overhead clear as a streetlamp, making the clouds look like black paper cutouts against the navy expanse. The sky threatens us with rain, but since the heater is out at my place, with my luck, I'm betting on snow.

But for whatever reason, my run of bad juju seems to have temporarily halted because a goddess by the name of Kendall Jordan is sitting in my truck with one hell of a banging-hot bod. And, holy shit, would I ever love to bang that body. But she's not the banging type. She made that abundantly clear when she accused my dick of having a "road show." She's funny as hell, though, I'll give her that.

We pull into the Johnny Burgers lot, and I slow down as we pass the front.

"Drive-thru or dine-in?" I ask, hinting at the game of Questions from earlier.

She leans over and inspects the place. Her hair drapes across her shoulders like a long black scarf, and her pale-gray eyes glow like those of a cat. Instinctively, I want to reach out and touch her, but I resist. I have a feeling I'll be doing a lot of resisting around Kenny in the very near future. She's not the type to voluntarily fall on her knees, and that alone makes me want her twice as bad.

I look over to the burger joint. The windows are painted with a snowy scene of Santa making his way down a chimney with burgers and fries bursting from his sack. Miles of holly garland outline the doors. I look for the mistletoe—no such luck.

Kenny blinks into the place with her long dark lashes, and the lights go out in the establishment before she can answer.

"I guess that's drive-thru," I say, pulling in, and we place our orders. Kenny hasn't said much, other than filling me in on Pennington's housing botch up. I'm not used to quiet girls. Moaning girls—screaming girls, now *that* I'm used to. Quiet worries me, makes me feel like I'm doing something wrong.

She reaches for her purse.

"No, I got it." I pay the girl in the window before Kenny can mime the offer. I catch her inspecting me with what I'm hoping to God is lust, but could just as easily be regret for ever setting foot in my truck, so I busy myself with putting away my wallet. "You're so damn good-looking it borders on illegal." I say it calmly, more as a fact than something engineered to land her in bed. I think both my dick and I have come to terms with the fact that Kenny Jordan isn't choosing *in* tonight.

She blushes a severe shade of pomegranate, and a sharp bite of heat cuts through me. I can't remember the last time I made a girl blush. Hell, I didn't know they could blush, at least not the man-eaters I associate myself with.

"Thank you, I think." She averts her gaze out the blackened window.

I take in her pale skin and perfect full lips. My heart pounds against my chest, telling me to knock this shit off or I might accidentally break it again.

The food comes through the window, so I hand Kenny the bags and drinks before heading to the overlook across the way. We can eat in peace on the cliff side with nothing but the Atlantic to distract us from ourselves.

"Where are we going?" Her voice spikes as if she suddenly fears for her limbs.

"Just across the street." I pull into the lot and land square in front of the wooden fence that separates us from a two-hundred-foot drop. "You can see the beach from here." I take a quick swig of my soda. "So, where are you from?"

"California. I love the beach. I practically grew up on one." She plays with the thin gold chain around her neck while stretching her gaze over the waterline. "I've never been to Massachusetts before. It looks nice from what I can see of it." She nods toward the windshield. "My mom really wanted me to get into Garrison." She unbuckles her seat belt and dips into the bag, handing me a burger. "You know"—she averts her eyes—"work on that M-R-S degree." She gives a sexy gurgle when she says it. "At least that's what she wants."

"M-R-S, huh?" A tremble of laughter rattles through me. "Good luck with that." I take a giant bite of the artery buster in my hand and wash it down with my drink. "Standing at the altar is the last place you'll find me. I'm pretty sure I'm not getting married." A knot twists in my gut, as if maybe I shouldn't have been so quick to shoot down any false matrimonial fantasies she might be entertaining—especially not if they involve me. I'm pretty sure I'd be happy to star in any damn fantasy she's willing to put me in.

She plucks out the fries and offers me one, so I accept. There's not a whole lot I wouldn't accept from Kenny at the moment.

"No altar for you, huh? That's because you're a player." She says it as fact.

I tick my head back a notch. "Who says I'm a player?"

I'm a player? Shit. I stare dumbfounded out the window a moment. That's what I've become. I guess bedding my way through the Greek alphabet, by way of sorority girls, will do that to a person.

"Yes, you're a player." She looks up at me from under those I-double-dog-dare-you-to-get-me-in-bed lashes as she sips from her shake.

My gaze dips for a moment, taking in her fully formed, round, incredibly soft-looking cleavage, and my dick perks to attention. I shift and place the bag over my lap in the event that things decide to get viral in my Levi's.

"I don't need a road map." She purrs it out low—all vixen and hell-on-heels. "You had ten girls hanging over you tonight. I think one of them digested your left ear."

I catch a glimpse of my slightly singed earlobe in the rear-view mirror. "I think her name was Gina, and in her defense, she was offering a demonstration of what she could do with her mouth." I tuck a smile in the side of my cheek, enjoying the color as it blooms over her face and makes her skin glow. "How about you? You play the game?" I ask mostly to see if I can get her to blush ten shades deeper, see if the color would bleed down her neck and light up her boobs like a pair of Christmas ornaments. Getting Kenny to emit an afterglow has become my mission in life. Besides, I already know that Kenny Jordan is far from a player and, unfortunately for me, that pretty much takes her out of the running for playmate. Too bad I'm not in the market for a girlfriend; if I were, I'd battle to the death to make sure it was her. "On second thought, don't answer. There's no way in hell you'd even know what to play with." This time I bury the smile and go for the cardinal-coated gold. My body ignites with heat just watching her light up a deep velvet crimson.

Her mouth falls open. "No, I'm not a player," she says it drawn out, incredulous at my taunt. "But I could be." She crimps a smile, and a tiny dimple implodes in her left cheek. "If I wanted to."

Hot fucking damn.

Her cleavage magically enlarges as she leans in, and suddenly I'm finding the need to readjust the bag over my lap.

"Although"—she touches her lower lip with her finger, sending my penis in full scale erotic assault mode—"I haven't really even kissed anybody except for the time I was drunk at my senior graduation."

"Really?" What the hell is wrong with the guys in California?

"Yeah, really." She traces the outline of her lips with her finger.

I'd like to do that for her—with my tongue.

"So I guess that means you're a virgin." Shit. Did I just go there? Looks like it's all systems go to make sure Kenny stays the hell away from me. Nothing like a little self-sabotage coupled with a jab at her virginity to make sure she's safe from my road show. Kenny needs some nice kid to sweep her off her feet, not me. I've got chains dangling from my bedposts for God's sake. Nope. There's not one nice thing about me these days.

"It's not a death sentence," she scolds. "Besides, maybe I will take my mother's unconventional advice. I could hang out with Pennington and see what happens." She makes a face as if it were the last thing on the planet she wanted to do.

I swallow a laugh. "I'm pretty sure Pennington isn't the one for you."

She postures seductively as her hips grind into the seat. "Well, I have to start somewhere if I'm going to become the female version of you, don't I?" She bites down on the smile waiting to take over, as if taunting me.

"Female version of me?" Intriguing concept, but I'm not buying it. I doubt she is either.

"Maybe I should turn things around for myself"—she gives an impish grin—"start taking advantage of all the fresh meat Garrison has to offer. You know, a social experiment."

"Social experiment?" I hold back a laugh. If I didn't know better I'd think she read my thesis. Has she read my thesis?

"Yeah, I can document my findings on what it feels like to become a female predator. They do exist, you know. The male gender doesn't own exclusive rights to sexual domination."

"You want to sexually dominate." I find this doubtful. Although if she's hell-bent on diving into a cesspool of STDs, who am I to stop her? In fact, I might even introduce her to the chains a little sooner than anticipated. "And, by all means, I volunteer to do the documentation around here." I'll be published by fall.

"I could be the next big player at Garrison," she says, stunned by her own admission. "I bet I can give you a run for your money."

"No, you can't." I take a quick swig of my soda. No use in placating her with false ideals. A kitten like her would be eaten alive in the most extravagant sexual fashion if left to the rabid bears on campus.

"Well then, I'll just have to prove you wrong." Her neck arches in a seductive manner, paper-white and long like a pillar.

She accepts the challenge as if I'd just issued a dare. I should set her straight, release her from the bondage of ever becoming anything like me, but my mouth takes a U-turn.

"So, I guess you'll need some pointers." I start up the car and back out of the lot without giving my conscience a chance to weigh in on the matter.

She leans as the car moves and her chest swells out of her T-shirt, making me hungry for far more than food.

"Where we going?" she whispers, worried by my sudden offer of assistance, I'm sure.

"To my place." I'll have her running for the nearest convent by the time I'm through with her. "It's time to get to bed."

2

THE EXPERIMENT

Kendall

*B*ed?

I watch as the moon lies over the water like a lover, the waves lapping the shore with their strange luminescent glow. Cruise weaves us down a deserted black highway with curtains of evergreens erect on either side. He's driving me to a yet undisclosed location to which he gleefully confessed happens to house his mattress. And I'm pretty sure after he has his way with me, there's a good chance he'll dismember my body.

I can't believe how stupid I am to get in the car with a stranger. They say never let an abductor take you to a second location—not that I've technically been abducted since I willfully entered the vehicle. Although in my defense, plenty of abductees have crawled into the passenger's side under the pretense of a burger and fries.

We drive out of civilization, just as I suspected, and into a black hole that eventually leads to a sign that reads CARRINGTON COUNTY then another less prominent sign reading ELTON HOUSE BED AND BREAKFAST.

"My mom runs the place," he volunteers as we pull in. "It was passed down from my grandfather." The muscles in his jaw tighten as he inspects the tall yellow structure. We turn down an offshoot and land in front of a small brick house tucked behind the B and B. "I have an extra room. The bathroom doesn't have a lock, but I promise I'll knock up a storm before barging in—maybe." He gives a devilish grin before killing the engine. "The room is yours if you want it, for as long as you need it."

"Thank you," I say, hesitant about this. "But I don't have any money for rent," I confess. And I'm pretty sure my scholarship doesn't cover shacking up with abnormally good-looking boys. But I guess one night won't hurt. He seems mostly sane. Although, I'm not sure I could take him if he decides to attack. I'll have to sleep with a stiletto at the ready should the need arise to put out an eye.

"That's all right. I'll let you cook me breakfast in exchange for room and board." He gravels it out as if he were the meal in question. "We'll call it even."

I follow him to the tiny porch as he lugs my suitcase. The air is icy as an arctic breeze, causing a cloud to form around our heads from the simple act of breathing.

Cruise glows with the powder-white halo surrounding him, and I give an impish grin at what might happen tonight.

He opens the door and flicks on the lights before taking a step back onto the porch.

"Ladies first." He waves me in.

It's clean inside. A large living room opens up to a kitchen filled with stainless-steel appliances and dark hardwood floors. Truthfully, I expected to find a colossal bong centered on the table like a vase, or possibly a meth lab sprouting from the sink. But to my surprise, there's no evidence of criminal activity.

"Nice," I say, making my way toward the U-shaped sofa. "Thanks for letting me crash on your couch."

"You won't have to. I have a bed with your name on it." His brows arch with an air of seduction as he leads me to a small room with an oversized bed. A maple dresser is set in the corner. The room looks harmless enough. Nothing to imply deviant behavior—no sign of rope or duct tape, so already I feel better.

"I'm in this one." He turns on the lights next door, revealing an unmade bed with a river of socks flowing onto the floor. There's an abandoned pizza box on the nightstand with a bevy of candy wrappers strewn over it.

I see his nightly conquests leave him famished, and his need for handy snacks outweigh any concerns he might have for nutrition.

A pair of chains dangle from his bedpost, and my stomach lurches with an unnatural level of excitement—or fear—maybe both.

"Bathroom." He nods behind me. "I'll get a fire going and warm the place up. Heater's out of commission, but I'll fix it." Cruise leans into the doorframe and examines me with a proficient thoroughness. His eyes lock over mine, and the hint of a corrupt smile plays on his lips.

God, he's gorgeous. I'm pretty sure a face like that and a bed less than ten feet away is a dangerous combination.

"So, what do you think?" He smolders.

"Um . . ." I'm concerned I've missed a boatload of clues that would have afforded a more experienced one-night stand aficionado the right to be testing out those mattress springs by now. "I think it's nice of you to let me spend the night." Really? *Nice of you to let me spend the night?* I'm pretty sure those words have never been uttered under this roof before. In fact, I'm betting niceties such as *please* and *thank you* have only been screamed under sexual duress in his deviant den, laden with chains and stale pizza.

He leads us back to the living room, and I take a seat on the sheepskin rug just shy of the hearth. I'm no detective, but I can deduce that the furry carcass I've planted myself on has seen some serious mileage in the soiled-with-sin department. Although, right about now, I'm so freezing I don't really care about the questionably defiled status of said dead creature. I'm so cold I might actually jump into the fire just to thaw out.

A bouquet of flames ignites in the small opening, and the room picks up a rosy glow.

"Thank you," I whisper as the heat curls around me.

"Anything for you." He growls it out with a perverse smile hedging on his lips. Cruise lands himself by my side. We watch the fire lick the air with lusty forked tongues while I try to surmise the definition of "anything" and the physical agility it might entail.

"So what happened last summer?" In the event that he thinks my girl parts might be a good repository for the hard-on blooming in his jeans, I thought I'd throw in the vague mention of his ex. "Rumor has it, that it was pretty harsh." I brace myself for the unromantic tragedy that's about to unfold. I'm thinking bare-breasted coeds are involved.

"Just your run-of-the-mill breakup. But everyone's got one of those, right?" He taps my shoe with his and scoots in. The thick veins in his arms protrude like cables, and his muscles bulge for no good reason. It makes me want to touch them and see what they feel like.

"No bad breakup for me," I whisper. "If you don't give your heart away, you can't get it broken."

His pale eyes latch onto mine. He holds my gaze, heavy as steel.

"No truer words were ever spoken," he says it low, sad, as if he means it, but too much.

Cruise softens and gives a little smile. He washes me with a delicate gaze, and my insides pinch tight.

There's something brewing inside him, inside me, and I've never felt this way before. It's probably just his hormonal super-powers having their effect on me—our pheromones conducting their obligatory exchange. I bet he slays women nightly with that same "broken heater" routine. I suspect he'll volunteer to keep me warm by way of body heat any moment now. Or at least I'm hoping.

"I can see why girls flock to you." I turn my face toward the fire in an effort to break the spell.

"Why's that?" He catches my gaze again, and this time it's impossible to look away.

"Because anybody can have you." I don't bother telling him he's gorgeous. I'm sure he's well aware from all the positive vaginal reinforcement. "You haven't known me for three hours, and I bet if I ripped my jeans off, you wouldn't turn down the offer." Crap. I think I just subliminally propositioned him.

"You're a smart girl, Kenny—beautiful, too." He gives the curve of a lewd smile and everything in me burns with heat.

I've never been called beautiful by a person of the penis before, and this pleases me with a strange intensity. It's as if I've needed it, craved it like a glass of water for my parched affection.

"So, when do we get to the ripping of the jeans?" he inquires with far more eagerness than expected, and a titter of excitement prickles through me.

"I take it you think my experiment should commence with you." Please, God, say yes.

"The experiment in which you attack the unsuspecting crotches of every living male on campus? Unless, of course, you plan on including corpses in your little jaunt on the wild side. We house those in the Health and Sciences Building." He gives a disbelieving smile. "Let the good times roll, Kenny." It comes out a dare as he peers at me seductively from under his hooded lids. A dirty grin forces his dimples to twitch in turn.

"I'm starting with Pennington, remember?" I'm quick to shoot him down. Pennington probably counts as a corpse. "Besides, it would make my mother's life if he were my first ex-husband. I think it's the cash payout that has her drooling more than some romantic notion that her daughter and the son of her once-upon-a-time best friend, go down in matrimonial flames together."

"Sounds painful."

"It will be." I take in his full lips, his high-set cheeks. He's driving me insane by way of his five-o'clock shadow. His lids hang heavy as he openly eyes my cleavage. "Although, I should probably get some experience under my belt before I go after a prize like Pennington. You know, practice the fine art of saliva swapping, among other things." God, how I would love to practice the fine art of transferring bodily fluids with Cruise Let-Me Deliver-You-from-Your-Virginity Elton.

He examines me an inordinate amount of time. Then he picks up my hand and presses his lips over the back, soft and warm. It sets everything in me on fire.

"I'm more than happy to offer up my tutorial services." He leans back and sweeps his eyes over me as if I were a meal, but there's a sadness lurking in them just beneath the surface.

"So, when do we begin?" I'm not sure I'm ready to give it all away right here in Massachusetts next to a blazing fire with a guy I hardly know, but a small part of me is begging for just that."

"Tomorrow." He gives a quick wink while helping me to my feet. "Why don't you get to bed?"

"Where you going?" My stomach bottoms out. He's probably got an entire stream of girls lined up for the night who are more than qualified to handle whatever he's willing to dish out—and because of my incessant need to preserve my virginity, I won't be one of them.

"There's a cold shower with my name on it," he says, walking away.

Cold shower?

I watch as Cruise disappears into the hall and the pipes squeal to life from the bathroom.

I can't believe a player like Cruise Elton wouldn't try to take advantage of me. It's obvious virgins aren't high on his to-do list tonight.

Maybe Cruise Elton isn't the player he makes himself out to be.

Deep down inside I hope he's not.

Cruise

In the morning, I wake with a start from a disturbing dream in which I'm drowning in a sea of long, soft limbs.

I'm not sure what I find so disturbing about it since it's otherwise classified as a typical Friday night. I wipe the sleep from my eyes and throw myself in the shower.

After, I make an effort to put on a pair of jeans that have actually seen the inside of a washing machine this month.

Kenny's door is shut, so I can only assume she's still here. I imagine her sprawled over the bed, naked, with her hair fanned around her like long black feathers. I'd love to see that in person. If she wasn't so damn sweet, I would have pressed a little harder to witness the sight firsthand.

I make breakfast for the two of us while a sea of dark clouds watches silent outside the kitchen window. They lie over the sky, heavy and full, like wool blankets ready to burst.

Kenny ambles into the room with her hair swept back in a ponytail. Her long T-shirt is tight over her chest, annunciating the fact that she's not wearing a bra. Not that I mind her beautiful round nipples staring me in the face.

The air sizzles, and the room sparks to life with her in it. Kenny manages to brighten the house with a glow all her own.

"Morning, sunshine." I give a crooked smile while jabbing at a mountain of bacon. I land enough on each plate to clog both our arteries decades before their time.

"Morning." She moans into the word. Her mascara is slightly smeared. She's sleepy-eyed and sexy as hell.

"You dream about me?" I land two fully loaded plates onto the table and dart back for coffee.

"I guess the more important question is did you dream about *me?*" She takes a seat and looks up with those diamond-cut eyes causing my mind to draw a fucking blank. Everything about Kenny feels like a dream, especially the part about not sleeping with me last night, which is mostly my fault. I've yet to corrupt a virgin, and I'm pretty sure I'm not starting with Kenny.

Her eyes drift to a pair of leashes by the back door, and my blood turns to ice because I know what's coming.

"So, where are the dogs?" She says it playfully, far too innocent to be faking. I thought for sure the vulgar nature of the leashes, the thick metal spikes, the red leather tassels dripping from the collar would set off the fact that they're exclusively for human purposes—or inhuman, take your pick.

"Are they outside?" She peers out the window still fixing her innocence on the prospect of a furry companion.

"There are no dogs, Kenny," I say, slightly amused. I lift my chin, and my stomach drops at how gorgeous she is in this slightly disheveled state of early morning glory. "Those leashes aren't for walking, young lady." I swallow a laugh.

"Looks like you run a pretty sophisticated playboy-for-hire ring."

Her eyes widen and that dimple goes off, melting my insides in a way I've never felt before.

"Is that my first lesson?" She breathes it out like a proposition. "Leather and lace?"

A smile digs into the side of my cheek. "You're not ready for that, sweetie." A heated moment passes between us as I raise my mug. "Merry Christmas."

"That's today! Well, tomorrow." Her face brightens. "I forgot all about the fact it's Christmas Eve. Merry Christmas." Her smile slowly diminishes as she runs her fork through her eggs. "It's weird, though. I've never been away from my mom or my brother, Morgan. He's out in Oregon on a baseball scholarship."

"I have a sister you can adopt for the holiday if you feel the need to rain down gifts on someone." Molly is a certified head case, but I leave that part out.

Kenny could slather me with gifts of the physical variety if she felt so moved, but I'm slow to bring up that prospect.

"I would love to rain down gifts on your sister. That is, if I had the money." She makes a face. "My neighbor is a stewardess and I was on standby for a cheap flight. She helped me get the ticket so I had to come. And here I am on Christmas, pretty much alone."

"Looks like Santa just left a perfectly good brunette in my stocking. You'll have to spend it with me."

"Well, if Santa insists." She runs her tongue over her lower lip, and my insides burn with a fire all their own.

The sudden urge to rake the table clean and take her right here crops up, but I'm quick to resist the craving.

"Looks like we'd better get a tree," I say, exhilarated by the idea of doing anything with Kenny. I take in the long river of ebony hair sweeping over her shoulder, her tan legs that ride up past her T-shirt, and wonder if she would ever want someone like me. "The tree—real or fake?"

"I want everything we share to be real." She winks a quick smile.

So do I. "Sounds like a date."

3

MAGIC IN THE AIR

Kendall

The Christmas tree lot is strangely jam-packed, on this, the final night to decorate overglorified shrubbery. Kids run wild with cups of cocoa while clusters of people stand around, talking and laughing. I get the feeling that this is what social gatherings will look like in the collegiate afterlife, once you gravitate outside the Greek system and procreation instincts kick in.

The clouds overhead wear dusty purple skins, yet somehow the evergreens still manage to lend their shadows across the pale dirt that spreads wide for acres.

"Last day at the tree lot is always a madhouse," Cruise says, navigating us through the melee. I watch as the muscles in his neck pop when he swallows; his jaw redefines itself with even the slightest inflection. He offers a soft smile to the kids who swim past us with glee, and that simple show of affection warms me to him. Everything about Cruise has my interest piqued, and it makes me wonder where these feelings came from. Had I been saving them up for someone like Cruise all along? Had my mother ever felt this way during one of her serial marriages? Maybe this is the magic that starts the ball rolling, then it evaporates, and you find yourself looking for an apartment with two kids in tow.

"It's the opposite back home," I tell him as we step through a cushion of pine needles at least a foot deep. "Everyone I know starts decking the halls the day after Thanksgiving—and the tree lots are bare two weeks into December."

"Sounds like home is a nice place." A plume of fog emits from his lips as he eases into a smile—this time it's all for me. He picks up my hand and leads me through the crowd. "You mind?" He gives my fingers a gentle squeeze.

"Not at all," I say as my shoes crunch over the discarded boughs. "We need to start somewhere if you're going to teach me your womanizing ways." I try to sound like it's no big deal, but in truth, I feel weak, nauseated, and extremely giddy at the prospect of holding his hand. It's electrifying—an honest-to-God high that rivals any narcotic known to man. The boys back home didn't have the power to make me feel this way. And I certainly don't have the desire to touch any part of Pennington, let alone his drunken frat brothers like I may have eluded. And since when did I add the fine art of lying to my personal resume? And for what? To trick him into some kind of twisted relationship? Although, someone like Cruise isn't interested in something long-term for the same reason I'm not. It never works out in the end.

I shake the thought loose.

"You'll be a man-eater by New Year's," he guarantees as we make our way through the crowd gathered by the register. "There's a special event today—local churches come out to buy trees for less fortunate families in the area. It's sort of a tradition around here."

"That's so nice." I like this altruistic side of Carrington County. I try to catch my breath as he leads us to the distal end of the property, and a clearing opens up with dozens of trees to choose from.

Cruise heads over to a tiny anemic tree with sparse needles and gauges me for a reaction.

I shake my head at that one. I don't tell him that's the same tree my mother bought year after year because it was all we could afford—that I dreamed of trees fat enough to eat up the living room, dripping with jewels and topped with a shiny white star. I suppose transferring my fantasies over to Cruise isn't the greatest idea, but I can't seem to help it. For some reason, I want him to be the one to make them all come true.

Odd, since I hardly know him.

"So, you're a size-matters kind of girl," he says it low, far too seductive for this early in the evening.

Soft drops of rain land over my scalp, and I hold out my hand, surprised to find tiny white flakes amassing over my fingertips. "I've never seen snow," I whisper the confession. "It's magic. It's beautiful."

"You're magic." He takes a step in until we're a breath apart. "You're beautiful, Kenny." He showers me with his gaze, watching as the snow freckles my dark mane.

Cruise leans in.

I can feel it coming.

My lips ache for him to do it.

My palms start to sweat, and my heart feels like it's about to jackhammer out of my chest—killing us both in the process.

"This one," I say, breathless, while plucking at the branch of a Douglas fir before I pass out from the idea of a kiss.

"Looks like we got our first tree," he says, never taking his gaze off me.

My insides bisect with heat at the thought of a relationship with Cruise that could string out into the unknowable future, spending Christmas after Christmas with his heart-stopping smile.

"Kenny . . ." His minty breath rakes across my cheek like a fire. "You mind if I kiss you?"

I shake my head, looking a little more than overeager in the process.

"It's Christmas." A smile slides onto his face. "And it's snowing. I think your first real kiss should be memorable." He washes his eyes over me with heartfelt affection. "I want to make everything we share memorable for you."

Good God, he's going to take me right here in the snow. I'm going to lose my virginity on the eve of Jesus's birthday in front of unsuspecting church folk. In just a few minutes, those children running wild will be screaming for another reason entirely.

"Merry Christmas, Cruise." I pant out of breath like I've just sprinted for miles.

He wraps his arms around my waist and pulls me in. I can hardly look at him. Cruise is far too gorgeous for me to ever comprehend.

"Merry Christmas, Kenny." His dimples dig in. "Thank you for my gift."

"What gift?"

"This." He closes his eyes and sweeps his feather-soft lips over mine before indulging in something deeper—something that feels so alarmingly holy and right it makes my insides implode with pleasure. I give an involuntary groan as his tongue flicks over mine, flirting, caressing. The exquisite exchange goes on for what feels like forever.

We kiss for hours, weeks, decades as the snow piles up around us. It tries to cool the inferno we've lit, but its efforts are impotent.

We're building a memory that can last a lifetime—two lifetimes. It's bliss like this with Cruise.

This is a Christmas wish come true.

One I didn't even know I wanted.

Cruise

Kenny and I leave the tree lot, one bushy evergreen richer, and enjoy the ride home, still hopped up on that lip-lock we shared. I've kissed my fair share of girls. I've logged some mileage with these lips, and swear to God have never experienced an out-of-body experience like the one Kenny just provided. Maybe it had to do with the fact that I'm aroused as hell at the thought of touching a virgin, guiding her down some dark carnal path, but whatever it was, it sealed itself in my memory as a holy-shit moment.

We arrive at the house and I pull backward into the driveway, trying to ignore the fact that I just took out the border garden my mother planted last spring. In my defense, a blanket of snow dusted the ground in the time it took to get to the tree lot and back. Parking in reverse was never my forte, although I'd never confess to being anything short of an ace behind the wheel.

I glance over at Kenny with her hair slightly wet from the snow and the skin on her chest quivering, and the breath escapes my lungs.

Damn, she's hot. I blink a quick smile and pat her on the knee like some perverted uncle.

"Let's do this," I say.

Kenny helps me drag down the furry monster that once stood proud as a card-carrying member of a forest but is now reduced to living room décor for all of one night. But I don't mind. I can't remember the last time I had a tree, with the exception of living in the bed-and-breakfast with Mom and Molly.

"It smells so good!" She inhales deeply as her lids flutter. She looks as if she were about to have an enriched sexual experience, and with me a good ten feet away, missing out on all the fun.

"Sure does. God's perfume," I say, dragging it into the house and leaning it against the wall farthest from the fireplace. No use in burning down our love shack before giving it the proper conjugal usage.

I step back and lose myself just staring at Kenny.

"What?" She bites down on her lip, and her hip juts out like she's making me an offer. For a girl who claims to never have had more than one drunken kiss, Kenny sure knows how to bring the heat without trying. And what the hell am I saying, conjugal usage? Kenny isn't one of the tramps I pick up on my nightly panty raids down on sorority row. I'm pretty sure this is one fountain of youth and beauty I won't be tapping anytime soon. The nice guy in me won't allow it. I'd like to take that part of me out back and knock the shit out of him with a shovel—bury him in the process for morphing into a bleeding heart without my permission.

Kenny comes in close with those pale sky-washed eyes, and I have a hard time catching my breath.

"Boy, you're quiet," she whispers.

"Just enjoying the view." God's honest truth right there. Kenny is a goddess who should be admired by the entire human race. "So what are we going to do with this thing?" I put on a tiny smile and try to pull her in the way I do with other girls. But for her, my heart skips a beat, and I'm not sure I like what this means—not sure I've ever felt this before.

"Come on." She pulls me down to the carpet, and we lean back admiring the tree's crooked form.

It's comfortable like this with Kenny. I push her shoulder playfully, and she reciprocates with a bubbling laugh.

"You kissed me," she whispers, looking up from under a thicket of lashes.

"Only because your lips were begging for it."

"You wish." Her cheeks fill with color like maybe they *were* begging for it after all.

Kenny locks those steel-colored eyes over mine and doesn't let go. For a second I envision straddling her—hell, her straddling *me* with that impossibly perfect body, her warm limbs wrapped around my back like a bow.

A wave of heat washes over me, and I glance down at the bare stump of the tree in an effort to deflect the hard-on in my jeans rising to salute her.

"You think we should decorate it?" She rakes her foot over mine, and an electrical jolt fires up to my groin.

Yes, with a condom, I want to say, not thinking of the tree. Instead, I opt for something more appropriate and likely to happen. "My mom probably has an entire crate of ornaments she'd gladly gift us." I tap her foot with mine and feel a surge bullet through me once again. I'm fascinated by the physiological effect she has the power to invoke. Obviously, sex with someone as physically charged as Kenny would kill me instantly. But what the hell, I say get the paddles ready, boys. I'm going in on a suicide mission.

For a moment, I envision myself stretched out on a gurney with my dick smoking.

I pluck my phone out and shoot a quick text to Mom before I get off track and end up dry humping the evergreen just to keep from going insane.

"Ornaments are just what we need." She shifts and appraises me as if seeing me for the very first time. She looks up at me with those bow-tie lips, and my insides come to life in a flaming ball of fire.

Shit. I'm not used to this. I haven't had a real girl over in so long—*ever* in fact, and it's quickly becoming obvious my body doesn't know what it's supposed to do with her. Hell, I know what it *demands* to do with her—and most of those things aren't legal in any of the fifty states.

"Tell me something about yourself," she says, lying on her back. "What turned you on to women en masse?"

I roll onto my elbow and take her in from this aerial vantage point.

"You're a beautiful species. Can you blame me?" I won't be overanalyzing my latest, not-so-greatest heartbreak with her anytime soon. Besides, I'm over that. This is the new me, the one that doesn't need assurances, just a pocket full of condoms and I'm good to go.

She adjusts herself and her chest ripples in all the right places, eliciting a groan from me in the process. I can feel the old me wanting to burst through and make Kenny my own in a far more intimate way than any of the long string of girls I've reduced to body parts in the last several months. But body parts in and of themselves are fun, and having your balls handed to you spiked on a stiletto, not so much.

"Well, I think *you're* a beautiful species." She nestles in a little closer. I can feel her gunning for another kiss, but she's too shy to go there on her own.

She kicks off her shoes exposing her glossy red toenails. Kenny rolls into me with her hip seductively hiked, her shoulder turned in until it looks as if she's downright posing. My body starts in on the shakes, and my breathing picks up pace. I lean into her like a warning and she doesn't resist the effort. Instead, her eyes enlarge, and her breathing becomes erratic, letting me know she wants it. I close my eyes and go in for the kill.

"So"—she bolts up as if waking from a bad dream—"we should roll some ideas around for our experiment. You know, set some ground rules."

"Our experiment?" I slouch after having my lips shot down like an incoming missile.

"Yeah, you know." She pushes her shoulder against mine and that same surge of electricity vibrates through my chest. "You're my fearless leader. You're going to teach me the ropes"—she ticks her head toward the leash on the floor—"literally."

"You really want to do this?" A thin rail of disappointment speeds through me. I thought maybe she'd cave, decide that she's a one-man woman and maybe, just maybe, that man could've been me.

"Yes." She pushes it out as if she's unsure. "I mean, only if you're interested. If you find me repulsive, I could look elsewhere for instruction." Her lips twitch under the duress of her words, as if she had meant it as a joke and had a reality check that stunted her ego.

"I definitely don't find you repulsive, and I'm not willing to relinquish my star pupil. Trust me, I'll have you bedding your way through fraternity row by New Year's."

She ticks her head back rebuffing the idea.

Knew it. She's a big phony.

A smile twitches on my lips, but I won't give in.

"New Year's?" She shakes her head. "How about Valentine's Day? That might be a nice touch. I'm sentimental that way." She gives an impish grin.

I'm quick to do the math. "Seven weeks without sex? What planet are you from?"

She opens her mouth to protest, and I place a finger over her butter-soft lips.

"I'm teasing." I trace the outline of her mouth as she arches back with pleasure. "I haven't forgotten your virginal standing. And believe me when I say, I'll prepare you well." I trace my finger down her neck, and she gives an uncontrollable shiver.

"I'd hate to take up too much of your time." She looks pained for a moment, like maybe she wouldn't mind taking up a little more of my time than she's letting on. "I mean, you know, I'd hate for the scoreboard on your bedpost to go stale because of me."

I drink Kenny down with her wide-eyed innocence, her spectacular level of vulnerability that sends my testosterone into overdrive.

"The scoreboard should probably take a breather. I was thinking about taking a break, anyway. That way I can hone in all my efforts on you." I stop shy of any sexual illustrations that were begging to fly from my lips. There's no way I'm going to feed her to the masses at Garrison or anywhere else. I'll simply teach her a thing or two about the male anatomy. Hell, maybe she'll like this slice of genetic pie enough to want to stick around—come back for seconds, over and over again.

"So, I guess you'll be my first." She leans in and her breasts ripple out of her low-cut sweater. I try to keep my eyes level to hers, but it's like holding up a battleship.

"I guess I will."

I'm mesmerized by this goddess before me. The idea of being with Kenny, of touching her heated skin to mine, burying myself inside her, sends blood rushing to places that will make for an interesting conversation in a few minutes, and I start to sweat.

What the hell has me so rattled? I do this all the time. It's practically a vocation I'm participating in on the side. I've completed a physical exchange with an indiscriminate number of women every week for the last seven months, and not once have I felt like a schoolboy about to ask the prettiest girl in school to prom. Kendall Jordan simply wants me to teach her the fine art of screwing her way around campus—nothing more, nothing less.

"Where should we start?" *Say "Bedroom."*

I lean in and wait for a reply.

"Maybe take it sort of slow." She winces. "Maybe we can start with a movie?" She shrinks a little when she says it, and I wrestle back a laugh that demands to bark from my lungs.

"A movie." I nod. Seated in opposite ends of the theater, I'm suspecting.

"Yes." She closes her eyes a moment. "Then, we'll round out the bases. What exactly are the bases?"

"First base." I run my finger over her bee-stung lips. "Second base." I drop my hand just shy of her left boob then back up. "Third base is holding me naked." I give the impression of a wicked smile. "With the lights on."

"Is not." She scoffs.

"It can be. Anyway it's just a step away from turning in your v-card, so use your imagination. We can employ the leashes if you like."

"No thanks." She's quick to reject the idea. "That's an advanced field of sexual aerodynamics I am far from ready for."

There's a brief knock at the door before it swings open. I keep meaning to take the key away from my mother.

Mom drops an industrial-sized, plastic storage bin onto the floor with the words *X-Mas* scrawled across the side. She gawks over at the two of us as if she's never seen a creature quite like Kenny before—and I'm damn sure she hasn't.

"You have company!" Her frizzy blonde mane has ballooned to twice its size, and she's donned her signature leopard print coat for the occasion. Kenny jumps up and is quick to greet her. I can't remember the last time Mom met a girl I was with, although technically I'm not with Kenny. I'm little more than a talking dildo at this point, but I accept the challenge. In fact, right about now, I'm feeling kind of lucky for hitting the party last night and embroiling myself in an agreement with one of the hottest girls on both the East and West Coasts.

I hop over. "Mom, this is Kenny. Kenny, this is Samantha, my mother."

"Oh please, call me Sam." Mom lunges into her with an awkward hug, and for the first time I do believe my mother is getting more action with a girl I'm "with" than I am. "Hey"— she dips into her purse and pulls out a little pink envelope—"I happen to own the hottest salon this side of New York City. Why don't you come down and get the works, on me!"

Kenny takes up the envelope and peers inside. "Wow, thank you! I've never been to a salon before. My mom usually cuts my hair." She plucks at an errant strand, and it shines like glass in the light.

"Dear God, child—you have been *abused!*" Mom rattles out a laugh that ends in a cough, which seems par for the course these days. She's running herself ragged, and if she doesn't watch it, she'll end up taking a nice long dirt nap to make up for the lost shut-eye. "Molly's with Brayden." Mom frowns at me. Brayden is my seventeen-year-old sister's boyfriend, and neither of us approve too much of *Brayden*. "I'm headed out to see Aunt Donna. Wanna come?" She presents the offer to both Kenny and me.

"Thank you," Kenny says, "but I promised my mom I'd spend it with her friend Jackie." She looks to me. "I told Pennington I'd be there."

"Jackie Alexander?" Mom arches a brow at the news. "Suit yourself. Sounds like a waste of a perfectly good Christmas if you ask me." She makes a face. "Ta-ta for now." She waves, making her way down the driveway and groans when she sees what my Michelins have reduced her marigolds to.

"I guess she doesn't care for the Alexanders," Kenny muses, tucking a lock of hair between her lips like a beautiful black rose.

I don't tell her that I don't think too much of them either— that I'm biologically one of them.

"I'll give you a ride if you want," I offer.

"Sounds like a plan." She glances up at the mistletoe hanging over the door and steps into me. "Butterfly or Eskimo?"

"Foreign import." I step in until I'm pressed against her. "I say we implement the French."

"Definitely French." She pants into the fog until it encircles us like a wreath.

I close my eyes and land myself over the soft pads of her lips. She swipes her tongue over mine, and I lose it. Her clean scented perfume lures me in like opium. I dig my fingers into her lush hair before indulging in a series of kisses far more animal than either of us had bargained for.

Seismic. Kissing Kenny shifts the landscape of everything I ever thought I knew about the lingual art in general. Kenny blows every kiss I've ever known off the map and pins her star high over the geography with perfect mouthwatering splendor. I've had sex that was less erotic. This was the pinnacle of wanting, a nirvana of passion—sublime in every way.

Kenny brings the magic, the miracles—her kisses are better than wine, and I can never get enough.

4

FAMILIAL FESTIVITIES

Kendall

Snow dances from the sky, dusting the windshield with miniature paperlike flakes as Cruise drives us up an elongated driveway in a gated community. The Alexander estate looks gothic with its cathedral windows and its upright stone lions just feet from the entry.

Mom and Morgan had texted this morning and wished me a merry Christmas. It was a nice gesture from both of them, but it made me feel a little sad that our family had been relegated to electronic well-wishes on the holidays, and incomplete sentences at that. But here we are at Aunt Jackie's, and I'm hopeful to have a down-home family Christmas for the first time in my life. Although judging by the grandeur, I'm guessing this will be anything but a homey holiday.

Cruise comes around and escorts me toward the tall mahogany doors. A pair of oversized tinfoil wreathes adorn the entry, managing to look slightly out of place among all the opulence. But honestly, the only thing on my mind this past hour has been those heated kisses. My face still burns from their fire. I can still feel his tongue in my mouth, bumping against mine, and I replay it over and over like some muscular memory.

Cruise gives a good strong knock, and we wait in awkward silence. He washes a quick glance over my body in a covert manner, and his chest expands.

I wonder if he's thought of those kisses—if he still feels me in his mouth and how I measure up to the long line of girls who have been there before.

Cruise leans toward me and fills the space between us with his spiced cologne. "So, Pennington"—he pauses—"asshole or douchebag?"

A voice emits from inside the house and the door rattles.

"Douchebag," I whisper.

Cruise locks eyes with mine while giving a brief nod. It's as if we're bonding right here on the porch over, of all things, Pennington's douchebag status.

I hope Aunt Jackie won't mind that I've brought someone along. Oddly enough, I know Cruise better than I do "Aunt Jackie."

The door swings open, revealing a woman dressed in gold lamé from head to toe.

"Well, look what the cat dragged in!" She sings the opera-like greeting. Her long black hair is frayed at the edges, and she sports an overprocessed tan that looks less Saint-Tropez and more Oompa Loompa. Her lips glow a pale pink as if she had smeared them with toothpaste, and her eyes are powdered a vulgar shade of indigo frost. "And who the hell is this hot little cutie?" She leans back on her heels—it takes a moment for me to realize she directed the question to Cruise.

"This would be your darling niece." Cruise fans a hand over me as if I were a carnival prize. "I'm just giving her a ride."

"Oh my *gawd*! Andrew, come here! It's Kendall! She's drop-dead gorg!" She pulls me into a rocking hug and does her best to smother me in her cushiony breasts. Her perfume lays over me thick and cloying like strong tea without any sweetness. "Look at you! All grown up."

I smile awkwardly at Cruise because mostly she's propagating a lie. She's never seen more than a dozen pictures of me.

An oversized chandelier drips from the entry, and the room opens up to a sitting area. A supersized white Christmas tree, decorated with clear lights and strategically dispersed red bows, sits in front of the bay window. It's beautiful in a sterile sort of way. I suppose once you amass a certain amount of wealth, you have sophisticated standards to abide by. Gone are the popcorn-strung Christmases and children's art from yesteryear adorning the mantle. It's as if the capital in your bank account bleaches the fun out of everything. Strangely, it's just this sort of opulence I had been craving my whole life, and now that I see it with my own eyes, I'd trade it for that tiny brick house of Cruise's and the bushy Douglas fir in a heartbeat. I might have already.

"Andrew? We're in the sitting room." She ushers us in haste toward a palatial room that houses a giant oil painting of Jackie and her husband as they hover over a younger version of Pennington—and speak of the devil. He strides in the room looking perfectly preppy—a wolf donning designer sheep's clothing.

My anger toward him actually managed to decrease significantly in the past twenty-four hours—especially since Cruise had the good sense not to dismember me. I'm thinking this whole thing with the Housing Department was the best botch up ever and I should be thanking Pen, so I've temporarily taken his name off the list of choice expletives. And even though I'm feeling charitable, I'll be quick to revert the action should Cruise turn into an ass by midnight.

"Dude." Pen high-fives Cruise before smacking me in the shoulder in a show of platonic affection just this side of battery. His eyes are glossed over, and he smells rank in an illegal sort of way, but I'll be the last to point out that tidbit of incriminating information now that I'm feeling charitable.

"Hon, your son is here." Jackie screeches at the top of her lungs until a middle-aged man with a spare tire appears in the arched entry.

Did she just say *son*? Is she talking about Pen or me? God—maybe they're all wasted. Maybe hitting the reefer is a long-standing Christmas tradition at the Alexander household.

"Dad." Cruise heads over and gives a hug to the man he just referred to as his father.

"My half brother," Pennington whispers, and holy shit his breath stinks like the exact illegal foliage I had mentally accused him of smoking.

And what's this half-brother business?

"And here's my future daughter-in-law." Aunt Jackie's voice hits its soprano register. "This one's all Pen's." She squeezes my shoulders tight. "I bet your mother we'd hear wedding bells long before graduation." She rattles me aggressively as if shaking the idea into my head. "And I never lose a bet." Her eyes get all wide and swirly like a cartoon character's and she manages to scare the shit out of me in the process. For a minute, I'm tempted to assure her she won't lose, even though I'm positive she will.

Andrew clears his throat. "She never loses." The friendly faced genetic donation station comes over and offers me a hug. He's far less caustic than his questionably better half, although, apparently, he's friendly as hell when it comes to women and generous with his sperm to boot. "How's your mother? I haven't seen her in years." His face lights up as if he wouldn't mind launching a few genetic missiles in her direction as well.

"She's good—just coming off a divorce." I say it a little too loud like it's an academic achievement or a laudatory honor that we might be moved to toast later. Nothing like making my own mother look like a loser in front of old friends on Christmas to start the night off right.

"Sit! Sit!" Jackie squawks. "Tell me everything. How's the dorm? And don't tell me the boys are cute because you've only got eyes for my Penny boy." She belts out a laugh while falling onto the sofa.

Cruise lands on the ottoman across from me and indulges in an all-encompassing grin because he so conveniently forgot to tell me he was giving me a ride to his father's house. That seems like it would have been a relevant nugget to share—yet he held onto it presumably for the shock factor. And judging by those soulful kisses he doled out, he rather enjoys getting a rise out of me.

"Um," I start, briefly losing myself in her shiny gold ball gown, "the dorm . . . actually—"

Pennington crashes next to me and wraps an arm around my shoulder. "She's just getting settled at Russell Hall."

"Oh, hon." Aunt Jackie touches her Cheetos-stained hand to her chest. Everything about her has an out-of-this-world appeal to it, from the foil-colored dress straight out of the future right down to the I-flew-too-close-to-the-sun radiation burn she's sporting. "You gotta get yourself in Delta Delta Delta. Your mom and I were both chapter leaders. We threw the best parties." Her eyelids elongate like frosted Easter eggs as she relives the memories.

"I will. I plan to." At least I did. I totally had my sights on Tri Delta until my housing options dwindled down to survival mode. "I'll have to wait until rush."

"Rush, smush." She fans her fingers in the air. "I'll make a few calls. Russell Hall is for losers. I'll have you home with family in less than a week." She punctuates it with a slap to her thigh. "Presents!" She jumps up and claps her way around the room, slipping again. Clearly she's dipped into the brandy-laced eggnog or broken into the special brownies a wee bit early—both perhaps.

Pen leans in. "Someone hit the rum balls a little too hard." His breath rakes over me, putrid and illegal. "Speaking of hard." He glances down at the rather nonexistent bulge in his khakis. "Dude, you are fucking *hot* tonight."

I straighten and shoot a look across the room to Cruise. Andrew sits on a chair next to him, talking about purchasing gold bars and moving to the Caymans. I hope to God he plans on taking Pen with him.

Cruise steals a glance my way, and our eyes lock. My stomach melts as he secures his gaze over mine.

"Okay!" Jackie gives an impromptu tap dance that ups the discomfort in the room several notches. For her sake, I hope Santa leaves an industrial-sized bottle of Ritalin in her stocking or at least a trial pack of Xanax. "I usually don't do gifts before dinner, but since we're all here . . ." She fans the room with her wine glass and a trail of merlot splatters over the floor. "What the hell, right?" She breaks out into a cackle while mopping up the errant vino with the bottom of her skirt.

"Cruisy." She tosses a small bag at him that looks rather plain compared to the glitzy boxes adorning the potbellied tree.

Cruise dips in and pulls out a brown leather wallet. He cracks it opens and plucks out a bill.

"Ten." He flashes a smile and is quick to thank Jackie and his father for his early inheritance. I get the feeling, if Aunt

Jackie gets her way, Cruise might be staring at the sum total of his payout.

"We really weren't expecting you." Jackie places us all in that awkward situation where she makes Cruise feel like an unwanted guest. "Pen, why don't you see what Santa brought?"

Pennington unwraps a rather ornate box embossed with silver snowmen. I'm kind of hoping Santa decided to be honest and deliver Pen what he most likely asked for, a roach clip. Instead, he pulls out a large leather bag with a strap and... is that a purse?

"You could put all your stuff in there." Aunt Jackie is quick to defend her androgynous purchase. "You know, your wallet, your phone . . . your shit. It holds a ton."

God, Pen is so wasted he might actually take his mother's advice and defecate in the butter-soft pouch. And I'm pretty sure "it holds a ton" is code for "gram." It's going to house his stash. Basically, it's a stashelle.

"Thanks, Mom." He rises and gives her a quick kiss on the cheek.

I guess "Cruisy" got off easy with a rather masculine-looking billfold and some spending cash at the ready.

Jackie lands a bright-pink box with a fuzzy green bow on my lap. It's so pretty and festive I sort of want to save it for the tree Cruise and I put up today and place it beneath it.

"Let's go!" She claps up a storm prompting me to wrestle with foil that refuses to tear. Jackie is more than anxious to show off her ode to Christmas commerce. I wrangle the box open only to reveal a duplicate of the purse Pennington just unwrapped.

"I . . . love it." Truthfully, I find it odd. Maybe Jackie was simply being frugal and this was a buy-one-get-one offer she couldn't pass up.

"Couple gifts, so soon?" Cruise glides into a half smile. He looks sexy as hell seated over there all by his lonesome, and suddenly, I want to head straight back to our soon-to-be love shack and round the bases in record time.

"You can never start too soon." Jackie ticks the air with her finger. "Time to break some bread." She motions for the lot of us to follow her.

Cruise waits for me and slings an arm low around my waist.

"You didn't tell me this was your family," I whisper. And after witnessing the fragile state of their sanity I can see why the aforementioned bit of biology was omitted.

"You didn't ask." His dimples depress. "And they're sort of not."

"I thought you said your last name was Elton?"

"It is, per my mother's brilliant discretion. I think she made a good move. Don't you?"

Aunt Jackie slips back in the room and spies Cruise's strategic limb placement.

She narrows her beady little eyes at me and clears her throat. "Your future husband awaits." It comes out cold, steely.

I wink at Cruise. "I believe he does."

———

Dinner at the Alexander estate is an asylum-worthy event. First off, a dining room painted a caustic shade of red and filled with bulky black furniture looks nothing short of satanic. Whoever thought pairing gargoyles in the four corners of the ceiling with angry-looking walls was a good idea might have been a little more than bat shit. I'm betting the loon in charge of this sanitarium is my very own faux aunt Jackie.

"Please tell your mother she's welcome anytime." Andrew, the saner and slightly more promiscuous of the two parental units, gives an assertive nod. "There's always a room waiting for her at our home."

Aunt Jackie clears her throat and cuts him with a death stare, like maybe there's no room at the exorbitantly large inn after all. Something tells me if Mom were to visit, she'd be lucky to find a manger with her name on it.

"Cruise, who's the latest squeeze?" She changes the subject on a dime and reverts our attention to Cruise's most recent penile endeavors.

"Just running through the Rolodex." He leans his elbows on the table and gives a sly glance in my direction. "Currently on J."

J is for Jordan. I give a private smile.

"You oughta get yourself deloused every now and again." Jackie dispenses her medicinal counsel without request. "Crabs aren't just for cookin', you know." She passes the sentiment through her teeth like a ventriloquist. "And watch out for that killer clap that's going around," she whispers. "I hear they've got a mutated strain that can make your balls fall off in the middle of the night. I got this spray upstairs in the bathroom—"

"And on that note . . ." Andrew rattles a little golden bell before Jackie has a chance to espouse the finer points of household disinfectants and their curative properties.

An entire army of scantily clad girls marches into the room at the flick of his wrist in what appear to be provocative French maid costumes. They break out in an odd variation of pornographic dinner theater that brings a whole new meaning to *Ho, ho, ho*. Who knew a burlesque show was in the works this evening?

Two of the younger girls openly drool over Cruise, and one slightly less-informed girl with her hair in a never-ending braid flirts with Pen by way of inserting her blossoming cleavage into his face every chance she gets. Lovely.

Once the wine has a chance to flow freely from our gilded goblets, which, swear to God, look as though they've been swiped straight from the Vatican, Jackie springs to her feet with a toast.

"To love!" She christens the room. "May we all find that special someone. And, dear God, I hope it's soon because I've got some lions that need to be girded." She titters from her more than slightly misguided analogy.

Odd toast, but since she herself is toasted, I'm willing to overlook it.

Cruise lifts his chalice in my direction. "To finding someone to love."

God—what I wouldn't do for that to be him.

In a perfect world, he wouldn't be a player, and I wouldn't pretend to be a hussy-in-training—because I sort of just want Cruise.

I blink into my admission.

In a perfect world, we'd both believe in love and fall into that beautiful pool of warm water together, headfirst.

"To finding someone to love," I say without losing his gaze. "At least for one night," I whisper just to play it safe.

Too bad one night couldn't turn into forever.

Cruise

The next morning, the sky breaks through just enough to add a blue luster to the blanket of snow that fell overnight. I wake up early right along with Santa and the elves to try and gut the heater to figure out what the hell is wrong with it. But mostly, it's to ransack the house for possible gifts for Kenny. It's been a good long while since I've been moved to gift someone with something other than my body. I'd give her the expensive-as-hell perfume I bought Molly, but I had Mom wrap it and put it under the tree at the house. Molly most likely ripped into it anyway.

I glance out the window at the Beemer nestled next to my truck. Jackie made a point to gift Kenny with a car she could borrow until she got on her feet. Typical Jackie, buying people off with my father's money—with the exception of me, of course.

"Morning." Kenny comes up unexpectedly and gravels it out in my ear with a moan. She's wearing the same T-shirt as the night before. Her legs spear out, long and lean, as if they were carved from butter. An image of her sitting on top of me filters through my mind—I can see her eyes partially closed, her neck arched with pleasure.

"Merry Christmas." I follow her out to the living room and hand her a bag of ornaments from Mom's bucket-o-holiday crap.

"Merry Christmas." She gives a shy smile.

I watch as she lands the bulbs on the tree, and I try to forget about the passing pornography that just swept through my mind. Can't help it, though. She's a fantasy come to life, and she just so happens to be walking into my living room with her hair dripping wet, her face scrubbed clean, without a stitch of makeup and still managing to look like a supermodel.

My phone vibrates in my jeans, and I pluck it out to find Blair's face smirking back at me.

Shit.

I'm quick to silence it and bury it in my pocket.

My blood runs cold from the visual. I haven't heard from her in so long—not that I care. I could go forever without seeing or hearing from her ever again.

"You going to get that?" She tilts into me. "I can leave the room if you want."

"Nope. Not important." Not important? There's a first.

"So, tell me all about your family." Her pale eyes light up as she dips into the bin and picks up the star. "I feel like we're related now. Is that weird?"

"We're definitely not related." The last thing I want to be is her brother. I'm gunning for something a little more . . . what the hell am I gunning for? I pause to take her in and wonder what I might be getting myself into. I haven't had a real feeling in months. Not quite sure how to categorize Kenny yet. "You and Pen though"—I give a slight nod—"that's practically bordering on incest."

"Can you believe Jackie had the balls to get us matching purses?" She gives a soft laugh, and her boobs bounce in rhythm.

"Yup. That's Jackie in a nutshell. The woman's got balls, that's for sure."

"So, what happened? She break things up between your mom and dad?"

"Nah, they were over before Jackie ever came into the picture. He did say he had one great love, and he let her get away—he said he always regretted that one. But Jackie, she's like crap on the bottom of your shoe. Once she shows up, it's pretty hard to get rid of her. Pen is all right though. For the most part, I hardly see them."

"Was that awkward for you last night?" She pulls her lips down and looks adorable as hell in the process.

She smells good, clean like watermelon and cucumbers. Her lips are full and slightly glossed. They're calling me over to them, but I resist.

"Nope, not awkward. I had planned on stopping by anyway. Jackie's nice enough, so long as I stay out of their way the rest of the year."

"Oh." She fondles the star in her hand and her features dim, so I plug it in and it glows through her fingers like magic. "Pretty." She holds it up a moment. "Was he around for you much? You know—was he still a good dad?"

I frown, upset that Andrew's crappy parenting has the power to dampen her Christmas spirit.

"He came to a few football games when I played. Saw him at graduation. He's been hitting all the right highlights. Pen's the one that reeled him in though. He got the tossing-the-ball-in-the-backyard version and the trip to Hawaii every year for summer vacation." I don't mention the fact that I could count on one hand the number of times my dad and I spent together, or the fact that "Jackie the Jackass" made sure to make me feel excluded the few times I was around. "How about you? What's your story?" She hands me a bag of giant red bulbs. I remember these. I used to think we were leaving fake apples for Santa and that's why he outright avoided us some years.

"Well," she begins, "my mom is vying for 'serial bride' of the century. My brother and I moved a lot—seven different schools. It was hard to always be the new girl. My dad is a lawyer in Oregon, where he lives with his new and improved family. I haven't seen him since I was four—he split from my mom long before that. Rumor has it I have six siblings. They live on a farm, and his new wife makes candles. My brother is at school up there, and I guess they're speaking again. So it's just me out in the cold." She purses her lips while untangling the wire from the frosted star in her hands. "I don't care, though."

I catch her gaze and hold it. Here we are, two wounded birds bearing our souls, pretending we don't give a shit. Kenny is the princess who grew up without a father telling her she was special, that she was beautiful, that she deserved so much more than a series of one-night stands.

"You care," I whisper, wrapping my arms around her waist without waiting for an invitation.

"Maybe a little." Her lips curve as she touches the back of my neck. "But that's over. I can protect my heart now that I know better—now that I know love never works out in the end. Right?"

My heart thumps unnaturally. I believed in it once and it didn't work out in the end, but trying to satisfy my body with a revolving door of girls isn't all it's cracked up to be either.

"Let's get that star on top of the tree." I hoist her up in the air and elicit a squeal from her in the process. She starts to slip and I place my hand over her bare thigh for support. My entire body enlivens touching her this way.

"I'm afraid of heights."

"Then you'd better make it quick." I tighten my grip and sit her on my shoulder. It feels good holding Kenny, touching her like this without decimating her body in a fit of smoldering passion—although, that's pretty damn high on my wish list this Christmas.

She lands the star on top of the tree and slinks down my body as if I were a pole. Her face lands next to mine, panting from the effort.

Kenny sighs into me. Her lips bloom into a perfect smile, and for the first time in a long while, I feel like I've done something right. Suddenly, I want to be the one to tell her she's special, that she's beautiful, that she deserves so much more than a series of one-night stands.

"Yesterday, at the tree lot, you gave me a beautiful gift." I meant for it to come out playful, but it burns from my lips as if I were stepping too close to the flames. "If you don't mind, I'd like to give my gift now."

"I've been waiting for it all morning," she says in less than a whisper.

I crash my lips over hers and dive in for one luscious exchange. The warm pool of her mouth draws me in, and I fight a groan working its way out of my throat—my jeans already cinching with a surge of desire.

I can feel the dark cave of my heart beginning to glow like that star on top of the tree.

If anything, Kenny has made me believe in magic again.

The next day, Kenny and I hit the gym. My longtime friend, Cal, owns the place, so I talk him into giving her an unlimited club pass. Kenny heads off to Zumba while I hit the weight room.

"So fill me in, dude." Cal tosses a towel over his shoulder and awaits the dirty details. I've made the mistake of filling him in with tales from the mattress, far too many times.

His head is shaved, and his body is ten shades darker than his face.

"When you going to dye that bowling ball that sits on your neck to match?" I lie down on the bench and start in on a series of lifts. "Spot me, would you?"

"Bowling ball? What are you talking about?" He ducks and jives until he catches a glimpse of his ugly mug in the mirror. "I'm a fucking work of art. Three different women offered to give me a blow job just this past week."

"Yeah? How's that working out for you? Is Lauren going to stand by and oversee the situation? Make sure they're doing it right?"

"Lauren." He balks at the mere mention of his girlfriend. "She's got a stick up her ass these days. Christmas Eve was a train wreck. She full-on expected me to pull a diamond out of my dick. And when I didn't, she raised all unholy hell. Now I'm paying for it, and I've got the blue balls to prove it. Speaking of train wrecks, you hear from Blair?"

"She called. I ignored." Strange. Haven't heard from her since June and out of the blue she's called twice. Both times I've managed to have the stones not to pick up. And now, Cal's calling her name out like he's trying to conjure her ghost.

"Saw her at a party up at Herald Hall. She must have asked a million questions about you. I guess things didn't work out with that douche from Dartmouth."

"Too bad." A searing pain jolts through my chest at the thought of Blair asking about me. Kenny and those hot kisses blink through my mind. Somehow, Kenny instantly made things better. She applied the salve over my soul with her own lips—began healing what a thousand girls before her could never hope to do. "What Blair and I had is over. If you see her again, you can be the bearer of bad news. She's the one who made that decision. I'm just backing her for once."

He holds his hands in the air as if it were a stickup, and the weights come crashing to my chest.

"Dude." He hoists the heavy metal off me and secures it to the post. "You take on way more than you can chew. That's been your problem since about the third grade. So tell me about this new one—the day pass. She Zumba for you in private? When you're through, go ahead and send her my way. I have a feeling Lauren is about to hand me my walking papers."

Something about Lauren giving Cal his walking papers doesn't sit right with me. Sure, he's always had a touch of asshole in him, but that's just Cal. I thought he and Lauren were a forever kind of deal. I guess Kenny is right—love never works out in the end.

"You can't have Kenny."

His face ticks back a notch. "Dude, you keeping her?"

"I'm test driving." For every dick on the planet, if she gets her way. "She's got this crazy idea she's going to be the female version of me."

He bobs his head. "Manwhore," he says without missing a beat.

"Thanks." I sit up and catch a brunette across the room openly molesting me with her eyes, so I turn to face Cal. "Kenny wants me to teach her the ropes."

"Teach her the ropes?" He starts in on a low-lying laugh.

"She's staying at the house, so I thought we'd take it slow. She's never done anything before, and I don't plan on taking advantage of her."

"What?" He jumps back at the insanity as if I'd just yanked off my balls in a show of dedication to my newfound celibacy. "You're Cruise Fucking Elton. Fucking is your middle name— remember? You've slammed more hot chicks in one season than most men fantasize about in a lifetime. Just because you've landed yourself a nice little fuck buddy doesn't mean she's gotta ruin your mojo. You're spermanating for the both of us, remember?"

"Relax, would you?" I hiss in an effort to get him to shut the hell up. God forbid Kenny walks in and hear the words "fuck buddy" being tossed around. "She's nice. I'm not instruct- ing her in that arena. The only thing I'm teaching her is the fact that I'm the last person on earth who should be anybody's role model. There are plenty of girls who act like me out there, and believe me, she's not one of them. I'll figure out a way to get that idea as far away from her head as possible. She needs a boyfriend, not a line of frat boys leading out of her bedroom."

"That's right. Tell her to stay off your territory. Get her the hell out of the house before she interrupts the line of sorority ass you've grown accustomed to."

I shoot him a look.

"About that—I'm taking a break."

"What?" His hands collapse over his head as if I'd just dropped some oncology-based bomb that involves his testicles. "Are you shitting me? You're taking a break because of this girl? This *Kenny*—the virgin, who's pleading for your instructional services? My God, it's like you're whipped!" He freezes. "You're whipped, aren't you?"

"I'm not whipped." I tick my head back a notch. "I hardly know her." Oddly, I know Kenny better than I've known any of the girls I've bedded like some fornicating marathoner these past several months.

"We need to find a boyfriend for little Miss Day Pass." Cal leans in, solemn, as if Kenny's relationship status had the power to unravel the universe. "I'm telling you, buddy, she's a fly in the ointment, corrupting the system. Ackerman House is throwing a New Year's Eve party. It's open invite to twelve different schools. That's twelve different kinds of collegiate ass to sift through, my friend. Do not forget your mission statement— bed, don't wed."

I glance up at him and shake my head. "You really need to stop living vicariously through my dick."

"You'd better grow a pair and kick the virgin to the curb before she digs her cute little claws into your back. The next thing you know, you'll be buying her flowers." He slaps me over the shoulder and takes off. "Believe me, she's nothing but trouble."

For a second, I envision her nails digging into my back, her legs wrapped around me like a vine. I can't wait for that moment with Kenny, but the truth is, she deserves a hell of a lot better than me.

Maybe she is nothing but trouble.

Maybe she's the exact kind of trouble I've been looking for all along.

5

CURL UP AND DYE

Kendall

The week rolls on, and both Cruise and I are finding a rhythm in the house. He cooks breakfast, and I make lunch. Dinner is on the fly and usually sponsored by Johnny Burgers. Cruise mentioned he needed to help out his mom this afternoon, so I'm running errands.

Driving on snow-slicked roads feels a lot like falling in love. Although I'm totally not falling in love—I'm falling in lust. That's all that really exists in this world. Everything else is simply an illusion born of self-inflicted desire.

I'm dodging some serious traffic, thanks to an entire slew of after-Christmas sales as I make my way back from Garrison. I made the mistake of checking on the status of my imaginary dorm room only to be informed Pennington fabricated the fact that he put me on a waiting list—turns out there isn't one.

I squeeze my hands over the steering wheel and pretend it's Pennington's little red neck. Speaking of the Alexander clan—I can't believe Aunt Jackie actually said Russell Hall was for "losers." Turns out, Aunt Jackie is nothing but a bully who kicked Cruise out of his father's life so she could slather all of the financial attention on her sweet Penny boy. Little does she know Pen is nothing but a stoner with a man-purse.

I pull into the Starbucks parking lot and speed into the cheery establishment to avoid the arctic chill. Much to my surprise, none of my warm-weather clothes are capable of keeping my body a toasty ninety-eight degrees. I've got some serious shopping to do and not a whole lot of cash to do it with.

"Kendall?" A friendly female calls from the corner, and I spot Lauren and Ally waving me over. I remember them from the Alpha Sigma Phi party. They're the ones I wanted to go home with, but fate stepped in and I ended up with Cruise instead. Wait, did I just say fate? I so don't believe in that. Fate is bullshit people force-feed themselves when they're too lazy to carve out a destiny of their own.

"How's it going?" Ally chirps as I take a seat.

"It's great. I meant to find you that night at the party. I guess Pennington missed the housing deadline, and now I'm homeless."

"As in park-bench action?" Lauren's eyes widen as if I'd just introduced smallpox to the vicinity.

"No, as in Cruise Elton action. He's letting me crash at his place, but I can't mooch off him forever."

They're quick to exchange glances.

"So you're on Cruise control." Ally sinks a knowing smile. "How's that working for you?"

"I hear he's hotter in bed than a forest fire." Lauren molests her necklace at the thought of Cruise burning up the sheets.

"I hear his dick is the size of a telephone pole." Ally's eyes expand the size of dinner plates as she awaits confirmation of the supersized theory.

Lauren points at me with her banana. "Stephanie Banks slept with him a month ago and dubbed him 'king of the triple orgasm.'"

Ally sucks in a breath and her face turns colors like maybe she's experiencing one herself at the moment. "That is freaking *insane*. Melissa Warbeck says he can do things with his tongue that qualify as criminally insane."

The two of them look at me as if I'm about to verify every sexual rumor Cruise Elton ever sponsored, and add a few unbelievable new ones to the mix.

"Uh . . ." Dear God. A triple? My entire body sighs at the thought of Cruise taking me down that unknowable path, landing me in a sexual-based euphoria with his rock-hard body pressed against mine. "Actually, we haven't done anything like that, yet." *Yet?* "Technically, we haven't had a first time, either," I confess.

"Really?" Ally's lips droop with disappointment. "So what's the deal?" She flicks her layered mane until it shags out around her face.

"I asked him to instruct me in his wicked ways." A devious smile plays on my lips. "I told him I wanted to be just as sleazy as he is when I grow up and asked him to teach me the tricks of the trade."

"Which consist of?" Lauren seems nonplussed by my ability to enlist Cruise as my personal portal to promiscuity.

"I don't know. It's like my mouth started moving without my permission, and before I knew it, I was asking him to lead me through the deep, dark forest of debauchery. The truth is—I sort of wanted to, you know, be with him, but I was too embarrassed by the fact that I've never been with anyone before." I shrug as though what just flew from my lips was morally sane. "I believe I referred to it as a social experiment."

"A what?" Ally squints at me with a level of distress reserved only for degenerate social scientists such as myself.

"Don't you get it?" Lauren knocks an elbow into her. "She's a genius." She diverts her attention back to me. "You're interested in him, aren't you?"

"Maybe a little." Okay, a lot.

"And you want more than a one-night stand." She asserts.

"That would be nice." True story.

"And because you're a slow learner, he'll have to do an awful lot of tutoring." She nods into the brilliance of my plan.

"I am a slow learner." I give a wicked grin. "And practice makes perfect, right?"

"Yeah, right." Ally doesn't look too convinced of said brilliance. "But Cruise is a sexpert in the field of moral depravity. You're going to have to really wow him in order for him to keep you around. Besides, do you really want him to touch you after the resident skanks he pleasures nightly?"

"He said he'd take a break for me." And I'm not above spreading rumors of a very bad rash he might have fictitiously acquired if he doesn't stay true to his word.

They take in a simultaneous breath as if what I'd suggested held serious security infractions for our great nation.

"He's taking a break?" Lauren's mouth falls open at the prospect. "Does his dick know about this? Look, you need to forget this whole idea and find yourself a good guy—someone who'll bring you flowers and candy."

"And triple orgasms," Ally interjects as though this very feature should land near the top of the list.

"Not everyone has an orgasm the first time." Lauren peels her banana without taking her eyes off Ally. "It's physiologically impossible. Besides, she's not there yet. Can't you see, she's a blank slate?" She reverts to me. "God, you're not even going to know what to do with that telephone pole." She sticks her banana in her mouth and maneuvers it in and out like she's tapping some sexual Morse code.

"Would you stop?" Ally snatches it from her. "I refuse to watch you perform a lewd act with fruit in public." She looks to me and closes her eyes briefly. "You can't be that blank of a slate. I mean, you've seen one, right?"

"Seen one, what?" I ask. "Oh! That. No, actually I haven't. Although, I did walk in on my brother once while he was using the bathroom but—"

"Gross." Ally mock vomits.

"Get this straight, Kendall," Lauren snips. "Brothers never count."

Ally pulls me in by the wrist. "It looks like a storm trooper," she asserts.

"Crap." Lauren bats her hand away. "Don't you listen to her. She thinks everything somehow reverts back to Star Wars. It looks like this." She holds out her banana, then proceeds to take a rather deep-throat inspired bite of the phallic fruit in question.

Ally groans at the visual. "Kendall"—she scoots in—"I wouldn't worry too much about your lack of carnal knowledge. Cruise is proficient in body language. I'm sure he'll teach you everything he knows."

That's exactly what I'm afraid of and hoping for all at the same time.

A pretty blonde wrapped in a bright-red coat strides in and takes a seat at the table behind us. She observes me with a cold expression, and I look away to avoid her uncomfortable gaze.

"In fact, don't worry about a thing." Ally goes on. "Cruise Elton will be a great teacher. And when he's through with you, we'll find you the perfect boyfriend—one that speaks at least three different computer languages because God knows you don't want to get saddled with a moron."

"Three computer languages." I nod absentmindedly, but all I can think about is the fact that not one part of me wants to get rid of Cruise Elton so fast. In fact, every part of me wants to keep him. "And what if it's Cruise I want as my boyfriend?"

Lauren sprays her coffee over her shoulder.

"You can't be serious." Ally scoffs. "That's like trying to tame a wild mustang. You need to be careful or you could get yourself killed."

"I don't know . . ." Lauren touches her finger to the rim of her cup as she considers this. "It's happened before. Cruise Elton once had very serious boyfriend potential. Is that what you're shooting for?"

"Maybe I am." I squirm in my seat at the thought of taming an apparently well-endowed mustang.

"Alrighty then"—Lauren raises her coffee and inspires Ally to do the same—"here's to playing the player!"

"To playing the player," Ally sings. "In the name of triple orgasms, may you take down Cruise Elton's heart and make it your own."

"Believe me, he'll never see it coming." Lauren takes a sip of her drink.

The thought of Cruise Elton as my own personal boyfriend stuns me.

I didn't see it coming either.

The girl in the red coat cuts me a hard look and dashes out the door.

After Starbucks, I decide to fill my afternoon with exploration.

The Happy Hair and Nail Salon sits nestled in the same strip mall as Starbucks, so I head over and decide to cash in on my hair and nail jackpot sponsored by none other than Cruise's own mother.

I watch as the artisan carefully paints my nails a candy apple red while another prods, pokes, and tickles mercilessly at my feet. Secretly, I hate getting a pedi. I hate having my toes scrubbed and molested, and every time they pull out the clippers, it feels as if I were having my nails chewed off by a rabid school of fish. There's nothing appealing about someone playing with your feet—unless of course, it was Cruise at the helm of the foot fondling. Speaking of which, I should have asked Lauren and Ally if there was something special I should be doing to ready myself for my impending conjugal union—like giving myself a wax in delicate places, or soaking in rose petals for thirty days straight. Not that I plan on waiting thirty days before getting down and dirty with the boy toy in question.

Am I really trying to trick him into boyfriend-hood? I'm not, am I? Tricking someone into a relationship is the earmark of a despicable person. I'm simply attracted to Cruise and, it just so happens, not to anybody else. A part of me wants to be a player—the girl with a heart of steel who couldn't care less about who I'm "playing" with at the moment, but it just so happens he's the only one I'm interested in sharing myself with sexually. Anyway, school starts in a week, and I'll probably forget all about my hormones like I have in the past. I'm studious that way, and professors and books rarely hold much sex appeal.

After an hour of listening to foreign banter that sounds like the aggressive plucking of guitar strings, I schlep myself over to a bona fide workstation near the front of the establishment.

A frail woman with burnt, frizzy hair plucks at my locks while inspecting them with great interest. She wears a purple frilly smock that bears the name "Boppy" emblazoned across the front, complete with sparkly jewels bedazzled throughout. Her blue fingernail polish is badly chipped, revealing a gardener's manicure just beneath the nail beds, and she's sweating profusely even though it's a balmy two degrees in here.

"Virgin!" She whoops it out like a fire alarm.

My God, can she really tell by looking at my freaking hair? I sink in my seat as a half dozen women flock over and pull my mane as if I'd suddenly morphed into a one-woman petting zoo.

"Give her a shag," one cries.

"A perm, but go spiral. She's got the length," another croaks.

I'm quick to scoff at the idea. I can attest to the fact that there shall be no follicular felonies of the permanent variety committed on my person this afternoon. The women admiring my virginal tresses have obviously developed a contact high off the ammonia congesting the air. Unless this quasi-dental chair they've hiked me up in has some magical time machine properties, and we've all been transported back to 1983, there's no way in hell I'm letting a spiral perm fly.

Boppy leans in. "I'm doing highlights." The overprocessed princess seizes me as if to ward off the angry villagers. "This hair is crying for some contrast, and would you look at those eyes? They're bedroom eyes, for God's sake. She needs bangs." She shoos the other women away like unwanted pigeons. "Don't you worry, hon. I'll have every man from here to Canada trying to drag you off to bed." She snaps her gum to annunciate the point. "Let's get you under the faucet."

"Oh, um, I washed my hair this morning. I think all I really need is a little trim off the bottom." The thought of her digging her less-than-hygienic fingernails into my scalp sends a rise of vomit to the back of my throat. I lean in and whisper, "It's my first time getting my hair done." A cloud of shame settles around me for no good reason.

"Oh. My. God." She backs up clutching at her chest as if I'd deliberately set out to break some indelible girl code. "You, my friend, are in need of the works. You don't worry about a thing." She slaps a pink plastic coat over my sweater and speeds me off to the sink. "This is gonna feel better than s-e-x." She belts out a laugh as the hose spits out a firm spray of heavenly warm water over my scalp, and I moan into the experience.

Oh God, it does feel good. Like triple-your-pleasure good. Not that I would know what that feels like, but still.

Boppy masticates at rocket speed while filling me in on the finer details of her boyfriend's professional cage-fighting career until something wet and hard flies into my eye.

"Oh my God!" She plucks it off and pops it back into her mouth. "Please don't tell! I swear you can come in anytime you want for like a year, but if my boss finds out I dropped gum on another client, my ass is grass and so is my rent. Believe me, I'll make sure you don't leave here until you are *satisfied*."

Gah! Her *gum*? As in the rubber cement she's been trying to wrestle into submission? *That* gum? That's the wet glob of goo that just fell in my freaking eyeball? I'm sure there are an entire litany of diseases I'm now eligible to entertain, like mono for starters, and the mainstay of the dead and dying the world over, hepatitis. I knew I shouldn't have come to the Happy Herpes and Molest Your Nails Salon. And now, she's going to try and *satisfy* me, whatever the hell that means. I will so throw her and her refried tresses down if she even attempts to initiate a "happy ending."

"I'm fine," I assure for the thousandth time as she escorts me back to mission control. She pumps up the chair until my stomach bottoms out from the g-forces she's exerting on me.

"Don't you worry." She combs my hair down the front of my face and cuts straight across in one clean hack attack. "Walla."

Holy shit!

Did she just hack off my hair and follow it up with a "walla"? Why does it suddenly feel like I'm back in fifth grade at Becky Zuckerman's house and she's giving my hair a "little body"—code for a fucking mullet.

Boppy fiddles with a rubber band that, honest to God, she just plucked from the filth pit that is her mouth, and flexes it over my head. She backs up revealing my new unicorn-inspired ponytail sitting on top of my head as I struggle to catch my breath. Clearly, Boppy is freaking insane. Clearly, her not-so-cute moniker comes straight from the fact that someone took her to task with a baseball bat. And now my hair is reaping the grave benefits of a fractured-skull trauma.

She begins mixing bottles and solutions as if they were potions while I plot my escape from this dungeon of disaster.

"We don't want to get any of this crap anywhere it's not supposed to be," she sings, ignoring the fact that I now have a miniature erect penis sprouting from my forehead.

"Where it's not supposed to be? Like my hair?" I'm only half-joking.

"Just some chestnut highlights. Nothing more, I promise."

She spends the next leg of a decade basting my hair with what looks like glue, then proceeds to wrap it in tinsel. Any moment now I'm expecting her to tune me like a radio and dial into the mother planet. Personally, all of this wasteful use of tinfoil is making me hungry for a Ding Dong.

She spins me into the mirror, so I can appreciate the full effect of her not-so-handy work.

"Oh my God!" It flies from my lips without meaning to. My hair has ballooned out two feet in every direction and it looks as though I've donned an aluminum afro.

"Here." She opens a jar marked "avocado" and slathers a green paste liberally over my face as her final descent toward insanity plays out right here on my person. "You'll be spit shined and ready to go. New Year's Eve, here you come, baby!" She lets a couple of hearty whoops rip for added affect. "Now all you have to do is sit under these lights for a solid thirty minutes." She pulls a set of octopus tentacles off the ceiling and surrounds me with a spray of blue and red bulbs. Suddenly, it all feels a little too electric chair for my liking.

I look at myself with my muddied face, the tiny follicular penis sitting erect on the top of my head and my hair splayed out like a tinsel factory exploded. I'm betting the electric chair is a tad less humiliating.

"I'm gonna take a quick lunch break." Boppy snaps up her purse. "I'll see you in a jiff!"

She spins the chair around, presumably so I won't be moved to inflict self-harm should I gaze too long in the mirror, and I'm met with a stunningly handsome, drop-dead gorgeous, very-much-aware-of-the-fact-that-I-look-like-an-ass Cruise Elton.

Just fuck.

Cruise

Oh shit.

I should probably busy myself pretending to look at paperwork, or answer the phone for the hell of it, or just run out the fucking door because my mother's incompetent salon has just turned one of the most beautiful women on the planet into a prime example of why other females should never set foot in the establishment.

A smile twitches on my lips as her mouth opens in horror. Great. Now she thinks I'm laughing at her. I'd better go over and say something.

"Kenny?" I ask in the off chance it's another coed who's mortified to see me.

She closes her eyes, and a tiny whimper escapes her throat.

"Have I mentioned I've never been to a salon before?" she squeaks.

I can see why, but I don't say a word.

"So"—she looks around as her eyes glitter up—"tell me about school." She presses her lips together, presumably fighting off tears.

A nervous laugh beats down my chest, and it takes everything in me to suppress the crap out of it. The truth is, I'm taken by her even in the Halloween garb she's currently imprisoned in.

"I'm a graduate student," I say, pulling up a chair. "I've got my sights set on a fellowship next year, with hopes to teach at Garrison someday."

"Really?" Her eyes glow a beautiful iridescent gray and my body feels as though it's fallen through a trap door, landed in a place where it's just Kenny and me on the other side.

"Really," I say. "Either that or I'll run the bed-and-breakfast."

She licks her lips, inspecting me. "You don't happen to know any computer languages, do you?"

Computer languages? "I know some JavaScript, C++, and C, but mostly that was for programming when my solitary goal in life was to become the world's most wanted hacker. That, and trying to rob my father blind of his millions. But in my defense, I was thirteen and he said no when I asked for a new bike."

She belts out a lusty laugh, and soon, I don't see the circus around her beautiful features. All I see is Kenny and the light that shines like a beacon from her heart.

"So you know three." She relaxes for the first time. "I actually don't know any, so your father's millions are safe from me."

"How about you? What are you studying?" An animalistic wave overcomes me, and I have the urge to do her right here in the salon under the red-hot spotlights brewing from above, tinfoil and all.

"Well, I'm on the five-year plan, plus I took a year off. Outside of striking a name for myself as campus bimbo, I'll be taking up airspace in the Liberal Arts Department. In fact, I was supposed to have received my schedule this week, but I keep forgetting to check my e-mails. I'm hoping I got all the classes I wanted. Art, English 102, Finite Math, and a class on gender relations."

"Study of men and women in society?" I perk to attention.

"That's the one." She darts a freshly polished fingernail in the air, and I imagine diving the digit deep into my mouth, grazing over it with my teeth.

"Bradshaw teaches it," I say, trying to drag myself out my sexual stupor before I find myself in a *hard* situation. "He's a good guy. But he's been sick, so they've got a TA covering it." I don't tell her that I'm the TA. That I'll be structuring a syllabus for the class later this afternoon because Bradshaw had a lobe of his lung removed last month.

"I just took it because it sounded like an easy A." Her eyes flicker like mirrors in the sun. "But with a TA holding down the fort, I'm sure I won't even have to show up."

Not show up? Sounds like she might be on the fifteen-year plan.

"Oh, I'm sure he'll make you work for your grade." I blink a quick smile. "In fact, I hear he gets inventive. He really likes to personalize the syllabus for each student's individual needs." Not really, but the idea came to me, so I run with it. I think I'll get started on her syllabus right away. I might even throw in a liability waiver—a hold-harmless agreement for the more acrobatic requirements she'll need to participate in if she intends on achieving that "easy A."

A half hour later the buzzer goes off, and about twenty minutes after that, Boppy drags her tail in from her break.

"Holy shit!" she snipes while scratching to remove the tin from Kenny's hair as if she were stomping out a kitchen fire. She throws Kenny under the sink with half the foil still glued to her scalp and starts sending up a string of prayers to the patron saint of fucked-up hairstyles.

After a good span of eternity, Kenny finally makes her way to the counter, or at least I think it's Kenny. Her face is scrubbed raw, with her eyes pink and watery like someone poured in vinegar. But it's the hair where the real trauma lies.

"Oh shit," I whisper.

"Oh shit is right."

She's good and pissed and, well, incredibly irresistible, even if she does look as if she'd magically aged about fifty years. I'm pretty sure she wasn't in the market for gray streaks when she came in.

"I look like a skunk."

I make my way around the counter.

"Kenny, the city kitty." I pull her in by the fingers. "Lucky for you, I'm into older women."

Her lips quiver like she might lose it, so I do the only thing I can think of to make the two of us feel better. I cover her mouth with mine and splurge on a kiss that drives me deeper into the insanity Kenny has me wrapped in.

On New Year's Eve, Ackerman House gyrates to raucous, loud hip-hop music that manages to pulsate through every cavity in my body. Swear to God, I'm about to find the volume control and turn it down about six notches, which probably highlights the fact that at the tender age of twenty-four, I'm too old for this shit.

Mercifully, the music dies down, and the next song belts out something a little smoother which my eardrums might approve of once they stop bleeding.

"So which one?" Kenny steps in front of me while eyeing a group of football players. Two of them are engaged in a mock fistfight that has them socking one another, hard as possible.

Tonight's lesson involves approaching potential hookups. Not that Kenny will be hooking up with the goofs running around this place. My lesson is specifically designed to keep her integrity intact.

Kenny went all out in the looks department tonight with her sky-high heels and a black miniskirt that shows off her luscious limbs. I don't think I can take much more of her walking around the house half-dressed, her wet hair, her braless mornings. If she doesn't give in soon, I'll fall on my knees and beg her to have her way with me. She's got me shaking just walking past her in the hall. We've done the movie and the dinner thing, twice. I think it's time to up the ante, lie down, and see if she bites. God, I hope she bites.

"Okay, see those two guys?" I point just past the jocks.

"The cute one with the football, and the buffed-out guy in a wife beater?" She licks her well-glossed lips.

"Nope." I redirect her to the lanky pair with their pants riding high on their waists. "We're going to start with those two. I want you to get at least six different numbers tonight. That should help you break out of your shell." And keep her woman parts safe from assholes that have an unnatural obsession with pigskin and wife beaters.

She struts around to my other side, and her hourglass figure weakens my defenses. Her hair still holds the strong scent of solution from Mom trying to correct the blunder her former employee proliferated. Gone is the gray. Kenny's hair sort of morphed to dark chestnut with highlights. Mom is damn lucky Kenny doesn't sue for emotional damages. She wore a hoodie for three days straight.

"Those two?" She balks. "Are you sure?"

"I'm positive," I whisper. "Now, get a move on, young grasshopper. I'll watch from the sidelines." I nod over to the super geeks in the corner until she ventures off in that direction.

A tangle of bodies filters between us, and I can't help but notice Kenny is turning heads. Before I know it, an entire herd of vulturelike horny-as-hell jocks surrounds her. Great.

"How's the virgin?" Cal shoulders up to me and hands me a beer.

"She's in the room, ass-wipe," I reprimand, cracking it open and taking a sip. "And things are progressing slowly. I haven't scared her off yet, if that's what you mean."

"That's not what has me worried. It's the fact that she hasn't scared you off, yet. What's going on? It's New Year's fucking Eve, and you're overseeing a vestal of innocence while other guys hit on her? I'm beginning to think you've lost your touch. Take her to task in the bedroom or boot her out the door. If you don't do her, I might just have to intervene and do her for you."

"Right. I'm leaving you now." I head toward Kenny to help her navigate the sheer number of drooling idiots who have amassed around her like zombies in some B-rated horror flick.

"Hey!" A pair of familiar arms wraps themselves around me. I glance down to find a brunette with her eyes half-closed already wasted into tomorrow.

"Donna." I think.

"Amber." She flashes a toothy grin.

Or that. "Look, I'm . . ." I glance over at Kenny and her band of aspiring bedmates, as she waves from across the room. She glances at the pale limb secured around my waist, and a hurt look flashes across her face. Kenny flips her hair and pretends not to care as she turns her attention back to the cute jock.

Shit. They're flocking to her, smiling like idiots, wearing their hard-ons right on their sleeves.

"Listen, Linda, I gotta go." I pluck her arm off and head into the crowd.

"It's Amber!"

I dig through a swell of bodies and every time I think I'm getting closer to Kenny, she and her throng of boy toys drift a little farther out of reach.

"Cruise!" Lauren, Cal's questionable other half, steps up, and I lose sight of Kenny altogether. "So are the rumors true? Cruise Elton has finally settled down? I hear you're trying out a live-in girlfriend for size." She gives her signature smirk.

"Nope, just a friend."

She mouths out an O. "Look"—she glances into the throng of bodies—"I'd hate to see anybody get hurt. Why don't you do everyone involved a favor and grow a pair—either commit or cut her loose. She's not at Garrison looking for heartbreak. I know what Blair did sucked, and I totally get why you took it out on the next five hundred vaginas that were at the ready, but Kendall"—she shakes her head—"she's not the same. Go easy on her, would you?" She melts back into the crowd like an apparition.

She's right. Kendall is different.

I pan the vicinity and find Kenny perched on top of the couch while six different guys vie for her attention.

Maybe I'm the one who should be vying for her attention.

6

A LESSON IN LOVE

Kendall

The music sinks into my bones with its annoying, jarring rhythm. The constant carousel of guys parading around me, wanting to give me far more than their phone numbers, is starting to grate on my every last sexual nerve. And God knows I can't breathe with this linebacker trying to suck an artery out of my neck every few minutes.

"Excuse me," I say, clawing my way through the mass tangle of flesh.

I haven't seen Cruise in hours. It's almost New Year's, and I've spent far too long drowning in the deep end of unwanted male suitors.

"Lauren!" I spot her over by the stairwell, and she gives a brief wave.

"You really packed 'em in tonight." She wobbles on her heels. "I thought you were trying to bag Cruise?"

"Shh!" I push my finger to my mouth in a panic. God, she's wasted, and she's going to ruin everything. "I was—I am. He sent me out on a mission, then I saw him with this girl, and I got all pissy and hung out with the football team." Basketball team, too, but that's beside the point.

"I did you a favor." She shouts it all whispery—employing the secret-keeping method preferred by drunks the world over. "I told Cruise to stop dicking around." She starts in on a tittering laugh and doesn't let up until she falls into my arms from the apparent hilarity of it all.

I'd ask why in the hell she'd say that, to Cruise of all people, when I specifically enlisted him in activities that involve his honorary member, but it's clear she's completely toasted. Normally, I'd be upset, but I opt to file this misstep under drunken debauchery. Lauren's too shitfaced to realize what she's done. It's the "dicking around" that I'm most looking forward to with Cruise.

I do a quick visual sweep of the area for her presumably sober BFF, so I can lovingly pass her along.

"Where's Ally?" It'll be midnight in less than five minutes, and if I don't find my smoking-hot roommate, who knows whose lips he'll be gracing with my New Year's kiss?

"Dear God." Ally magically appears and helps me land Lauren in the stairwell. "I can't find her boyfriend." She shrugs into me. "Lauren thinks he's cheating." She leans in. "She's totally paranoid. He is so not cheating. Have you seen him? He's lucky he has Lauren."

"Right." I hope to God it wasn't Lauren's boyfriend who tried to give me a necklace of hickeys. I may or may not have accidentally kneed him in the balls to make my great escape.

"Oh look, there's Cruise." She nods behind my shoulder as her eyes swell the size of grapefruits "Never mind. Let's get Lauren to the car instead."

"Never mind what?" I try to spin around, but she secures me by the wrists. "Oh, I get it. He's with some other girl." I give one bionic pull and wrangle out of her death grip in time to see

Cruise heading in my direction sans any female appendages. I lower my chin and do my best to seduce him.

The countdown begins, and Ally jumps on the nearest jock.

"Just in time." I beam as he strides over. He gives the slight glimmer of a smile, but overall, he looks a little ticked as if some emotional altercation had just occurred. I cut a glance behind him, and a girl with strawberry blonde hair douses me with a look of venom. She sears me with a fresh brand of hatred and my stomach pinches as if I'd genuinely done something wrong.

"Three, two—one!" The crowd breaks into cheers and screams.

Cruise softens into me, molding his body to mine. He latches onto my gaze, and we meditate on one another for a brief moment. Cruise dips in with a grin. Our lips crash together in one hot, delicious kiss. His tongue maneuvers through my mouth, slow and deliberate. He holds the slight taste of beer and spearmint, and his warm, familiar cologne springs my senses to life. This was no frat boy trying to pick me up for the night. This isn't Pennington from whose touch I would repel. This is Cruise, and something about the way he kisses me, the way our bodies sway in time—it's as if we were meant to do this all along.

Happy New Year, Cruise. But I don't say it.

I don't ever want this special brand of magic to end.

Cruise races us home at speeds that exceed the sound barrier. I'm positive this measly cloth seat belt is not going to prevent me from testing the windshield once inertia insists I meet my untimely demise.

He lands us in his driveway and whisks around to my side before I can ever get out of the truck. Cruise helps me along every inch of the way as if I'd morphed into a hopeless geriatric.

I race him to the door, completely smitten with this playful side of him.

"Are you drunk?" I giggle into him as he unlocks the door. I turn on the light and bounce inside still reeling from the heavenly kiss he graced my New Year's with.

"Nope. Not drunk. I'm hopped up on something altogether different," he says as he follows me in and bolts the door behind him.

Oh God, he's thinking with his little head—and as much as I find this exciting, I'm scared to freaking death.

"Aren't you going to ask what I'm hopped up on?" He lowers his chin and approaches me with a seductive prowess I haven't seen in him before. Well, maybe that first night when I was still a prospect, but I thought I took that off the table in a roundabout way. Didn't I? Weren't we saving my deflowering for some nebulous point in the future? I was sort of hoping heart-shaped boxes and sappy greeting cards would be involved. Perhaps an "I love you," but I don't really believe in that. Do I?

"I'm pretty sure I can guess what you're hopped up on," I say, rounding out the coffee table as he hedges in on me from the other side.

"I'm pretty sure you can't." A wicked grin slides up his face. His brows dip in a sharp V, and he looks beyond gorgeous in a demented I'm-going-to-chase-you-around-the-furniture kind of way. He darts in my direction, and I retract. "Every one of those guys tonight wanted to do just this."

"Well, then, aren't you the lucky one?" I squeal as he pulls me in by the waist, landing us both on the couch.

"I guess I am the lucky one." His chest rises and falls in a dramatic fashion, and I can feel his breath gently caressing my chest.

I wonder if this is what it would feel like to be lying next to him, his body writhing over mine in a fit of passion, then nothing but the afterglow, the breathing that commences as we stare into one another's eyes.

"Kenny?" Cruise doesn't move. He simply drinks me in with those watery pools, and I melt at the sight of him.

"Yes?"

"What do you want from me?" There's earnestness in his tone that I haven't heard before, something far more honest than the playboy that resides inside him.

For a moment, I consider telling him I want only him and that I think we should get to know one another because I think we could have something special, but I chicken out. I seriously doubt happily ever after is in the cards for me or anybody else for that matter.

"Teach me how to use my body." In all of my twenty years, that single sentiment is perhaps the saddest to ever pass through my lips. Although I have no intention of prostituting my mortal instrument to every, and any, male at Garrison, those very words only seem to highlight how immune I pretend to be from love. The concept itself might be alien, sure; I may not have had the greatest examples, but something is brewing in me, and it's all for Cruise. An entire volcano of desire is percolating deep down inside me, and I only want to experience it with the wonderful person holding me right this very minute.

I gaze into him and run my finger down his cheek while his stubble tickles my flesh.

I want to tell him that I'm bubbling—ready to burst to life for the very first time—that everything is new again in this strange springtime in my heart. I'm falling, and it feels so very right.

Cruise brings my hand to his lips with a forlorn expression.

I've managed to douse all the joy he exemplified only moments before.

"Okay, Kenny." He presses a kiss born of sadness against the back of my hand. "I'll do anything you want."

I wish I could be honest with Cruise.

I wish I could be honest with myself.

Cruise

Teach me how to use my body.

I pour over Kenny in all her inordinate beauty and wonder why in God's name she would choose this path. Who hurt her so badly that she thinks nothing greater than a string of one-night stands waits for her?

I get up and start a fire before we freeze to death. The night riffles through my mind like a disorganized filing cabinet, shaking out the events in random order. Kenny and I arriving at Ackerman House, the sea of hard-ons surrounding her, then Blair showing up like some twisted nightmare. The last time we stood face-to-face was the day she declared everything I thought I knew about us null and void and asked for my blessing to move on with her new Mr. Uptight Right. Tonight she wanted to talk, to start the New Year without any bitterness. I simply told her I wasn't bitter and walked away.

It was Kenny I wanted to talk to, to be near. It was Kenny and all of her beautiful glory I wanted to surround myself with. Then her lips gave that mile-wide resplendent smile, reducing me to nothing, and I kissed her right there. I wondered if Blair was watching—if she thought it was some kind of perverse revenge kiss. A part of me was sad for her because I knew the truth. I was kissing someone special, someone I'm falling for a lot harder and stronger than I ever did for Blair.

Kenny lands on the sheepskin rug as the fire roars to life. I pull two more rugs from the corner and blanket the floor with the fleece of three dead sheep, discards from the bed-and-breakfast. Something about the irony doesn't escape me. There's definitely something dead inside both Kenny and me if we can't pinpoint love, if we can't figure out that it just might be staring us in the face. And here I was all amped up to tell her how I felt when we walked through the door, but those weren't the words she wanted to hear.

"Second lesson." I let out a quiet groan as I land beside her. She's got her top hanging so low her cleavage bulges out like perfect twin mounds.

"Second?" Her eyes sparkle like cut glass as she reclines onto her elbows.

"The kisses were first. Which, by the way, you've mastered, but I highly suggest we practice to keep your skill set high." I give a devilish grin and sweep my lips across her cheek just enough to tease her. "But tonight, we're advancing to the fine art of touch." I run my fingers up her bare thigh then slowly up her skirt until I round out the searing skin of her bottom. Her lids close partway, and her chest rises and falls in one quick motion.

"I don't know." She rolls into me. The slight curve of her mouth lets me know she approves. "What about all those phone numbers? You said get six, and I got twenty." Her teeth graze over her blood-red lips, and my jeans cinch at the crotch.

"You were trying too hard." I hold back a laugh. "Besides, other people don't count."

"No?" She watches me with that diamond vision of hers. I can feel her wanting me, trembling to have me. I want to string it out—make it hurt until she abandons her efforts at becoming anything that remotely resembles the predator I've morphed into.

She picks up my hand and rubs slow circles on my palm.

"This sounds personal," she whispers, her eyes heavy with either lust or fatigue. I'm hoping for the former.

"It should always be personal." My fingers land firm on her thigh. I run my thumb under the lip of her underwear and trace over her hip. "Take off your clothes," I whisper it like a dare.

"No." She bows into the word as if she never had any intention of doing something so vile.

"You're going to make a lousy one-night stand." I bury a kiss into her neck in lieu of a laugh.

Kenny bubbles with a string of giggles. She arches into me and I lay over her, my body conforming to hers.

"I like tonight's lesson," she murmurs in my ear. "Touching."

I sit up and pull off my shirt, leaving my arms extended for a moment while she rakes me with her eyes.

"All right." I slip back over her and dot a row of kisses straight down her chest, stopping just shy of burying myself in her cleavage. I've envisioned at least a thousand times what that would feel like, lost in the soft pillow of her flesh. Kenny has me shaking with a hard-on ready to rip from my jeans. "Next lesson will be conducted with considerably less clothing. And believe me, you have nothing to be shy about."

"Neither do you." She runs her fingers over my shoulder, soft and unsure.

I gently take her hand and run it down my chest, never breaking our gaze. Kenny interlaces our fingers. She closes her eyes as I pull her lower, inch by inch, until we crest the hard ridge in my pants and she gives a soft moan. Her hand escapes mine, and she cups me over my jeans. *Dear lord, yes.* She lets her fingers glide over me soft and achingly sweet. I glide my hands under her sweater, and I slip them over her breasts, feel the lace of her bra, and trace out her hard nipples underneath.

Kenny pulls me in and crashes her lips over mine. Her mouth is ripe with the taste of strawberries as she delivers her sweet, juicy kisses. Her tongue strokes over mine, slow and easy, as if we had already logged a decade of doing exactly this. I could spend an eternity holding Kenny, her lips and body welded to mine. Her cool hands slip into the back of my jeans and dip into my boxers. Kenny relaxes her fingers over me and gives a gentle squeeze. It takes everything in me not to move her hand around to the front, introduce her to the physical part of me that craves her most. Her bra unhooks beneath my fingers, and I move my heated hands over her bare stomach until I feel her quiver beneath me. I glance down at her beautiful face. Her lids are closed and she licks her lips in anticipation as I cup her breasts full with both hands.

Kenny takes in a sharp breath and bucks beneath me. Her lids flutter with ecstasy as if this simple act of loving her made her dizzy.

I lay my lips over hers as we indulge in a spastic war of limbs. Kenny tastes and feels as if she were made just for me.

Kenny is stabbing at my heart with her being—molding herself over my existence.

Something amazing is happening—something meaningful and real.

Monday afternoon, Cal and I run side by side on the treadmill in the overcrowded equipment room. Every person on the planet has meandered into the gym today, trying to work off that extra slice of holiday pie. A couple of girls across from us have all but resorted to smoke signals to let us know they're interested, and for the first time in a long while, there isn't anything in me that's up for a hot and sweaty quickie at the gym. Now, if it were Kenny initiating the offer, I'd take her right here in the middle of the room, with an audience, if she wanted.

"Kenny thinks 'touch' should act as an extended lesson." I marvel at my dumb luck. "But for whatever reason, she's still hell-bent on continuing with her experiment," I say out of breath, trying not to shout too loud should the girls across the way be moved to eavesdrop. I wouldn't put it past Blair to set her eyes and ears in my midst.

"Touch, huh? Maybe she could give some pointers to Lauren. Can you believe she thinks I was cheating on her New Year's Eve?"

"You tell her you were with me?" I flinch at the thought. After I saw Kenny surrounded like a pageant queen on parade, I hauled ass outside for a pity party and ended up confessing to Cal that I had more than a few feelings rolling around for Kenny—that surprisingly, they weren't solely tied to my balls' incessant urge to release some pressure. I used the L word for the first time in a good long while, out loud, and not even my own ears could fucking believe it—still not sure I do.

"Yeah, I told her I was with you." He catches the worried look on my face. "Relax, I didn't rattle off any of that bullshit you were shoveling." He wipes down his forehead with the towel draped around his neck. "I thought you swore off love and traded it in for, I believe the quote was, 'quick and dirty ass.'"

I try to shake the accuracy of his words out of my head. "I thought so, too. Don't worry. You're not the only one who's disappointed in me." I don't tell him that I saw Blair at Ackerman House—that she wanted to talk, that I essentially blew her off and fused my lips to Kenny instead. I don't want to drag Blair into every conversation. I want her and the ghost of who we were hidden in the back of the closet. I wish I could burn it down, torch every memory we ever made. And now, here she is, showing up just when things are shaping up in my life. Figures. She probably doesn't feel she did enough damage the first time around.

I drain the rest of my water and end up spilling the reserve down my chest.

"Watch the equipment, buddy. That's a three thousand dollar machine you're desecrating. You think getting your heart ripped out of your ass hurt like hell, wait until I come after you for restitution. How's the bed-and-breakfast going? Business mistreating you much these days?"

A groan escapes my throat at the mere mention of that money pit. "I handed the reins back to my mom last summer when I ditched my sanity. I should swing by and glance at the books."

"Wear safety goggles. Those books have a way of trying to knock you out. I should know. Hey, school starts tomorrow. You ready to begin instructional duties?"

"Yup. Already found my favorite student."

"No way."

"Yes," I say, exhilarated by the thought. "Wrote up a syllabus just for her."

"I bet you did. You fucking perv." He says it with a marked sense of pride.

"I wouldn't have it any other way."

Pennington struts in with his thin frame puffed out, his glazed expression that lets me know he's already high as a kite at this early hour.

"I bet he rolls his joints with your daddy's Benjamins." Cal spits out exactly what I was thinking, and I give a little laugh. Then an idea comes to me.

7

THE DATE

Kendall

After Zumba, my limbs rebel and quietly petition to secede from the union of my torso. Okay, not so quietly. Every muscle in my body is on fire and rioting in protest to my sudden faux interest in fitness. I hit Starbucks afterward as a show of affection to my poor earthly frame. I thought about asking Cruise to join me on my quest for the perfect cup of Joe, but I'd hate for him to think I'm clingy and needy. The last thing I want him to feel around me is like he can't breathe. But God, how I'd love to smother him—preferably with my chest.

Snow covers the ground in smooth, sparkling sheets, a visual treat that I'm in no way prepared for. It's as if the landscape of my heart had magically transformed into a fairy tale much like this new world I've touched down in. Cruise is the sparkling magic. He's adhered himself to that secret place inside me that I once denied existed. He's molded himself perfectly over my heart, my soul, my marrow. And now I can never let go. How will I ever tell him the truth? That I don't want twenty boys on speed dial—that I only want one. And that he just so happens to be the one in question.

Carrington County glows a resplendent shade of lavender, dressed in a winter wonderland that, up until now, I had only seen in movies. I don't know what possessed my mother to pack up on a whim and move clear across country—trade paradise for smog and traffic. The fact that my grandmother passed away around the same time she graduated might have played into it, but still, now that I see how nice everyone is here and how stunning the scenery is, I never want to go back to California. Although, I guess if she didn't hit the West Coast, she would never have met "the loser surfer" she hooked up with and spawned my brother and me.

I glance inside Starbucks and the line looks incredibly long, but I venture in anyway. The thick scent of roasted coffee lights up my senses. God, I love this smell. If this out-of-body experience I've been enjoying with Cruise had a fragrance, this would definitely be it. They should have a coffee named after him— Kisses with Cruise. I'd drink it down by the pitcher—get on my knees and let them pour it down my throat with a beer bong.

A group of cackling girls walks in behind me, and I'm quick to secure a place in line. I glance over the counter and don't see any sign of Lauren or Ally. Honestly, I can't remember which one works here.

I hope Lauren's okay. Last I saw her, she looked heartbroken over the idea her boyfriend might be cheating.

A vision of Cruise with that girl in the thigh-highs he almost took home that first night shoots through me, and a wild pang of jealousy cinches my stomach. Just the thought of him touching her, his oven-hot hands searing over her flesh the way they did mine makes my heart drop like a stone.

I shake the thought away and distract myself by counting the people ahead of me. If they each take five minutes, then I'll safely be here a solid hour.

"Next!" a friendly voice calls from over the counter, and Ally waves at me. The line moves briskly now that two baristas are at the helm, and I'm at the counter in less than ten minutes. "How's it going?"

"Great. I can't get over how gorgeous the world looks covered with snow." I dig out my wallet. "Venti iced mocha."

"Iced, huh? You really are from California." She leans in. "Hey, that girl in the corner over there . . ." I follow her gaze to the back, where a teenage girl sits. She has a tissue pushed into her face, and it looks as if she can't stop crying. "That's Cruise's sister, Molly," she whispers. "Maybe you can see what's got her so broken up. She's been sobbing for the last half hour."

I take in a breath at the sight of her. "Oh, I totally will. I know how it feels to be crapped on by kids at school. I bet she's dealing with some serious bullying issues. High school is nothing but a hotbed of bitches."

Ally belts out a laugh. "I'll catch you at school tomorrow, where there will be very few bitches, I promise." She writes something down on a napkin and slides it toward me. "Call me when you're free, and we'll get together."

It takes another few minutes for my coffee, and all the while, I inspect Molly from afar. She's stunning with her dark blonde hair, her pale, smooth skin—gorgeous doe eyes. My heart breaks seeing her back shudder as she sheds her not-so-silent tears.

I take up my drink and make my way over, nervous at the prospect of crashing her tearfest but totally dying to meet her and, hopefully, make her feel better.

"You mind?" I point down at the empty seat beside her— half-afraid she'll bolt now that I'm here.

"Nope." She moans and drops the wad of tissues to the table like she's making a statement. Her heavy-scented perfume creates a toxic cloud in the vicinity, sandalwood mixed with unripe fruit. Maybe it's not people upsetting her. Maybe it's the fragrance offense that she's committing.

"I'm Kendall," I offer. "I'm actually staying with your brother." She looks much prettier up close, and here I thought that was impossible. "Is everything okay?"

"Brayden Holmes is a dick." She announces it like a fact, and her cheeks depress with an impression of a smile.

"Boy trouble." I say it mostly to myself. If it were pissy girls I could've given her sound advice, all of which I've thought long and hard about, but never truly implemented. But people with hanging appendages are involved, and seeing that I've never handed my heart to anyone on a silver platter, I don't have the first clue how to help her.

"It's over, so there's really not a problem." She spits it out with a viral level of angst reserved for high school girls the world over. And judging by her visceral reaction, it is *so* not over.

"Can I ask what happened?" I can't help but feel I've just dived in over my head. She probably caught him looking at someone, and now she's heartbroken.

"He tricked me into sleeping with him, then dumped me for some slut named Tracy Schaffer."

"Holy shit!" I bounce back in my seat. "We need to tell Cruise. He needs to beat the living crap out this... this... Brayden person." I'm panicked at the thought of someone taking advantage of his little sister like that. And I had no idea we were going all the way in our conversation or I may have opted to forgo the meet and greet for another time, like after she clawed Brayden's eyes out and was staring down the barrel of a prison sentence. No wait. Preventative measures need to be taken to ensure neither she nor Cruise lands behind bars. Once cooler heads prevail, I'm sure we'll think up a way to inflict bodily harm to the jackass without leaving forensic evidence behind.

She snatches my wrist so quickly she nearly knocks my coffee off the table. "There's no way in hell we're telling Cruise anything." She grits it through her teeth. "He'll know what a loser I am, and then he'll tell my mom, and they'll both kill me." She heaves into a spontaneous sob, and for a second, I wonder if it's all an act.

"Of course they're not going to kill you." *They are so going to kill her.* "Did you use protection?"

"I'm on the pill." Her eyes enlarge as I writhe in front of her.

"You're on the pill?" I'm horrified by this. There's no way I'm going to be able to keep all these secrets from Cruise.

"Yup. In fact, I just ran out. You think you can give me a ride to the free clinic? It's all the way downtown, and I'll probably freeze if I try to hoof it."

"I . . ." Fuck. Should I be giving her a ride? "I guess."

I hope to God it's me Cruise doesn't kill.

———

The Carrington Free Clinic is situated in the seediest part of the downtown district. Two derelicts seek shelter in the alcove of the entry, and one of them has decided to spell his name on the wall with a creative spray of urine. I'm quick to usher Molly through—ready and willing to implement my ninja moves should he decide to get creative in other ways with the disgusting hose in question.

We land inside and I let go of a breath I didn't know I was holding.

The interior is a dingy gray, the color of dead skin. A row of plants on the counter has wilted to yellow wisps as the sick and the desperate for birth control gather en masse in the tiny petri dish of a room. I'm sure sixteen different strains of the flu are merging in our lungs as we step deeper into the hotbed of infestation.

Molly yanks me in by the jacket. "Are you sleeping with my brother?" she asks, almost as an afterthought.

"No." I pull my arm back. Grabby little thing. "Molly, you don't have to sleep with boys to have a relationship with them." That doesn't change the fact that I've made it my singular goal in life to bed Cruise Elton ten different ways before Valentine's Day. That's a personal ambition I don't plan to make public anytime soon, especially not to his seventeen-year-old sister. "Sex isn't a sport."

A hurt look sweeps across her face. "I do it 'cause I like it." She struts over to the front desk fueled with anger and attitude.

I pull up behind her as she writes her name down on the roster.

"Did you like the public boo-hoo fest you held in Starbucks?" I ask. "Because in case you haven't figured it out, the asshole at point A led to the bawling at point B." Maybe not the kindest tactic I could have employed, but something tells me Molly here isn't the dainty flower she wants me to believe she is.

She wrinkles her nose. "Look, I like Brayden. He's special." She rolls her eyes like he's really not. "This thing he has with Tracy Tramp-Stamp Schaffer will blow over. It always does."

"Oh my God, he's done this before?" I take in her watery blue eyes. Her chin is trembling like she might lose it right here in front of an entire waiting room of people infected with sore throats and STDs. Molly doesn't say a word; she just stalks off and takes a seat in the back.

"Ma'am, would you mind signing in?" The gal behind the counter holds out a pen. "There's a line forming behind you."

"Oh." I glance back at the angry mob waiting to accost me if I don't move out of the way.

The pill? Should I be on the pill? Cruise and those heady kisses spiral through me, and I'm numb just thinking about them. Yes, I should very much be on the pill. I jot my name on the roster and find a seat next to Molly.

My phone buzzes in my pocket. It's a text from a number I don't recognize.

Cruise here - set up a double date for tonight at seven. That OK?

Double date? Everything in me warms at the thought of officially dating Cruise. For sure, I made the right decision to get on the pill.

I text back. **Better than OK!**

I can't wait to take my relationship with Cruise to the next level. And dating, well, I guess that throws my experiment out the window. I'm totally fine with that. I didn't really like lying to him to begin with.

"So what do you think of my brother's deformity?" Molly smirks before relaxing into an exaggerated sad puppy face. She's a peach, this one.

"What deformity?" If Cruise is deformed, every man on this planet should be so lucky.

"You mean he didn't tell you about his accident?"

"What accident?" A rush of heat explodes in my chest at the thought of anything happening to Cruise—past or present.

"He got his balls lopped off after eating it on a motorcycle when he was sixteen. Don't worry, they saved one on ice and re-attached it. He can have kids and stuff one day when he's ready to pollute the world with his seed. Too bad it chopped his dick in half, though. Horrible disaster." She clicks her tongue to an-nunciate her false sense of pity.

The memory of that bulge in his jeans comes to mind, and my face floods with heat. God, if that was half, he must have been the size of a snake. I swear it was as long as my arm, and I thought *that* was a deformity. Not that I believe one word out of his little sister's not-so-precious mouth.

The only horrible disaster around here is Molly needing to be on the pill in the first place.

                    ⌒

The nurse calls Molly and me to the back at the same time, and we each get stowed away in our own closet-like rooms. I take off my clothes and ready myself for a checkup. I secretly hate the gynecologist. I hate having myself spread-eagle in the name of medicine and vaginal well-being.

I lie back and examine the photos of some bodybuilder strewn across the wall. They're all signed and everything. His frame looks freakishly large, and the muscles bulge from his body like a cloud made of flesh, as if someone had blown them up like balloons. I try to imagine him lying over me, crushing me with his truck-like weight.

Rumor has it, pumping their muscles up like that is lethal to the size of their joystick.

A gentle knock erupts as the door slides open, and a tall, handsome man with a fake bake comes in flashing an ultrabright smile. He's completely buffed out. His muscles balloon from his shirt, and I can practically make out the curves from under his coat, and hey, it's the same guy from the pictures.

"Is that you?" I marvel, pointing at the testament to all things steroid.

"That's me." He gives a chuckle while reading over my chart. "Precautionary." He nods. "Usually, girls wait until they've had many sexual encounters under their belt before wising up and taking it upon themselves to get on the pill." He looks up and blinks a smile. "They're not smart like you." A goth-looking nursing assistant pops into the room and gives a little sneer. "We can start now," he says, motioning for me to lie down. "Go ahead and slide to the end of the table. Put your feet in the stirrups."

"What? Where's the doctor?" I cinch up my legs until my knees meld together.

His features smooth out. "I'm the doctor, Kendall." He taps his nametag, which proudly boasts, Dr. Gaines.

"I want another one!" I sit up in a panic. "I usually have a woman." I've *only* had a woman gynecologist. In fact, I didn't even know it was legal not to. What the hell kind of health care practices do they have in Massachusetts anyway?

"I'm the only one on staff today," he says with a peaceable smile.

Shit! What have I done to Molly? Hopefully, she ran screaming and didn't let some body builder parading around as a doctor examine her. God, Cruise is going to hate me after this and most likely have me arrested.

"We're really busy today." He gives a little wink. "I promise to be gentle."

A wink? Really? Is that what they teach male doctors in med school? Or maybe it was the wrestling ring. He snaps on a pair of rubber gloves, and I slip my feet into the frozen stirrups, dying to get this over with.

Think of Cruise, I tell myself. Think how amazing it will be to finally have his one-balled, half-penised body inside me.

I let out a string of involuntary giggles no thanks to Molly and the exceptional bullshit she tried feeding me. Forget Cruise, I'm going to kill Molly for planting such phenomenal crap in my mind. Of course, she was lying. Right?

Afterward, I get dressed, and Sally from *The Nightmare Before I Lose My Virginity* leads me to a room down the hall.

"We're briefing all the first-timers." She gravels it out like a threat. "This will take about twenty seconds."

The small office is crammed with six other girls, and holy shit—one of them happens to be Molly.

I speed on over.

"I thought you said this was a refill," I hiss.

"I never said those words. I said, I 'ran out.'" She pinches a smile, and her dark brows peak in a malevolent manner.

"Ran out of what?"

"Patience." She spits it in my face.

I take in a breath, shaking at the thought of being tricked into getting her on the pill of all things.

"Patience? I've run out of exactly that," I warn her.

We sit through a quick debriefing, but I'm so hopped up on my newfound insanity I don't hear a word they say. Afterward, I practically drag her out into the blizzard-like conditions, so I can drill her a new one in peace.

"What the hell was that about?" I ask as she makes her way to the passenger's side of the car.

I unlock it, and we get in.

She dusts the snow off her sleeves before answering. "Look, I owe you one. Okay?" She shakes her head as though I should be grateful for her divisive services.

We drive home through stunted silence. I'm sure Molly is secretly doing the happy dance at what a live idiot I am—and I can't think straight to formulate two words because she happens to be right.

I drop her off at the entrance to the bed-and-breakfast.

"Molly?" I call to her just as she's ready to slam the door.

"Yes?" She gives a sweet smile, looking all of twelve in the process.

"Do yourself a favor—wait for someone special. Trust me, he's not roaming the halls of your high school. And if he were, he wouldn't be sleeping with some girl named Tracy, or Stacy, or anybody else. He'd only have eyes for you. Don't give away something you can never get back, save it for someone you love and who really loves you, too."

Molly sighs, expelling an entire plume of breath from her lips.

"Yeah, whatever." She slams the door with a marked finality and runs toward the glorified hotel.

If I didn't know better, I'd swear I was starting to believe in something that just a month ago I would have bet was nothing but a myth.

Love.

I guess it really does exist.

Yeah, whatever.

Cruise

The snow bears down on us as we make our way into the Cineplex 10, where our respective dates are waiting. Kenny looks hotter than hell in her denim jacket, skinny jeans, and heels, but unfortunately, judging by her blue limbs and purple lips, she's about to turn into the world's cutest Popsicle. I did happen to notice she's lacking in the winter-coat department. If I didn't need every dime to eat I'd help her out. Might just do that, anyway.

"So who's Pen bringing?" She glows as she looks up at me.

A cold chill tingles through my spine at the idea that Kenny thinks she's my date.

Before I can rectify the situation, Pennington speeds in this direction with Monique hot on his heels. Her hair flows down her back like a flame, and she's wearing those thigh-highs she's famous for. I've seen her in them a couple times with nothing else but a smile.

Shit.

"Oh my gawd!" Monique lunges at me with a running start and hikes her legs around my hips. She leaves me physically spinning, already dry humping me in the foyer of the theater. "I have missed you!" She pokes her finger in my stomach before dipping down to my crotch. "But I've missed *you* even more," she sings.

"Whoa!" I set her down, almost afraid to glance at Kenny. Her lids hang low. I can't tell if she's pissed or about to cry. She wraps an arm around Pennington, and it's only then I notice they've both accessorized with their matching purses. Something about it rubs me the wrong way, even if it was accidental.

"I guess it's me and you, Pen." She says it sultrily, like she means it, and begins to nibble on his ear. Her teeth graze over his earlobe, and she cuts me a glance before moaning into the endeavor.

My stomach clenches just witnessing the unholy encounter. That should be *my* fucking ear.

Shit. This isn't going as planned. And what the hell did I plan anyway? Driving her wild with jealousy so she could hone in on any feelings she might have for me? And now Pen and his extracurricular cartilage are getting all the attention.

"Let's do it." I pull Monique in by the shoulder and lead us over to the ticket counter.

We all agree on a horror movie, *The Damned and the Restless.* I suppose I'm the damned tonight for shoving a perfectly good Kendall Jordan in my horny little bro's direction. Monique would be the restless in this equation since she's already felt up my crotch a half a dozen times, no matter how hard I try to evade her efforts.

"I'm buying." Pennington volunteers like it's some heroic effort on his part. Nothing like being financially emasculated by Pen to further toss the night into the crapper.

Kenny looks over her shoulder at Monique and outright scowls. For a second I think the claws are going to show, but Kenny reverts and twitches out a charitable smile.

Do I detect that Kendall Jordan is, dare I say, jealous? My adrenaline kicks in at the prospect. I sling an arm over Monique's shoulder, inspiring her to snuggle in deeper. I believe this is feeding in beautifully to my original misguided intentions. And, since we've already met up with the green-eyed monster before getting out the gate, I'd say the evening is off to a pretty damn good start. I'm hoping at the end of the covetous rainbow lays a pot of golden affection. And right now there's nothing more I want than Kendall Jordan's affection.

I gaze into Monique and moan. "Popcorn?" I'd hate for Kenny to miss the real show, the one in which I accidentally drive her into my arms. I jab an elbow into Kenny. "What about you? I'll spring."

Her perfect pink mouth falls open as she takes in the body slinked around mine.

"Pennington, what do you think?" she asks, latching onto him with her long slender arms as my insides explode into a ball of acid.

"For you?" He slips his hand around her waist far below her hip, and I see her fidget, trying to keep him from hitting pay dirt. "I'd buy the left side of the menu if you wanted." He dots the sentiment by planting a kiss in her ear.

Who the hell kisses someone in the ear? Idiot.

Pen loads us all up on enough junk food to proficiently rot the teeth out of our skulls before the movie's over. I specifically told him I didn't want any. The last thing I want is to look like a charity case, but I end up hauling all the crap to the theater.

Kenny leans into Monique. "You guys mind if we sit by you?"

My heart thumps a little faster at the idea of Kenny wanting to sit together.

"We can trade Gummy Bears and Sour Patch Kids." Kenny nods at the python currently strapped to my hip as if this confection-based currency were the sole purpose of securing proximal seating arrangements. And sadly, it very well could be.

I lead us over to the middle right, my usual landing place. I don't care what anybody says, it's the best place to see a movie. I let Pen slide in first, then Kenny, and I'm quick to file in after her.

First of all, I'm not that into horror flicks. If I really want to scare the crap out of myself, I'll consult the file marked student loans. I nearly shit a brick the last time I looked at the running total.

Monique dips her hand under my shirt and slips those icicles she calls fingers inside. There's nothing wrong with Monique. In fact, she happened to be at the gym and overheard the conversation when I was setting things up with Pen. She practically volunteered to be my date. I've slept with her at least twice, although the details are fuzzy. All I remember is her hair falling in my eyes while she rode me like a stallion.

The theater dims to pitch and I envision Kenny riding me like that—her long, glossy mane whipping me softly.

I move my jacket over my jeans in case my spontaneous salute to Kenny decides to cause a scene.

I look over and note she's stealing sideways glances every chance she gets. Monique's hand flops like a fish over my leg until it bounces onto my crotch, and I shift away in the event that she feels inspired to help me release a little tension. I don't need much deliberation to know I'm not going there again with Monique, tonight or any other night.

Kenny cinches her lips and slides toward Pen. His hand slithers over her shoulder, landing square over her tit like a freaking missile shield.

Crap.

My breathing grows erratic by the minute because I'm about to beat the shit out of my brother for feeling up my girlfriend.

Did I just call Kenny my girlfriend?

First I'm talking love, and now I'm on the brink of some romantic commitment? I glance over at Monique—the lust-driven look in her eyes, her legs already parting with the invitation. I could have her if I want to. I'm sure there's an empty corner or bathroom stall just waiting for the two of us. It's obvious she'd be more than up for the challenge. But nothing in me wants to play that game again. It was empty, shallow, and made me feel like I was falling down a bottomless pit with no comfort, no rest, and for damn sure nothing a box of condoms could cure.

The movie drones on and Monique begins gnawing at my ear, inspiring me to deflect her efforts. I have no clue what the hell is going on with the movie because all I keep thinking about is how the fuck long Pen is going to act like some human boob warmer.

Kenny looks over at me and catches my gaze. She glances down and makes a face at the vile limb in question until she delicately removes it from her person. I give a little smile as my entire body exhales with relief.

Monique dives her hand between my legs. I'd better douse this fire before Kenny tries to one up us in the movie-make-out department and turns this into some kind of copulation relay.

"You mind?" I say it nice enough, but there's never a good way to tell someone to stop trying to have sex with you.

Kenny leans toward me, and I shift in her direction until our shoulders rest up against each other. I drop my hand low, hoping she'll do the same. Her fingers brush up against mine until they slowly interlace, and my heart races like a sixteen-year-old about to get lucky at prom. Holding hands in a dark theater with Kenny outweighs every public sex act I've ever committed. This is gratifying, satisfying, and intensely erotic all on its own.

I'm in love with Kenny.

There it is.

I've broken the worst promise I've ever made to myself, to never fall in love again. But Kenny is definitely no Blair. She's a million times better. For once, I'm thankful things ended the way they did for me last summer, or I wouldn't be sitting here holding hands with the only girl on the planet I want to be with.

She gives my hand a squeeze and rubs tiny circles over the top with the warm pad of her thumb.

Kenny Jordan is by my side, and all is right with the world.

If I didn't know better, I'd think she was starting to have feelings for me, too.

8

THE SYLLABUS

Kendall

Early Tuesday morning, on what will officially be my first day at Garrison, I pull back the curtain and catch a glimpse of the dark, angry sky. The brooding clouds, all dressed up and nowhere to go, lie stagnant overhead like a layer of black coals. The evergreens stretch their branches toward heaven in hopes of bursting the pregnant sacks, but are impotent to the challenge; and the earth remains dry, thirsty for something that might never come.

The sun has no hope in a place like this. I'm not sure I can get used to a world without sunshine, but the snow, the friendly footprints of the birds and squirrels stamped throughout the roadside, more than make up for the lack of sun. Then there's Cruise. The way his smile widens when he sees me, those brilliant flashing teeth that would make pearls ashamed of their color, the five-o'clock shadow affording him that perennial bad-boy look. He reduces me to dust and ashes without even trying. There's no doubt Cruise Elton is unforgivably sexy. How I long for him to be mine. How thirsty I am for his body and soul to want me the way I desperately want him. I wonder if that shower of affection will ever come. If it will ever be genuine or just some lesson on how to score a home run.

The double-dating debacle runs through my mind. I'm such an idiot for thinking Cruise would ever want to be my date. But he sort of was in the end, and that's all that matters. I can still feel his fingers relaxing over mine, warming me with his palm, the current that ran through us, alive and anxious. Cruise and his affection seem as innocent as a downed power line thrashing in a pool of water. Loving Cruise will only hurt in the end, cause irreparable damage if I'm not careful. But I'm not all that interested in being careful anymore.

I walk out of the room and find a note on the kitchen table. "Have an early meeting. See you in class."

I'm pretty sure he meant at school. I doubt I have any classes with a graduate student.

I rush through my morning routine and put on the warmest clothes possible. It looks like a nuclear winter out there. God, I hope those classrooms at Garrison have the heaters turned up full throttle.

I step outside and the icy wind knifes through all four layers of clothing like a sickle hacking through weeds. My skin enlivens from the blowtorch effect. This is what I imagined love would be like, the beauty of the landscape luring you in then the surprise of the flames as you burn under the guise of your own foolishness.

And, as foolish as it sounds, I wish Cruise would step into that fire with me. God knows I'm looking forward to the burn.

I'd do anything to melt with Cruise.

Garrison University is a superhighway of bicycles, bodies, and brick buildings as tall and ornate as cathedrals. A tower sits in the center, erect, proud, and, well, in every way a monument to all things phallic. A giant metal-framed globe sits on top, declaring it the tallest structure on campus. I gaze at it an inordinate amount of time and wonder how frightening it would feel to be perched on top of its skeletal frame, how fragile the world would look from that vantage point.

I move through the crowd and soak in the people, the luxurious landscape that puts to shame the tiny junior college I went to back home. The stone benches with students sitting beneath the trees, expensively dressed girls with tall leather boots, warm wool coats, and supple leather handbags. I keep forgetting most everyone at Garrison is a child of privilege, save for the few like me who managed to score a scholarship. But I'm here. I've escaped the soup kitchen that was my mother's home, the dreadful beat-box neighborhood where she landed us time after time. And now, Morgan and I are both quasi-independent, freeing my mother of the lead shoes we had been for the better half of two decades. Here I am at Garrison, officially on my own. It feels as if the next step I take will usher me over the threshold into adulthood.

I love it here. I can finally breathe.

Then there's Cruise, who perhaps is the best thing Garrison, Carrington County, and Massachusetts as a whole have going for them, at least in my eyes. Everything in me soars at the prospect of seeing Cruise today, as if living together could never be enough.

Bodies begin to thin out, and the bicycles whirl by more spastic than before, so I hustle over to the liberal arts building for my first class of the day, Gender Relations. I hike my way to the second floor of an overbright building. Everything looks new and immaculate inside with its glossy white walls and floors to match. The walls are devoid of the graffiti and informational posters I've grown accustomed to at my last school. The hint of fresh paint lingers in the air—the scent of pine cleaner layered just beneath that.

Room 228A. This is it.

I peer inside. It's nearly full with row after row of students crammed behind tiny desks, the same ones they had at my old JC. I'm not sure why this surprises me.

A girl swoops inside, and I slide in after her, taking the only other seat available, in the second row. I hate sitting anywhere near the front. It's the not-so-fun zone, because everybody knows your odds of getting called on go up astronomically. My backpack hardly fits at my feet, and I find this more than slightly irritating. For some reason I thought the forty-thousand-dollar price difference would add some square footage to my seating area.

The professor stands with his back to the class. He's tall, dressed in a tweed jacket and brown cords—looks nice enough. He busies himself writing something on the chalkboard. Chalk. For sure I thought they'd have those interactive whiteboards gracing this institution of overpriced learning. My mother used to joke that you could replace the S in Garrison with a dollar sign. It's nothing but the best at Garrison, she would chime. But even my JC had the slightly more appealing whiteboards to tool around on.

The professor remains diligent in his primitive communication endeavor as a trail of dust snows down from his fingertips. God, he looks gorgeous from behind. He sort of reminds me of Cruise the way his hair narrows to his neck in neat waves. In fact, the way he just jerked his shoulder reminds me of a muscular twitch I've seen Cruise demonstrate on more than one occasion. I would know. I've been watching Cruise Elton like a freaking hawk these past three weeks. I've memorized his nuances, studied them like it were a new field in science; his breathing pattern could keep me mesmerized for years.

He turns around and inventories the population until he lands right on me with that killer smile.

A breath gets caught in my throat.

Shit!

It *is* Cruise!

I straighten in my seat, completely caught off guard by the fact that I've been secretly devising a plan to sleep with faculty. It feels innately dirty and oh so delicious all at the same time. I give a private wave before sinking in my seat a little.

"Love." He steps away from the blackboard and reveals the word scrawled out in large block letters. "Welcome to Gender Relations. Professor Bradshaw is out indefinitely, and until he's able to reprise his role I'll be stepping in. You can call me Cruise, or Mr. Elton, if you feel so moved." He glances up at me and the curve of a wicked smile ignites. "Master, if you like."

Half the girls in class have a Cruise-gasm at the innuendo.

A thin girl with a razor-sharp haircut leans in and whispers, "Can you believe this?" She looks completely unfazed by Cruise's godlike qualities and sudden desire to be addressed in such an egotistical manner.

"Nope, I can't believe this at all." I give a wry smile, never taking my eyes off Mr. Elton.

God, he cleans up nice. He even shaved for the occasion—he's wearing a tie and shiny brown shoes, which totally make him look official and everything. To think I came this close to raking up against one of my professors. Not that he's a bona fide professor. He's more of a sexy fill-in, but still.

A wave of heat spreads through me as he passes out the syllabus. He hands a thick stack to the girl seated to my left and one to me before moving on.

Gender Relations: Spring Semester Syllabus
On Your Knees
Tongues and Tickles
Art of Whoredom
Touch Me, Tease Me, Lick Me, Please Me
The Fine Art of Moaning
Skin on Skin
Ask and You Shall Receive
Strip Xbox
Body Frosting
Role-Playing and Erotic Fantasy:
    A Journey into Mental Imagery
Show-and-Tell
Master and Servant
Sex Video

Sex Video? What the hell is this? Porn 101?

Oh my God, this is completely perverse. Cruise is going to get himself sued or fired, or worse. Obviously, he's got some sex addiction if he plans on living out these scenarios with each one of us. I scan the room quickly, expecting half the class to burst out laughing or screaming, but they don't say a word.

The extras get passed in my direction and I gloss over one.

Gender Relations: Spring Semester Syllabus
Read: *The Great Gatsby*

Essays and quizzes are listed, and I take a paper for myself before shooting a look to the not-so-funny man in question. He's got his arms folded across his chest, and he's leering at me with his lips curled to the side. He's so enjoying this, I can tell.

It's illegal and unethical to proposition a student, let alone gift her with incriminating evidence should she be moved to initiate legal action. But I'm not. I'm moved to see what the "Fine Art of Moaning" might entail. The rest of the class fades to nothing as I negotiate the deep recesses of my mind and envelop myself in a warped fantasy that involves a whole lot of vocal cords and very little clothing.

"Good morning." Cruise paces until he sits on the edge of his desk. "I'd like to open the class with having each of you introduce yourself and share your position on love in the sensual, sexual sense. And why, outside of the preservation of the species, do you feel it continues to prosper as the single most valued human desire."

He starts in the front, and most students give a dry, rather morose view on sensual love. Three girls in a row give an expository on how love degrades women and reduces our gender to nothing more than a sexual porthole of pleasure, and I nod in agreement.

Cruise twists his lips as he considers the words of the last girl. You'd think Cruise himself had just knocked the feminist movement back three full decades the way the girl in the bright-pink rain slicker cut him off at the balls for implying that love was the "single most-valued human desire."

Things are falling to shit quickly, and a part of me feels sorry for him. Although, I'm still a little miffed he didn't tell me he'd be morphing into my teacher in the literal sense since he was already sort of filling that role anyway. Plus, that whole sexual syllabus just makes me roll my eyes, even though I plan on going over it in detail as soon as I'm alone. I have to admit, "Role-Playing and Erotic Fantasy: A Journey into Mental Imagery" does sound interesting.

"Ms. Jordan?" Cruise calls from the front, and I spike up in my seat.

"Yes? Oh, right, love. Um . . ." I pull a strand of hair over my lips the way I do when I'm nervous, and consider it a moment.

"Your views?" He leers into me with those bedroom eyes, and my stomach bottoms out. "You could share your past views, present views—that is, if they've evolved at all." He says it low with the deep register of his voice, while smoldering at me openly in front of the class. Something about this forbidden foreplay lights an inferno around me, makes me choke on the prospect of every item on that syllabus occurring in real time.

What am I saying? Cruise Elton looks at *every* girl that way. And to think otherwise is only setting myself up for a spectacular fall.

"I think love is nothing but a fallacy propagated by the greeting-card industry and a billion-dollar bridal enterprise that feeds into the fantasy of every little girl." I say it a little louder than called for. "I think the divorce rate in this country is solid evidence that love and all of its trappings are nothing more than an illusion supported by fairy tales that promise 'happily ever after' in a world where neither *happy* nor *ever after* truly exists. At the end of the day all that really remains is high-octane lust— enough to fuel a rocket ship. But it still doesn't make it real."

His cheek cinches to the side and his dimple goes off, but no smile. He manages to melt me in the process anyway. There's that high-octane lust I was talking about. It's as if my hormones were insisting on making the point for me.

"Perhaps, Ms. Jordan"—he locks me in with a heated gaze—"you simply haven't met the right person, yet." He moves on to the next student, but that cold-steely look he gave makes me shudder. Why do I get the feeling I've just done something terribly wrong—like stomped out the rosebush of our love before it ever had a chance to blossom.

The thin girl next to me clears her throat before giving an answer. She turns to face me fully. The harsh lights from above annunciate the fact that she's sporting a rather burgeoning girl-stache as she frowns. "I'm sorry for you." She says it short and simply, and my face burns with color. She reverts her attention back to Cruise. "My parents have been married for almost thirty years. They say 'I love you' and kiss each other hello and good-bye. They've raised four kids together, and they still go out on dates." She cuts me a look as if I'd just slashed open the bellies of a hundred newborn puppies. "I believe in love because it exists. I don't take other peoples' failures and make them my own. I will find love, and it will prosper."

A stunted applause comes from the back of the room and builds until the entire class is roaring and cheering, spontaneously jumping to its feet, with the exception of a well-beaten-down me.

The class goes on that way with everyone declaring themselves Team Love, while I seem to be garnering more than my fair share of dirty looks. You would think I were secretly spearheading a matrimonial apocalypse, or I've made it my personal crusade to take down Valentine's Day.

The class ends and bodies drain from the room. I wait until the last of the stragglers dissipate before making my way to the front.

"I see you've outfitted me with a syllabus tailor-made for your sexual pleasure." I mean for it to come out peppered with humor, but it comes out a sad admission from the one who all but declared herself anti-love. Anyway, that's basically how I introduced myself to Cruise, so he shouldn't be surprised.

He glances up at me from behind his large mahogany desk, looking dangerously sexy as he takes off his glasses. He walks over, wraps his arms around my waist and holds me for a long span of time. I take in his scent—memorize the girth of his body entangled with mine. He feels safe, nourishing, and hearty. It's as though I'd hungered for Cruise my entire life and now I have the vitamins, the essential minerals I need to survive. All along I had been anemic in the very thing I decried—love. Cruise was the iron my marrow so desperately needed. He kick-started my body again, put God's own breath into my soul, and I had the nerve to deny him right to his face, openly calling these feelings budding inside me a flat-out lie.

A ragged breath escapes from me, and then the unthinkable happens. Tears begin to fall, and I'm weeping a river over his freshly pressed dress shirt. It's as if I've carried a weight around with me my whole life, a heart of lead and granite. And today, in front of God and Cruise and about fifty of my newest peers, I dropped it. It lies shattered at my feet because I don't want it anymore.

I do want to believe in love. I want all of its trappings, and if it costs me my sanity and a very good divorce lawyer, so be it.

I pull back and gasp at the mess I've made of Cruise. His shirt has turned to velum, and his skin glows beneath. Two necrotic butterflies stain his once-pristine dress shirt, and I'm mortified at what I've done.

"I'm so sorry," I say, gently tapping the mess with my fingers. God knows I can only make things worse. It seems to be my specialty.

"Come here." His dimple goes off as he buries a smile in his cheek. Cruise exudes affection for me. All of his formidable lust pours out like oil, spilling its riches right into my soul. He leans in and blesses me with a soft peck, then dives in for something deeper, kissing me thoroughly, fully, and intensely on his quest to leave no lingual stone unturned as his tongue warms mine.

Cruise pulls away and his mouth opens as if he's about to say something—say *it*. A breath gets caught in my throat at the prospect, and I wait, but it never comes.

I wonder if *it* ever will.

Cruise

Kenny.

I don't remember ever walking around campus with a goofy grin on my face when I professed to love Blair. In fact, quite the opposite, I dragged my ass all over town like a beaten-down wuss with my tail between my legs—hardly smiled at anyone. That was a relationship filled with death and dying. I lived out each of the seven stages of grief every day, and twice on Sunday. I should write her a thank-you note for letting me out of the tower and escaping exorbitant legal fees somewhere down the line. However, her father is a notorious divorce attorney and would have probably only billed me my half. Looks like I avoided having my ass handed to me twice.

I hustle over in the direction of the administration building. A puff of fog illuminates the campus, soft as a gas lamp. Kenny has lit up my world. She peeled off the layer of hurt I've been hiding under all these months, filled me with her presence, and now the entire universe glows under her beautiful light.

Horton Hall comes upon me with its arched Roman colonnades, and I run up and duck inside. It's warm and, suddenly I have the urge to take off this thick ape suit I've strapped myself into. But Kenny left her calling card on my chest, and I'm certain the board would have its curiosity aroused at the sight of those tragic smudges.

Back in September, I applied for a fellowship, and now the committee has called me in. I'm amped as to what it might mean—hopefully dollar signs. If I get it, I might actually afford to feed myself, and Kenny, too. I'd move heaven and earth to have her stay at the house forever even if she thinks the concept of love is just an illusion. Kenny is a dove with a broken wing, and I want to be the one to help her mend it.

In the office, members of affluent academia line the periphery with the dean of graduate admissions, the dean of doctoral studies next to him, as well as Professor Bradshaw—and, holy crap, he looks like a corpse.

"Cruise." He stands to greet me, and I take his hand in both of mine, afraid he might keel over and explode into dust. He's lost about fifty pounds, and he hardly had it on him to begin with. His skin is pale and thin as parchment with dark circles beneath each eye. If ever there was death on the move, it's encapsulated in Bernie Bradshaw. I'd ask how the chemo is going, but I think I know.

"Did you enjoy your first class?" He gives a pleasant smile as he lands hard in his seat.

"It went great. Better than expected. I appreciate the opportunity."

"Fantastic," Dr. Barney, dean of admissions, interjects. "I hope you'll appreciate this new opportunity that's about to come your way. You might even call this your lucky day."

I glance at the three of them. I'm a lot of things—lucky isn't one of them.

"Unfortunately for Garrison"—Dr. Barney offers a morbid nod—"Professor Bradshaw has decided it's best for him to step down at this time."

"I'm sorry to hear that." Shit. Knew it wasn't good.

I swallow hard. Bradshaw has been a mentor to me. He assisted in structuring my thesis, tailoring it for a surefire admit to the doctoral program.

"Cruise"—Barney leans in—"we'd like to know if you'd be willing to take over for the rest of the semester?" He glances over at Bradshaw. "We realize you signed on to help out with a few classes, but this would mean running the course on your own. Professor Novak volunteered to oversee the situation. Technically, it will be considered coteaching. Although, Professor Bradshaw assures us you're more than capable of running the show on your own. Your passion for gender studies hasn't gone unrecognized. However, we understand you have your own course work to tend to, and should you decline, we would certainly support you either way."

A surge of adrenaline races through me. *Hell yes*, I want to shout, but somehow manage to remain subdued.

"Should you accept"—Professor Bradshaw expels the words as if he were utilizing his dying breath to birth them—"you'll have the tuition of one course credited to your fellowship as income this semester." He withholds a smile and tilts his head back with pride.

"I got the fellowship?" A credit for one course no less?

"Congratulations." Dr. Barney bears his yellow fangs, and I'm more than glad to see them. "As a part of your doctoral studies, we'd appreciate it if you would continue teaching the class in the fall as well. It will be a pleasure to watch you grow as you, yourself, become an esteemed colleague right here at Garrison."

"Thank you." My heart lets off a few irregular beats, like it's misfiring. It all feels surreal. Kenny and now the fellowship? I've got a gut feeling someone upstairs is making more than his fair share of errors, but I'll be the last one to point it out. "It's an honor to be considered. I accept."

The three of them stand, and I shake their hands in turn. I pull Professor Bradshaw into a half hug and accidentally brush up against the bony protrusions of his spine.

"I won't let you down," I whisper. "I promise."

His bushy brows lift, revealing a network of green and blue veins beneath his onion-thin flesh. "You'd better not. There were far more qualified candidates, but I knew you had the fire in your belly. You'll carry out the program much better than any of those dry wells. Just remember"—he clasps both his hands over mine—"believe what you teach. What was the topic today?"

"Love."

"Do you believe in it?"

Kenny blinks through my mind.

"More than ever."

———

I bolt out of the administration building feeling like I've just won the scholastic lottery because, holy fucking shit, I have.

That stupid grin takes over as I head into the stream of bodies rushing to class. The ground is dusted with a layer of snow, and the first thing that comes to mind is Kenny and her serious lack of winter clothes. I'll take her shopping to celebrate. I've got an entire semester's worth of loans I don't need to worry about, and even though I'm sitting under a mountain of financial duress, I'll gladly treat Kenny to something that can keep her pneumonia-free for the next several months. Hell, I might even take her to dinner. Although the fellowship still doesn't change the fact that I'm a little low on spending cash at the moment.

I sweep my eyes over the vicinity, hoping to see her, and with my newfound luck, I just might.

I scan every dark-haired girl as far as the eye can see and none of them even come close to the beauty that Kenny holds. Kenny is an exotic flower in a sea of common houseplants.

All last semester, I sat at the University Bar and Grill and listened to Cal rate girls in ratio to how many beers it would take for him to sleep with them. I never once found them exceptional, but that night at Sigma Phi when Kenny walked in, I couldn't take my eyes off that face—that mind-blowing body; her heart-stopping beauty was alarming in every good way. She openly defied my thesis on the heresy of love at first sight. I knew then I had to have her, if only for a night. A lifetime seemed like an impossibility. And now, it doesn't seem like enough time at all.

I stop just shy of the bookstore and glance at the corkboard filled with requests and opportunities. A bright-yellow sign catches my eye.

NEED $200? NOT SHY? WE WANT YOUR BODY!
CONTACT PROFESSOR WEBBER. ART DEPARTMENT.

I tear a fringe off the sheet, with a number on it, and tuck it in my pocket. I think I just found Kenny's new winter coat and boots.

A familiar head of blonde hair catches my attention from inside the bookstore and I peer in to confirm my worst nightmare.

Blair. She rocks steady on her heels while browsing the literature section. She peers out from over her book as though she's been eyeing me all along.

I turn and head in the opposite direction.

Shit.

She can't be here. She transferred to Dartmouth to follow the idiot whose dick she impaled herself onto before she officially dumped me.

I take a deep breath, giving one final scan of the campus for Kenny before taking off.

Blair can't be back.

Garrison isn't big enough.

9

RUN INTO YOUR ARMS

Kendall

The fine arts building is situated on the outskirts of campus. Its large circular architecture is reminiscent of an igloo if, in fact, an igloo was designed to stand seven stories tall.

I stumble into the giant studio in which the artful study of the human body is conducted, and after experiencing countless miniature desks that progressively seemed to get smaller throughout the day, a cavernous open space is a welcome change of pace. Benches are laid out in lieu of miniaturized workspaces with easels situated in front of each one. A charcoal pencil lies at the lip of the unit, along with an eraser that looks as though it's made from a giant wad of gray gum.

After spending over four hundred dollars on fewer than five books for only two of my classes, I'm hoping the accessories list for this class won't break the bank. My scholarship strictly covered tuition, so books, and my nonexistent dorm, are the only things my mother is taking a loan out for at the moment. I'm pretty sure it isn't going to thrill her to know she's spiraling into debt for coloring supplies. Although, technically, the loan is mine since I promised I'd pay back every dime.

The thin-lipped girl from "Professor Elton's" class sits two seats over to the left. Perfect. She'll probably be moved to overanalyze my work, and all roads of critical interpretation will inevitably lead to the fact that I gave love the middle finger. And, really? Who the hell cares about my opinion? Well, apparently, she does.

A girl with a svelte red coat zips in and fills the space between us. Already, I like her for acting as a buffer between me and Miss I-Will-Find-Love-and-It-Will-Prosper. Let's see who's so hot on love after a few volatile divorces and a bitter custody battle that spans states or, God forbid, countries. One day she'll add divorcée to her personal roster of achievements and will mark my words as the only truth she's ever known. Of course, my mother never referred to herself as a divorcée, she simply said she was "out on parole." And the whole custody battle never materialized for her either since, technically, both parties would have to *want* the child for those evil shenanigans to ensue. My father was far too busy procreating with the candlestick maker to deal with the family he left an entire state behind.

The girl in the crimson coat turns and gives a curt smile, so I take the initiative.

"Kendall." I offer her a quick handshake. Everyone at Garrison has been so nice. Back home, life was all about hard looks and keeping to yourself, but here, everyone feels like family. "Liberal Arts."

"Blair Lancaster." She pulls her cheeks back without a smile. "Journalism, but photography is my passion."

There's something strangely familiar about her, and I just can't seem to place it.

A loud shuffling comes from the front as an older woman makes her way to the center of the room. She wears a long damask coat with a vomit-inspired color palette and layers and layers of beaded necklaces, as though she robbed the accessories department at the mall and decided to don all the loot at once. There's an overall bohemian appeal to her, and innately I know this is Professor Webber. Her wiry red hair sprays out in every direction, and it's not until she turns my way that I realize she's taken liberty with cosmetics that should be restricted exclusively to Broadway plays and Halloween. She hands out a syllabus without so much as a hello, and I gawk at the list of essential supplies.

"I'm going to need a storage unit to house all this," I muse. "And to make nine trips from the bookstore to lug everything."

"Tell me about it." Blair cuts a glance my way. "But I bet a pretty girl like you has a nice strong boyfriend to help out."

I make a face before turning the paper around and gasp. The list goes on for another entire page.

"This is going to cost a fortune," I say, mostly to myself. "She is aware most of us have yet to outfit ourselves with a six-figure income."

Blair scoffs. "You'd think the only thing we really need, to sketch a bunch of nude models, is a number two pencil."

"Nude?" I swallow hard. I can't do nude. I'll laugh, or cry, or run out of the room screaming. I'll have human private parts permanently seared to my inner psyche, and who knows where this will take my nightmares?

"What did you think this was?" She tucks her chin in and gawks at me, appalled by my naïveté.

"Um, art . . ." I take in a quick breath. Shit. Study of the human body literally translates into drawing the human form? "I thought it was statues and stuff."

"Nope." She picks up her pencil and points over to the center of the room, where a middle-aged man and woman emerge without much fanfare, outfitted in thin purple robes.

Oh crap.

I have a feeling their bare legs and arms are all signs of over-exposed things to come. They slip off their makeshift kimonos and reveal a tidal wave of flesh before neatly folding their robes as if it were perfectly sane to do household chores in the freaking nude with a live audience of newly emancipated minors.

They're naked!

Naked.

I turn away as if I'd just witnessed a horrible car accident, complete with gallons of blood and severed limbs, only it's miles of wrinkled skin and age spots in places where the sun should never ever shine.

I sneak another quick peek.

Bits and pieces!

Bits and pieces!

Shit! Shit! Shit! I knew I should have read the class description a little more thoroughly. I was so worried about not getting a full load that I glossed over the specifics. And the fact that I was a transfer student meant I would be left with the crappy classes the rest of the student body didn't care for if I didn't act fast. I thought for sure I made safe choices, unlike the dicey decisions I've engaged in since my arrival, like asking my newfound professor to tutor me in the fine art of one-night stands—and for damn sure I wasn't gunning to stare at geriatric penises for an hour straight, three times a week, in the name of art of all things.

"You can stop freaking out," Blair whispers. "He's completely turned the other way."

I peer over and confirm her theory. He's older with a hairy back and a furry ass to match. I don't really mind all the fur, seeing that it creates a simian effect, and that sort of takes the edge off the whole naked human thing. To his left sits an equally garmentless woman, woefully seasoned by time. Her heavily puckered face boasts a thousand wrinkles that wink in and out as she frowns. Her copper hair is in need of a touch-up at the roots as evidenced by the four inches of silver sprouting from her scalp. And I'm betting she's had enough experience with the Unhappy Hair and Nail Salon to know to stay the hell away from that place. Her skin is dutifully leathered, leaving her unusually smooth and perky breasts to glow like lanterns in contrast to the rest of her.

"God, it's like her boobs never aged," I whisper to Blair.

"I bet half the boys in the class are hitting DEFCON five with their erections right about now," she sneers, and we share a laugh.

"They should've mentioned the arousal factor as a disclaimer for the class. Not that I'm even slightly aroused."

"Not with that beefcake you've got lying around." She glides her pencil across her paper with a marked aggression. Beefcake? She probably has me confused with someone else. Technically, I'm not with Cruise, although he does more than qualify for the beefcake category.

Professor Webber scuttles over. "Start with the model closest to you." She leans in over my shoulder, inspiring me to pick up my pencil and quickly sketch out something that loosely resembles a cat. "I'd like the models to rotate positions," she booms over at the two human skin sacs, and they shift in their seats.

I wait until she scissors by before leaning into Blair.

"Let's hope he doesn't offer us the full frontal," I say, attempting to sketch out his form. He's hunched over and his head is tilted to the side. If I didn't know better, I'd swear he were coming to the conclusion that this was an egregious error in judgment.

"You act like you've never seen it before." She gives a disbelieving look.

My mouth opens to say something, but a shy smile cinches up my lips instead.

I suppose it's odd to find a virgin in the masses, so I don't volunteer that I'm one of the defamed mythological creatures. Instead, I happily trace out the half-moon spread in front of me and try not to dwell on the fact that he's slightly adjusted himself and now I can see his belly. I simply won't look below the fold and safely avert all trauma.

"You know they pay a fortune for these models," she purrs.

"Oh, I'm sure they're volunteers." I'm quick to shoot down her fiscally unsound theory. "There are probably miles of perverts willing to ingrain their junk into our delicate gray matter. I wouldn't be surprised if the nudists on display are having some heightened sexual experience on our behalf. I once watched this special about people who got off looking at feet all day long. Swear to God, every time I see a man glance at my stilettos, I run the other way."

"You're funny." She says it drily like she doesn't really mean it. "But I happen to know for a fact that the Art Department at Garrison pays two hundred bucks a pop to anyone who wants to strut their stuff." She shrugs. "It beats flipping burgers. The catch is you're only allowed to model once a semester."

"Are you going to do it?" I'm completely intrigued, and for a brief moment, I imagine her perched on one of those cold, steely chairs sans the paper-thin robe.

"Maybe." She looks to the ceiling a moment. "How about you? I bet it'd more than cover the cost of the art supplies. You'd practically make money on the deal."

Two hundred dollars? Forget the art supplies, I could pay Cruise for room and board. Take him to dinner for a change.

"Well, I was sort of thinking of getting a job at Starbucks." True story. Plus that way I could hang out with Ally and sip lattes for a few hours each day, and it wouldn't feel like work at all.

"At minimum wage?" She balks. "This is practically a semester's worth of paychecks in one short hour. It almost seems too good to pass up. She probably doesn't have any spaces left, though."

The elderly gentleman shifts just enough to expose us to more of his goodies, then I see it.

Gah! I close my eyes tight and slowly peer from around the side of the easel. I was half-hoping he'd be cleverly holding a book or a magazine or, hell, even a cigar to cover up his spare appendage, but dear God Almighty, he is loud and proud. Well, actually, not so loud, more like a whisper. It's sort of a nub—dehydrated at that, and no bigger than a fun-sized candy bar. Are they really that tiny? Dear God, it's almost invisible. Lauren said it was like a banana, so I'm actually sort of disappointed. And for sure the storm trooper theory just went out the window. Maybe he needed the money to get one of those prosthetic jobs? Or maybe he had it hacked? You hear about all kinds of pissed-off wives who go after their cheating husbands with a hatchet. Or maybe it was just your run-of-the-mill, not-so-fictitious motorcycle accident.

The visual assault goes on for an hour solid, and to my horror both the male and female models stand around afterward speaking to the students like it's some twisted social mixer with an optional dress code.

"So, are you going to talk to the professor?" Blair incites the two-hundred-dollar question once again.

"Doubtful. I don't have the guts to do something like that."

She pumps her shoulders. "Two hundred dollars can make someone pretty brave. Besides, it's easy cash."

"Are you going to do it?" I fully examine her for the first time. She's pretty in general. Her mid-length hair is perfectly curled and sprayed into position, making it impervious to the constant windstorms that reside outside these walls. She wears a simple strand of pearls and perhaps a little too much foundation in a shade that gives her an unnatural orange glow.

"I will if you will," she offers.

"Maybe I will," I say.

Blair escorts us over to Professor Webber and fills her in on the fact that we're willing to expose our youthful flesh in exchange for two hundred hard ones. She's quick to pull out her planner at the prospect of two potentially nude coeds.

"Only a couple more female slots left. I've got next Monday and the following Friday wide open." She looks up at us, impressed by our decision to bare it all in the name of artistic enlightenment. For a stunt like this I should be guaranteed a B in the class for *baring* it all. But I'm gunning for an A, so it really doesn't matter.

Blair looks over at me nervously. "I'll take the following Friday."

"So I guess it's Monday for me." That gives me almost a week to chicken out of the idea. "Wait, Monday the nineteenth?"

"That's right. Is that a problem?" Webber's fuchsia lips pull into a line.

"No, it's not a problem." It's my birthday.

I'll simply be wearing the same outfit that I did twenty-one years ago on that very day—my birthday suit.

———

I come home to find Cruise still in his suit jacket, his wire-rimmed glasses. God, it's as if he were a total fake these past few weeks and now his real self has emerged as some perverted academic.

"Professor Elton," I say as I walk past him and pull a bottle of water from the fridge. "Oh, I'm sorry. Am I to call you master? I can't remember. I haven't quite memorized the syllabus yet."

"So you're upset?" He bleeds a nefarious grin as if this pleased him on some level. His eyes secure themselves over me with that *get in my bed* seductive stare.

"Why would I be upset? I'm always pleasantly surprised to learn the person guiding me in the fine art of physical debauchery is also employed as faculty at the school in which I'm attending. I guess that makes you legit." I don't smile, laugh, or leave any room for doubt concerning my slightly ticked disposition.

God. It just occurred to me he's probably been using me for his thesis this entire time. No wonder he offered to document my journey. I've unwittingly become exhibit K for "Kenny."

"So did I score a place on your thesis?" I ask point-blank. "If an exposé on my soon-to-be-departed virginity is going to be made available for publication, I should probably be alerted to the fact. Unless, of course, you're aware of some legal loophole that will exempt you from any litigious endeavors I might throw your way." As if I would ever sue Cruise. Well, maybe for being too damn sexy.

"I've yet to document your soon-to-be-departed virginity." His lids close halfway, letting me know he can make my virginity depart a whole hell of a lot sooner than I bargained for. And the way he's leering at me, I might be open to the idea. "I wasn't planning on mentioning you in my thesis, Kenny." He presses out a dry smile. "And, as much as I like to consider my foray in fornication as field study on some level, I've collected more than my fair share of data. I'm turning in the keys to the carnal kingdom."

Turning in the keys? Maybe Cruise Elton is boyfriend material, or maybe he just wants me to believe he is. This is all probably a ruse in the name of continuing his promiscuous blind study.

"That's too bad." I strut in front of him with an air of false confidence. "Rumor has it you hold a black belt in arousing the female anatomy." Did I just say that?

A husky laugh escapes his throat as he makes his way over.

My stomach cinches at the thought of Cruise using me all along as some sort of immoral barometer.

"So," I whisper as he warms my senses with his cologne, "I guess once I start sleeping around, I'll be tearing down all sorts of gender barriers." I say it in a lame attempt to spice up my résumé in the event that he reneges and labels me Slut Number Three or something equally degrading. "I mean, women get a horrible reputation for sleeping around, and men get called a player, which basically amounts to a term of endearment. I guess you can say I'm striving for fornicating equality." God, you'd think I was angling for a prized position in his pornographic term paper.

"Fornicating equality." Cruise comes in close with his eyes heavily lidded as if he has a serious boner to contend with, and he's about to recruit me for the alleviating efforts. "I think we should advance your training." He rasps it out low while breathing an invisible fire over my skin.

"I suppose this is where the sexual syllabus comes in handy." I tug him in by the collar and do my best to get him to kiss me. "Which of the many perverted points would you like to try out first? Master and servant? Professor and student?"

His cheek pulls back, and his dimple depresses, approving of my scholarly seduction.

"I was thinking something more along the lines of show and tell," he whispers, stepping in until his body warms mine.

For a second I think of telling him all about my adventures in art class, but he wraps a solid arm around my waist and the moment passes.

Cruise Elton looks beyond gorgeous in his scholarly suit and glasses, and the embarrassing incident that took place in his classroom comes flooding back to me. I can't believe I managed to hang myself with a noose crafted from the finer points of love, of all things, in front of a jury of my peers and my scorching-hot professor. Which reminds me, I'm still a little miffed at the big scholastic reveal.

"Show or tell?" My head rolls back involuntarily, and I snap out of his spell of seduction. "Neither." I break loose from his embrace and take off down the hall.

"Where you going?"

"To bed."

"What about me?" It comes out a plea on his behalf of his blossoming crotch.

"You can take a cold shower."

The alarm clock blinks mockingly at me, two A.M.

It's so freaking cold I'm about ready to jump into the refrigerator to warm myself. Honest to God, I'm beginning to think this whole broken heater thing is a ruse to land me on his mattress. And God knows I've thought long and hard about hopping into Cruise Elton's bed tonight, pride be dammed.

So what if he didn't confess to being my professor? He probably thought it was funny. I bet he had a good laugh printing up that secret syllabus rife with perversion.

I'm sure the "Art of Whoredom" was meant to give me a good chuckle and not at all alluding to the pact I entered into with Satan himself. Not that Cruise is Satan. He's more of a sexy alien who's rumored to have a penis the size of a lightning rod and the superpower to make women scream with pleasure on three different occasions in a very short span of time.

My body writhes at the prospect. I close my eyes and envision Cruise pouring those molten-hot kisses all over my body, his searing hands traveling at the speed of light, then dipping down in all the right places.

A rustling sound emits from behind the dresser.

I freeze and cease breathing to hone in on the mystery noise.

A loud scratching comes from the wall—and HOLY MOTHER OF GOD, IT'S TRAMPLING IN THIS DIRECTION!

I let out a muffled scream and bring my knees to my chest so fast I knock the air out of my lungs.

Shit! Shit! Shit!

The undeniable pitter-patter of vermin feet shuffling over the hardwood floor electrifies the room.

I bolt for the door only to smack into it at a hundred nose-breaking miles per hour.

"Shit!"

Locked!

I jog in a spastic manner while fiddling with the handle in the event that the gigantic mutant rats decide they want to scamper up my legs en route to gnawing off my face. Honest to God, if I lose my virginity to a fucking sewer dweller, I'm going to scream all the way back to California.

I break out of the rat tank and make a run for Cruise's bedroom. Thankfully, his door is wide open, and I manage to avert a second unfriendly run-in with pine that most likely would have ensured emergency rhinoplasty.

"What the hell?" Cruise jumps up on his elbows as I dive under the covers. He lifts the comforter, and a seam of moonlight falls over his bewildered, more than slightly gorgeous face. "Kenny?"

I let out a breath. "Is roll call really necessary?" On second thought, this is Cruise.

I scoot into him as close as humanly possible in the event that the vermin takeover decides to spill into his quadrant of the house. Cruise lets out a warm breath on my neck as he spoons alongside me, cradling me with his strong, bare arms.

Gah! What if this was all some evil ploy to land me in his bed naked? Of course, I'm not naked, but I'm willing to bet good money (which I'm currently deficient in at the moment) that Cruise Elton is.

I reach down and touch his equally bare leg, thus confirming my theory and pull away from him as if he were on fire.

"You're naked." It comes out accusingly as though he planned it all along.

"I won't bite," he purrs, reeling me back by the waist.

"I bet if I ask real nice." It comes out sarcastic because we both know he's not above an orthodontic assault if the situation warranted it.

"In that case, I'll do anything you want." He nuzzles his face into my neck, and I can feel his stubble grazing against my skin, his soft lips as they pull along in a slow hot line. "Are you wearing a jacket?" He pulls back the covers just enough to reveal my odd selection of nighttime accoutrements.

"Yes, I'm wearing a jacket—and a sweater, and a T-shirt, a pair of sweats, and tights, and two pair of freaking socks. That's what happens when you move to the Northeast. You wear your closet to bed, so you don't cryogenically freeze overnight."

"But think of how well preserved you'll be in twenty years."

"You're phenomenally funny, Professor Elton."

"No, I'm not. I'm an ass." A heated breath escapes his lungs.

Something in my chest loosens at his well-timed, self-deprecating remark—and just when I was gearing up to discount him to the playboy rack once again.

He rolls onto his back, and I carefully take him in.

The room glows the faintest shade of blue, and thanks to the moon and all its reflective glory, there's way too much light for comfort. I stare down at his body, his rippling abs, his muscular V-shaped waist. The sheets artfully cover his telephone pole, and I breathe a sigh of relief. Knowing me, I would probably run screaming and land in bed with the six-foot rat taking up residency on the other side of the wall.

Who am I kidding? With Cruise lying here like the Sultan of Seduction, it's almost too much to bear.

"What brings you for a visit?" He runs his gaze down my ridiculous state of dress. Perfect. I'm pretty sure I'm the least sexy woman to have ever graced his bed.

"The rats of Massachusetts have gathered in my room for a statewide conference," I whisper in the event that their tiny ears perk up at attention and they decide to migrate here. "You, my friend, have an infestation of the vermin variety."

"*Every* rat in Massachusetts has congregated in your bedroom?" His left dimple goes off, mocking me, and suddenly I find his vexing good looks annoying as hell.

"That's right," I say accusingly. "And I bet you've been planning it all along."

He belts out a laugh that startles me.

"You got me." He holds out a hand. "I had a big meeting with all the rodents in the neighborhood and orchestrated the entire event. I've got an alligator working its way through the sewage pipes as we speak."

"No way." I cover my ears. "If I listen for one more minute, I'm going to pee standing up for the entire next year."

"I'm teasing. I assure you the throne is still a safe place to rest on your laurels." Cruise sits up and pulls me to my knees. "Clothes"—he drills into me with those lucent blue eyes—"on or off?"

My heart beats erratic, and my mouth runs dry. With everything in me I want to say off, but the only thing I'm able to squeeze through my vocal cords is a choking sound.

"I heard off," he whispers, unzipping my jacket and removing it from my person. He cinches a smile as he lifts my sweater and T-shirt from me in one slick move. My arms stay frozen in the air as he grazes over my bare chest with his eyes. He gives a tug at my sweats, and I wrap my arms around his neck as he peels them away.

He looks at me, unsure of what to do with my underwear then runs his thumbs inside the elastic, and his breathing picks up at a quickened pace.

His warm hands round out my bottom, and I gasp at his touch.

Cruise Elton strips the underwear from my body, and I don't do a damn thing to stop him.

Cruise

The moonlight rinses out the room in a blue wash, sanitizing us from the trappings of reality. Everything feels dreamlike in this altered state. I try not to lose it as this erotic fairy tale unfurls around me with Kenny playing a starring role as the princess.

Kenny didn't say a word as I peeled off her clothes. She wasn't exaggerating when she rattled off the clothing inventory a moment ago. Every last thread was present and accounted for.

It's too bad about that pest-control problem she's having.

Best two dollars and ninety-nine cents I've ever spent. The lady at the pet shop thought I should purchase at least three, babbling something about the social nature of field mice—and who was I to refute her theory?

Kenny shivers as we lie side by side, so I pull her in, touch her soft skin against mine, and everything in me pumps to life.

A part of me wants to apologize for not fixing the heater, but the truth is I managed to fix it Christmas morning. I thought for sure she'd crave a little body heat by now. If I didn't buy the damn rats, we'd probably have frostbite to contend with by midterms.

I lie next to her, trying to steady my breathing, and for the first time in a long while I'm unsure of what to do next.

"Boy, you took everything off, swift as a magician," she marvels.

"Practice makes perfect." Shit. I'm not sure if bragging about how many times I may or may not have disrobed a woman is a good thing right about now. Besides, this isn't any other woman—this is Kenny.

"I'm naked," she whispers as if alerting me to some shameful secret. I pull the covers over the two of us and nestle her bare bottom into my stomach.

"I won't tell if you won't." I twist my hips away from her in the event that I accidentally introduce her to my hard-on and send her running for weaponry. She's got to know I've got one, right?

"So, now what?" She eases into me until her back fuses against my chest.

I close my eyes and drink down her warmth, her amazingly fucking soft skin—the way her bare chest rests on my arm and sears me with pleasure.

"You make the next move, Kenny." I trace out her ear with my lips. God, I hope she turns in the right direction.

She spins around and takes a deep breath. Her hands land over my chest, and she moves her fingers in soft, smooth circles.

"Show me what to do," she whispers. "I'll do whatever you want."

Whatever I want.

I swallow hard as I pull her in, and this time my bodily protrusion greets her by gliding against her thigh. Kenny's dark hair stains the room like a shadow, and her pale features glow, soft and luminescent like a tissue-covered lamp.

"You're so beautiful." I press a kiss over her cheek and linger. Kenny would do anything I wanted. I could have her right now. I could bury myself inside her, put an end to this aggressive buildup brewing inside me once and for all and explode with relief from the pressure. But Kenny deserves to have someone say those magic words to her, one of which is the very word she declared war against in class this morning. I suppose I'm a big enough asshole to take her anyway, screw good morals and integrity, but I can't—not with Kenny.

"I think tonight's lesson is snuggling," I say, gently rolling her into me until we're spooning again.

"Snuggling?" She burrows her hair, scented with flowers and vanilla, into my neck, and her skin burns an erotic hole right through me. I close my eyes, taking in the ecstasy and the misery as if she were writing a poem over me with her flesh.

I let out a dull moan and feel the vibrations hum through her body as if we were the perfect conduits.

"Snuggling," I whisper in her ear. "Once you have your way with all those hundreds of guys, you might want to catch a breather after. Maybe catch some z's." Just the thought of her bare skin touching anyone else's is enough to send me into a rage.

"Oh, right." There's a marked disappointment in her voice. Like maybe she wanted me to take advantage of her, but was too shy to ask.

Tonight's endeavors are entirely up to her. If she wants, she could still turn this ship around and navigate my dick into the harbor where it desperately longs to dock. I have a condom at the ready. God knows my entire existence is crying out, screaming at every cell in her body to want me as badly as I want her.

But Kenny doesn't make a move.

And neither do I.

I hold Kenny all through the night, watching as the moon radiates its beams over her like a love song. I would spend every night like this if she let me. If I'm lucky, the mice will breed, and she'll never want to be two feet away from me. But I don't want our first time to be the result of manipulation on my part.

In fact, I want to put it off until after I tell her exactly how I feel.

And hopefully, she'll feel the same way, too.

⁓

The next afternoon at the gym, without consulting my better judgment, I decide to share a few details with Cal.

"You let her decide what to do, and she laid there like a limp rag?" Cal extends his hands, and the weights shift to the left. "Sorry."

"No—she let me decide. And I decided not to. Besides, that isn't what she wants."

"Of course it's not what she wants. That's precisely why she didn't ask for it. She's probably gay. Face it, you've got the wrong anatomy."

"She's not gay. She's just young, sweet, and innocent. She needs to be in a committed relationship."

"You tell her how you feel?"

"Not yet."

"What the hell are you waiting for? Those three little words have been uttered time immemorial in order to secure young, sweet, 'innocent' ass." He takes the weights and hoists them onto the bracket. "Man up already, would you? I'm getting frustrated listening from the sexually deprived sidelines. If I wanted to experience a dry season, I would focus on my own sex life."

"Maybe I will man up." I pluck the towel that perpetually hangs from his neck and wipe the sweat off my face.

"Guess who came in yesterday and purchased a membership for the year?" Cal sits on the bench across from me with that I'm-not-shitting-around expression he gets during tax season.

I don't need to play twenty questions to know it's Blair. "What the hell is the deal with her? She's at Garrison, too."

"She told Lauren things didn't work out with her and lover boy. She says she's back for the long haul—that she wishes she never left. Rumor has it she's got her sights set on a familiar old boyfriend—or was it fiancé?"

"Nope, not fiancé." I get up and head out of the room. "She didn't say yes."

And, after meeting Kenny, I've never been happier.

10

A DOZEN LONG-STEMMED HEARTACHES

Kendall

On the Sunday before I bare far more than my mortal soul in art class, I decide to brave the snow and grab some coffee with Lauren and Ally.

Lauren called, said there was some kind of relationship emergency and that she needed a hot brunette with a great body ASAP. To be honest, I didn't like the sound of it.

Cruise has been helping his mother with repairs all weekend at both the hair salon and bed-and-breakfast. I'm not sure how he magically morphs into a handyman once he leaves the house, and yet the heater remains mysteriously irreparable. Although I'm not complaining. I've spent the last week lying naked in his arms with his protruding affection jammed firmly against my thigh, and, well, okay, it might have slipped in a more intimate location a time or two, but he was quick to reposition himself.

I'm sure he's long given up trying to have his way with me. He probably thinks I'm asexual, that I'm not even remotely interested in him or men in general. But the truth is, I'm ready to cave. I'm one heated breath away from turning around in the middle of the night and diving into his delicious dimples. I don't care if he impales me with that power line between his legs or if it manages to jet right out of my throat in the process. Everything in me cries for his body. I'm not sure what I'm waiting for. But God knows I'm waiting for something.

Per rules of the universe, Starbucks is packed wall-to-wall with bodies. You'd think the only working heater in all of Massachusetts was right here in this shop, and if Cruise's home and the classrooms at Garrison are any indication, it just might be.

The thick scent of coffee seduces me with its slightly burnt aroma, and I inhale deeply as I get in line.

"Kendall!" A loud, rather abrasive woman's voice hails me from the front. I spot Aunt Jackie waving and head on over.

"Guess who I talked to today?" she asks, offering me a big rocking hug. Her perfume and hairspray launch an assault on my senses and for a moment, I lose the ability to breathe.

"Pen?" I haven't seen Pennington since our botched double date. I can't believe he had the nerve to bumble his way to second base while in a public establishment. Of course, I had the nerve to molest Cruise's hand while on a date with Pen, so I guess we're sort of even.

"No, silly." She flicks her wrist, and her diamond-encrusted tennis bracelet threatens to fall off. There's something about the way Jackie presents herself that scares me a little. Maybe it's her obvious fake lashes. I've been known to don falsies on occasion myself, but these in particular look like she plucked the wings off some poor unsuspecting butterfly, way too transvestite for this early in the afternoon. Or maybe it's the heavily penciled eyebrows that give her that perpetual look of surprise, or the thick black outline of her lips—a look I thought was canceled along with *Baywatch*. Nevertheless, the sixties are calling. They want their go-go boots back. "I talked to your mother!" She beams. "You'll never guess what she said."

"She's getting married?" I ask, averting my eyes at the thought. If that's the case, I think I'll skip the nuptials and cheer from the sidelines once the dissolution is on the horizon. A heavy feeling overcomes me at the thought of her racking up another tally mark in divorce court. I hate the thought of Mom getting her heart broken once again.

"Bitter much?" Jackie puts in her order while I wave at Ally. "Make it two!" She turns back to me. "I've got this," she whispers without even asking if I wanted a double espresso. But I'm more than thankful. At the rate I've been mismanaging my anemic funds, I might have to familiarize myself with the local soup kitchen in less than a week.

"So"—I turn to Aunt Jackie, ready to end the big mystery as to what my mother could have said—"what's the big secret?"

"The girl is lonely." Jackie makes a face. "She got that stewardess friend of hers to get her a ticket. So she'll be out for a visit." She punctuates it by tapping me on the nose.

Lauren breezes in and trots on over. Her dark hair is whisked across her forehead and her mascara looks smudged as if she's been crying.

"I'm so glad you came." She pulls me in by the elbow. "We desperately need to talk."

"Um . . ." I look back at Aunt Jackie. "It'll just be a minute."

"Take all the time you need. I'm leaving," Jackie insists. "She'll be coming out in a couple weeks, so you might want to make arrangements."

"Is she staying with you?" I ask as she heads toward the door.

"I'm having the house painted. She's all yours, hon. We'll do dinner!" And with that, she walks out into the snow-covered world. A younger man with a goatee takes her by the waist and gets her settled in the passenger seat of his dated Monte Carlo.

"Who the hell is that guy?" I whisper mostly to myself. "And who paints their house during blizzard conditions with no end in sight?"

"Who cares?" Lauren pulls me off to the corner. "I think my boyfriend might be seeing someone else." It speeds out of her. Her glassy eyes blink in quick succession as her cheeks explode a bright shade of pink.

Ally comes up from behind. "That two-timing asshole!"

"Shh!" Lauren hops up and down in a heightened state of panic. "He's on his way."

"Perfect," Ally snipes. "I feel an accident coming on with a boiling pot of coffee. We'll fry his balls and see how far that gets him with the ladies."

"No!" Lauren darts a finger in the air. "No frying of the balls. Get back behind that counter. I'm going to have Kendall hit on him and see how he responds."

"What?" Now it's my turn to jump out of my skin. "I'm not hitting on anybody. I don't even know how to do it." True story. I tried to hit on Cruise, and now I'm sleeping naked next to him in the hopes of tricking him into liking me. God only knows where I'll end up with her boyfriend.

"Pretend he's Cruise and flirt," Lauren instructs. "Just be your cute little self, and he'll fall all over you." Her face crumbles at the thought.

"Then what?" I clutch at my chest in horror. I suspect third-degree burns will be called for in the event that he goes for our poorly hatched plan.

"Then"—Ally twitches—"I scald him and make sure his future endeavors in procreation are physiologically futile. We burn the bastard."

Knew it.

"I don't even know what he looks like." Shit. I'm nowhere near ready to pick up strays at coffee holes. By definition, Cruise is doing a lousy job of directing me in all things hookup.

"He's bald and looks like every single stranger your mother ever warned you about," Lauren says, pedaling me to the back of the store. "Just picture him asking you to look for his lost kitten while luring you into a windowless van."

A small cry escapes my throat. "God, Lauren, you are so going to owe me for this."

"Done," she says, ducking behind some foliage.

I take a seat at an empty table and wait for a tall, bald predator to walk through those doors and see if I qualify to be his sex kitten.

Cruise

The smell of rust and hairspray fumes pulls me out from underneath the bathroom sink.

I look up at my sister who's wielding a can of toxic hair glue like it's a lethal weapon.

"You mind?" I bury my face in my armpit and take a deep breath. I'd rather inhale the remnants of my deodorant than asphyxiate myself with the vaporous shit Molly insists on suffocating me with. "I'm going to die of lung cancer one day, and it's going to be all your fault," I say, tossing my wrench back in the tool bag.

"Sorry, but I have to look perfect." She twirls the curling iron in her hair, and a series of vapors emits from the wand. I'm pretty sure it's not supposed to smoke like that. I've held down the fort more than a few times at the Crappy Hair and Snail Salon where the new logo should be "We'll age you thirty years!" Not sure why Kenny never lawyered up. My mother is damn lucky she still has a roof over her head—me too for that matter.

"What do you need to look so perfect for?" I say, getting up and dusting the rust off my jeans.

"I got a date."

"A what?" I look at her in the mirror. Her face is painted like a Kabuki doll, complete with bright-red lipstick, and her hair is twirled in perfect ringlets like she's going to prom. "You can't go on a date."

"Says who?" Her bright-pink nails maneuver the curling iron around another stray lock.

"Says me."

"You're not my dad."

"You don't have one, so I sort of am." I bend over to pick up my tool bag, and she knees me solid in the balls. "Shit." My head dips to my thighs as a blinding pain spreads through my body, slow and searing like molasses on fire. "Moll," I say, following her agitated footsteps down the halls. "I'm sorry." I pound against the door. "Can I come in?"

"No. I *hate* you!" The soft sound of sobbing emits from the other side.

"I'm sorry." I wiggle the doorknob until it unlocks. Nothing ever works around here, so it's no big surprise I can manipulate the bolt with a flick of the wrist.

Molly lies on the bed, crumpled and broken. She depresses her face in the pillow as her back heaves in a wild fit of tears.

"Hey." I go over and sit on the edge, rubbing her shoulders with my deep regret. "I just don't want to see you getting hurt, kiddo. That's all." Shit. Could I damage her any more than I already have? It's not her fault her dad is a screwup. He landed in the pen five years ago on a cocaine bust that ended with a body, and now here I am, rubbing her face in it. "You really like this guy?"

She twists around and looks at me with those tear-filled eyes. Her lipstick's smeared, and her neat curls have exchanged themselves for a ball of frizz. She might very well be transforming into a beautiful young woman, but all I see is that six-year-old who used to follow me around like a puppy—wish it were still so.

"Yes, I like him." She straightens her legs, and I'm shocked to see they almost dangle off the bed.

"Does he treat you well?"

"No." She doesn't hesitate to answer.

"Then what the hell are you doing with him?"

"I don't know. I just want him to like me. I want him to tell me he cares about me—that he loves me, but he never does. He just slobbers all over me and pretends like that's enough. At least buy me a freaking flower before you stick your tongue down my throat."

"You know I'm going to have to kill him."

Her eyes slit to nothing. "Touch him and I'll arrange the need for a brand-new set of tires and repeat the effort."

My stomach sours at the thought of anyone hurting Molly— cheating on her. All she wants is a few kind sentiments and flowers.

She might as well be talking about Kenny and me.

"Look, I gotta run." I lean over and tousle her hair. "Do me a favor and give this guy the cold shoulder, will you? Stay in and catch a movie with Mom. She could use the company. And don't let anyone stick his tongue down your throat, or I'll have to track him down and rearrange body parts."

"Where are you going?"

"I've got some shopping to do."

***

Flowers. I give a little laugh as I stare down at the bouquet of bright-red roses I picked up from the florist. I wanted it to look special, not like I swiped it out of a plastic bucket off a street corner, so the florist peppered in a bunch of baby's breath, and it looks like a song came to life right here in my hand.

I tried to text Kenny to see where she's at, but she didn't answer. I figured I'd hit a few of the usual haunts before waiting it out at home. I'm amped and ready to tell her how I feel—that she's the most beautiful woman I've ever laid on eyes on, that her inner beauty outshines the stars, the moon—makes them look like amateur hour when it comes to phosphorescence. Then I'm going to say it. I'm going to say those three little words I haven't uttered in so long—and for the first time ever, I'm finally going to mean them.

The Beemer is parked right outside Starbucks, amassing snow an inch deep over the windshield, so she must have been here a good long while.

I park and brace myself before getting out of the car—hell, before imparting such a life-changing statement. Everything about the two of us will change in that very moment. She'll either say it right back or laugh in my face.

A flurry of snow greets me as I make my way inside. The flowers feel foreign in my hand, like I've donned a costume and this is just some prop. It doesn't feel real. My heart drums out a vicious beat as I pan the establishment. I spot Ally behind the counter, and her jaw drops. I tick a quick hello before scouring the crowd and spot Kenny off in the back.

My stomach bottoms out.

Kenny has her arms wrapped around the waist of a familiar looking, bald-headed bastard—Cal.

She belts out a laugh and her neck arches with pleasure in a way I thought it only did for me.

Looks like Kenny is taking the game to a whole new level—flying solo with Cal, of all people. And here I didn't think she had it in her, that she secretly may have wanted only me.

A little girl walks in with her mother. Her long hair, those large brown eyes with the slight look of hurt in them remind me an awful lot of Molly.

"These are for you." I hand her the flowers and dart back to the truck.

———

She didn't come to my room last night.

I glance out the window bleary-eyed as the sun crests the hillside, casting an eerie tangerine glow over the mounds of snow that piled up overnight. I lie back down and throw my arm over my eyes, trying to block out the dismal light, the world—reality in general. Kenny had seemed so innocent when I saw her that first night at the party. I knew she wasn't coming home with me to heat the sheets, but she held the oxygen in the room, and I damn well needed to breathe. I was floating on the wreckage from my last heartbreak and Kenny was a beautiful island that emerged from nowhere, one that I longed to explore. And now I'm petrified that what I really came upon was a volcano ready to blow my world to pieces. If I thought Blair and her blatant F.U. after years of being together was bad, then I have a feeling Kenny is going obliterate me in the worst way possible.

I didn't think I could feel pain so deep from someone I've barely known a month. I never knew I could have my heart ripped from my chest and set on fire by my sheer desire to have someone who has no real interest in me.

This afternoon I'll be wearing nothing but a smile in Kendall Jordan's art class. I know for sure she's enrolled in it because I double-checked her schedule last night.

I'll have to put on that invisible suit of armor I've donned since last summer when everything went to shit, just hoping to make it through the hour.

I could always not go—forfeit two hundred big ones. Technically, I'm staff, so I shouldn't be so eager to shed the stitches, although Professor Webber made it a point to let me know graduate students were her primary pool of applicants. Besides, I should probably get back in the game—start tearing through that industrial-sized box of condoms I've got stashed in my nightstand. Kenny was just a misstep. I let her get too far in my head, and if I keep trekking in the same direction, I'll turn into one big emotional pussy.

After a quick shower, I don't bother getting dressed. Instead, I wrap a towel around my dripping wet body and venture into the kitchen.

"The heater worked last night!" she marvels, and my heart sinks like a stone.

I fired it up while she was gone, hoping she'd come to my bed willingly.

My chest grows heavy. Kenny managed to deflate my ego with one prick of her tongue. I was nothing more than a heater. And last night, when she didn't need my services, she didn't bother to show.

With all my heart and soul I wish she wanted me. A part of me wants to weep like a schoolgirl at the thought of Kenny getting it on with Cal or any other asshole that happens to rub up next to her.

My lips twitch a mournful smile. I want to look away, pull my gaze from hers, but she's hooked me, reeled me in with those sea-glass lenses.

"Look at me, Kenny." I glance down at my body. "I want you to see every part of me." I grab hold of the towel cinched at my waist, and her lips part, her eyes magnify in size at what I'm about to do. She shakes her head ever so slightly, apparently mortified that I had ditched "good morning" and went for the carnal jugular before she could down her coffee. I open the towel, slowly and methodically, exposing her in full to every inch of my being.

Selfishly, I don't want Kenny to see me for the first time in front of strangers while she tries to sketch me with shade and light. Selfishly, I wish she *wanted* to see me, to have me all for herself.

She turns away, quick as a hurricane, and spills the contents of her mug in the process.

"Shit, Cruise. Good morning to you, too." She lands her cup hard on the sink and leans toward the window.

"Lesson of the day." I come up from behind—adhere myself to the curve of her body and don't bother to pull away once I feel myself grow. "I want you to see me like this," I whisper almost ashamed of what I'm asking her to do. "You don't have to touch. Just look." It comes out sad, forlorn because I know deep down inside she won't—that I don't deserve to have her look at me.

"Cruise . . ." She turns her head into my shoulder. She doesn't say anything, and for a minute, I think she might cry, that I might turn into a giant pussy and join in on the sob fest.

I offer a gentle kiss to her cheek, and our lips find one another for the first time in a week. It's as if she were afraid to kiss me lying in my bed, as if my mouth were the portal to unspoken treasures, and once she entered she could never leave.

That visual of her touching Cal on the collar, laughing at whatever flew from his lips, rolls through me like rancid fat, and I pull away.

"I guess I'll see you in class," I say, cinching up my towel.

She takes a breath, never taking her sad eyes off mine. "I guess you will."

11

THE BIG SURPRISE

Kendall

It's my birthday.

I arrive late to Professor Look-at-Me-Naked Elton's class and take a seat next to the thin-lipped girl who greets me with her traditional snarl.

Figures. It's going to be a crap day all around, I can tell.

I came so close to telling Cruise that I have feelings for him. That I don't want to pretend to play this sick little game I thought was cute a few short weeks ago. That I actually want to engage in a monogamous relationship with him and do everything with his body that he would ever want, but the words wouldn't formulate on my lips. Technically, it was his fault for sidelining me by asking me to conduct a body scan before breakfast. Hell—who am I kidding? I would have inhaled his body *for* breakfast, but a part of me is holding back. If Cruise doesn't want just me, then I suppose I shouldn't want him in that way—and, frighteningly enough, I think I still do.

"The finality of love." He belts it out like a song, looking hotter than a bonfire in his dark corduroy jacket, his inky jeans, and cowboy boots—my heart lurches just laying eyes on him.

To hell with it. I'm jumping into his bed tonight and having myself a nice little birthday. He's wearing cowboy boots for God's sake. The man doesn't fight fair.

"Today, I thought we would touch upon the vulnerability we face once we've fallen in love." Our eyes meet, and he gives a quick wink. Obviously, he thinks love is a joke, and only he and I are privy to the punch line. "Can anybody tell me why a person becomes vulnerable when experiencing love—especially for the very first time?"

Miss Thin Lips spikes her hand in the air like she's about to have an accident. Personally, I'm rooting for the accident.

"Cheryl." He nods with a prolonged blink.

Ha! She is totally getting on his last nerve.

She clears her throat and cuts me a look as if she'd heard. "It's because love embroils its participants in a psychological power exchange that takes place once you trust someone with your heart." She wiggles proud in her seat after dispensing the armchair psychiatry. "If I were to fall in love with someone, and he broke that sacred trust, I would be forever wounded and therefore protect my heart from ever being crushed in such a violent manner again. Naturally, I would build defenses. I might even resort to meaningless sexual exchanges as nothing more than a device to satisfy myself—there wouldn't be any real love involved because I would probably stop believing in it."

Cruise leans against his desk. His face blanches as he considers this. It's as though he realizes she diagnosed him so correctly he's only now aware of the fact that his manwhore ways were nothing more than a ruse. In the end, that's probably all our affections will be reduced to, a meaningless sexual exchange— nothing more than a device to satisfy ourselves—no real love because we don't believe in it—only now, I think I do.

Cruise takes a breath. "So the power exchange is what creates the vulnerability between sexual partners, and when the balance is disrupted, it crushes the weaker of the two units."

"Not necessarily." Cheryl straightens at the prospect of conducting a lecture all on her own. "The power exchange doesn't need to have sexual underpinnings. It could take place with a child and its parents. Plenty of girls are victims of deadbeat fathers, and statistics show that girls who grow up without a paternal influence in their lives seek male attention in other ways. Any stripper in the country can testify to this."

Cruise cuts an involuntary look in my direction.

I know what he's thinking—that I'm rife with daddy issues. He thinks he's pegged the very reason I've decided to descend into whoredom, no thanks to the malnourished wealth of information next to me, espousing her not-so-sage wisdom. And, sadly, both he and she would be right.

"Kenny," he says it low, robotic, "you look like you have something to say."

I take in a sharp breath. "I guess it's true." I look over at Cheryl and watch as her skeletal frame gloats in my direction. "Like any stripper in the country, I can testify to this. Funny thing, it was one of my stepfathers who enlightened me to this morsel when I was twelve."

"That's all right, Kenny," he says it lower than a whisper, as if I've shared enough already. Cruise is trying to talk me out of carrying on with the verbal massacre of my adolescence.

"He already packed his things and was hauling his suitcase out the door." I take in a ragged breath. "He and my mother had a really big blowout. I remember . . . he shouted, loud as he could, that I'd grow up to be a tramp just like my mother." I hold Cruise's glassy-eyed stare for a very long time. The room, the other students, they melt away like snow—it's just Cruise and me having an intimate conversation regarding the tumultuous state of my inner child. I had lifted my skirt and bared my shame to everyone in the vicinity. I don't see the point in stopping now. "That's why I did it. I held onto my virginity like a very sharp knife. I'd cut anyone who came close to me because I wanted to prove the bastard wrong. I wanted to show the world I would never end up like my mother. I ran from anything that even remotely resembled love and made damn sure it never found me." Until now.

Cruise closes his eyes. A seam of liquid seals over his lashes. He turns to the board and takes out his aggression on a tiny piece of chalk as he scrawls out an assignment.

"Give me a short essay on the vulnerability of love." He pulls me in with a volatile stare as everyone busies themselves with the task at hand. "Kenny, can I see you in the hall a minute?"

I take him in like this, the well-dressed authoritarian with his glasses firmly in place, his hair slicked back nice and neat. I think I like the sweaty version, the midnight rendition who presses his stubble into my neck while his hard-on pleads with my body to find it a home.

"No," I say, and get to the business of writing an essay for my professor.

———

So far, I've had a pretty shitty birthday.

I've managed to avoid Cruise on at least two occasions since my impromptu confessional. First, after class, when he tried to tackle me like a defensive lineman in the hall and again in the library, where he tried to flag me down, but I simply made a beeline for the stacks. Who knew that hidden among rows and rows of dusty old textbooks you could find such an odd assortment of carnal perversion, ranging from blow jobs to hand jobs—covert coitus with pants slightly sagging, the skirt perfectly adjusted. It was practically a Kama Sutra performance piece in there. They should seriously consider renaming it "The Raunchy Reference Center."

I begrudgingly make my way to the art building, where Professor Webber meets me near the door, a purple robe in hand.

"You're late." She bites the air as if I'd intentionally decided to show five minutes past the hour to stage some grand entrance because God knows I want to bare my breasts in style. Which reminds me, I meant to shave my area this morning, but was waylaid by Cruise and his sudden need to flash me.

It's probably not that bad. It's not like I'm out to impress the peanut gallery. In fact, the less appetizing I look, the less likely I am to score unwanted phone numbers once the hour is through.

Webber scuttles me off to a dressing room, and I'm quick to strip to nothing. I glance down at the dark triangle spraying out over my thighs and gasp at my unkempt oversight.

Gah! I'm a *bush*. This is horrible. This is far worse than I thought. Not only am I slightly out of shape and my boobs have picked this day to sag like oversized water balloons, but I have the Butchart Gardens sprouting from my ass—quite literally.

Crap.

I'll have to take the cash and catch the next flight back to California after this debacle, or I'll be risking some horrific nickname, like Bushzilla, Pubic Enemy Number One, Magic Carpet Ride, or Carnal Curtains, which will haunt me the rest of my natural days. I suppose after this, I'll owe everybody here one big "pubic" apology.

"Let's go, let's go!" Professor Webber herds me from the makeshift closet.

I don my robe and file in behind a man in purple, staring down at his feet as we conduct the walk of shame to our respective seating areas. It didn't occur to me until now that the metal stool I'll be displaying myself on will feel like someone tucked a glacier under my bare bottom, at least for the first few minutes.

From my peripheral vision, I see his robe fall in a lavender puddle to the floor.

I take a deep breath. What in the hell have I gotten myself into? Taking off my clothes in public? What's next? Strip clubs?

Okay. Relax. Nobody is going to care what I look like. This is in the name of art. The entire class is probably thrilled to have some youth to contrast the geezer standing next to me.

It's like ripping off a Band-Aid. I just need to do it and not put too much thought into it.

A cool breeze hits me as I pull back the robe. I feel the fabric release from my shoulders and trickle down my body with a pronounced finality. I pretend to inspect the chipped polish on my toes when really I'm trying my hardest to die from mortification because right about now death seems the only plausible way out of this mess.

"Kenny?"

I glance up at the familiar voice.

Standing before me is a very gorgeous, very surprised, and very much naked Cruise Elton.

"Shit!" I cross my hands over my chest and knock my knees together.

It's him! Where the hell is the geezer?

I do a quick once-over and suck in a breath.

Double shit! I just saw it! Right here in front of at least forty-five different witnesses, I've just laid eyes on Cruise Elton's package for the very first time.

My stomach cinches. My eyes drift right back to where he hangs long and lean down his thigh, and in no fucking way did he ever get it chopped in half in some motorcycle accident.

"Take a seat." Professor Webber barks out the order and both Cruise and I are quick to comply.

Cruise settles into his chair, never taking his eyes off mine. He gives the tiniest hint of a lewd smile, and I can feel my entire body flood with heat.

I scowl at him. Damn pervert. I wouldn't put it past him to shake this kind of delicate information out of poor wire-haired Webber. Although, I suppose, he could be in the market to turn a quick buck.

"God, she's turning beet red!" someone shouts from the periphery.

Professor Webber lets out a few viral claps. "Don't be afraid to use color."

Great. Not only will I be a hairy bush, but I'll look as if I were about to catch fire; I'll be the burning bush. And right about now, I'd do anything for a gallon of gas and a couple of matches to put an end to this misery.

I glance back over at Cruise, and my eyes dip down his chest. It's smooth and as wide as a building. Cruise takes immaculate care of his body. He would never show up for strip-beyond-your-skivvies day and not be courteous enough to manscape his scrotum. Speaking of which. My gaze dips a little lower, slow and sweet like honey, and I see a sparse line of dark brown curls that leads down from his belly button, a neatly hedged treasure trail, and then an enormous fold of skin lying over his thigh, and . . .

Oh. My. God. It's *growing*. It's rousing to life slow and lethargic, like a giant waking from a very long slumber.

Cruise needles me with the beginnings of a nefarious smile. He's blooming to life, and it's all for me.

The entire class breaks out in a viral gasp as if Cruise were doing something insanely unnatural, like levitating or swiveling his head 360 degrees. But this is completely natural, and perhaps the best part is, it's directly in response to yours truly. I hope.

Cruise digs in a smile and his dimples ignite. I want to dive into them. I want to dive into Cruise, use him as a covering and a shield. My eyes roam back down his body, and I take him in, fully formed and beautiful as his body pridefully salutes me from too far a distance to fully appreciate.

Cruise Elton just gave me the best birthday present ever, and he doesn't even know it.

Cruise

Kendall Jordan is a real live wet dream. And if I'm not careful, my dick is going to alert the authorities, because I'm a thousand percent sure having an erection in public, while seated in front of the student body, is something akin to a felony.

I drink Kenny down with her creamy-white skin, her pink lips like cherries. Her chest swells like two perfect cantaloupes; the dark hair buried between her legs is like a sea of ripe currents, and suddenly I'm very fucking hungry for cantaloupes and currants.

I try to absorb what's happening. That somewhere in the innocence of trying to purchase a winter coat for Kenny, I've put my new position as professor on the line and now, in a sudden turn of events, I'm not only naked in front of strangers, but in front of the woman I love. And I do love Kenny. Come hell or high water, I'm going to let her know tonight. Whether or not she decides to speak to me afterward is entirely up to her. She didn't care for the fact that I kept my status as faculty from her. I'm guessing spontaneously exposing myself in her art class is something she would've liked to have been clued in on—especially in the event that she was about to shed a few layers herself.

Professor Webber steps in and looks right at me. "Good job," she whispers. "Never in all my years of teaching have I seen something like that before. Have you considered a career in the adult film industry? You have serious equipment that shouldn't be ignored."

I shoot her a look. I don't feel the need to propagate the fact that I'm well-endowed. I've long known it's an anomaly. The last thing I want is to freak Kenny out and send her running for vaginal cover, opting for less amply gifted men to contend with, like Cal and his nonexistent member. Which reminds me, I've yet to beat the crap out of him.

"Turn around so the rest of the class can see you." Webber motions for us to face the other direction, and my dick retreats from its performance position. It's like it's trained to stand at attention whenever Kenny is around.

I try to settle my gaze on the clock on the wall. Nothing like staring down the minute hand to make the time crawl by.

A blonde in a red coat smiles at me, and everything in me freezes.

Blair. If there's one thing in this world that can kill my hard-on faster than a wrinkled hag suggesting I try my hand at porn, it's my ex-girlfriend.

Just when I didn't think things could get any worse.

I can feel her looking at me, burning a hole through every square inch of my body with her unwanted stare. Blair had her chance with my flesh, and she wasn't interested in keeping me or my dick around, so I don't know what makes her think I'd be desperate enough to let her back in my life. Although, if Kenny weren't here . . . if I never gave her all of my power without her even knowing it, would I want Blair back? I'm quick to deduce a flat-out no.

The hour finally draws to an excruciating end with my manhood rendered temporarily peniplegic thanks to Blair and her libido-killing lasers.

I pick up a robe and cover Kenny from behind, brushing her hair with a kiss that could have easily been mistaken for nothing more than the simple act of passing, even though none of the ways I love Kenny can be classified as a simple act of passing. Everything about the way I plan on showing her my affection, both physically and emotionally, will be nothing short of well-engineered.

"I believe you dropped this." Blair pipes up from behind, and I take my robe from her before whipping it on. "Good show." She tilts her head into me.

Kenny has already made a beeline for the dressing room, so I don't mind unleashing a little bit.

"The show wasn't for you, Blair. Nor will it ever be." I don't wait for the shocked look to register on her face. Instead, I dart into the room where I left my belongings and do a quick change, so I can catch the woman I love before she races back to the West Coast for good.

───

"Hey, beautiful," I say, catching up with Kenny outside the art building. The evening sky encroaches overhead, desolate and grim with ominous clouds that hold a soft-blue patina. "You strip here often?"

"Not as often as you salute the queen." She gives an impish grin. Her hair whips around her neck in long, dark sheets. "It's my birthday."

Everything in me breaks for Kenny. She fidgets with her backpack, and her perfectly painted nails shine like sirens. Her sweater slips off her shoulder, and her bra strap is showing. A part of me wants to fix it, fix everything for her. But she's sexy as hell and perfect, and there isn't a thing about her I want to change.

"Why didn't you tell me it was your birthday?" A strong ache pulls in the pit of my stomach. Everything about today must have been pretty lousy for her, starting with me attacking her with my towel, the sad confession about her stepfather's words, then the finale—baring her perfect body to fifty different students when I wish to God it were only me in that room with her.

Professor Webber makes her way outside, flagging us down in a panic. "I'm glad you're still here." She hands us each a check. "You're both welcome back, anytime. Of course, you'll have to be paired together. Your chemistry sizzled off the page." She winks over at me before darting into the unseasonably cold evening.

Kenny and I emit giant white plumes with our heavy breathing as if we were on the cusp of discovering something far more intimate about one another than our bare bodies could ever reveal.

Kenny waves her check in the air. "Food and rent." She tries to hand it to me, but I won't take it. Kenny did that out of obligation to me. She wanted to help. "I thought maybe you could call someone to look at the heater, but it somehow magically fixed itself this morning." She shrugs.

My stomach hardens like a stone when she says it. She wanted to repay me—help me fix the furnace I wouldn't turn on in hopes she'd keep landing in my bed night after night. I'm worse than a predator, and I hate myself for it.

"Well"—she wraps an arm around my waist. I can feel her shiver as she tucks in close—"let's get me to a bar and celebrate the fact that I can legally inebriate myself. God knows I need a stiff one." Her eyes spring wide as she realizes her Freudian gaff.

"Beer or wine?" I ask, trying to keep a straight face.

"Oh, honey, I think this calls for something much, much *harder*."

I tick my head back a notch as I take her in. Kenny is a vixen in a league all her own and she doesn't even know it.

Maybe that slip wasn't so Freudian after all.

In fact, I do believe Kendall Jordan just propositioned the hell out of me.

"Happy birthday, Kenny." I press in a gentle kiss, soaking in all her beauty as I pull away.

"Thank you, Cruise." She bats those doe eyes at me and reduces me to a big ball of hormones just begging to detonate.

I'm going to tell Kenny that I love her on her birthday.

Who knew?

The night glows in hues of purple and navy with fresh snow on the ground as we head out to properly inebriate Ms. Jordan. I followed Kenny home, so I could fulfill my role as designated driver.

The University Bar and Grill glows like a pumpkin lit up on Halloween with all the same devilish intent that particular night conjures—along with an assortment of pornographic implications thrown in for good measure.

"Drinks!" Kenny hops up and down. I've never seen her take a sip of anything remotely fermented or manufactured in a microbrewery, so the fact that she plans on hitting something hard amuses me on every level. I predict I'll be washing out vomit from the inside of my truck in about three hours.

We walk up to the pub and I lay my hand over the frozen door handle, pausing for a second.

"You want to talk about what happened in my class?" I can feel my Adam's apple rise and fall as I swallow. "I know that had to be tough for you."

"It's my birthday." It comes out far sadder than expected. "Maybe some other time." She reaches up and cradles my face for a moment, and her lips part as if she's about to say something profound, but nothing comes. I'm not sure what I expected. Hell I know what I wanted, but what I want and what I get seem to be two different things on a consistent basis.

I open the door, and the scent of perfume and tequila wafts over us, creating an intoxicating combination. A blast of rock music hits us like a volatile force field as we engulf ourselves in the questionably upright establishment. We play bumper bodies as Kenny leads us to the bar in haste as if she were afraid they might run out of liquor before we get there.

This was the place to be on any given night when I was keeping myself physically entertained—dick kicks is how I lovingly referred to the time I spent trolling these unsacred halls.

"Sex on the Beach!" Kenny chirps to the bartender before she hits the stool.

"I can make that happen," I shout over the live band that's busy destroying a perfectly good set of speakers. Hell, I'd make any fantasy come true for Kenny.

Her tongue runs over the top of her lip, and she intensifies her gaze into mine like a promise.

"Looking forward to it." She relaxes her elbows on the bar and rocks steady to the music.

"So what are you looking forward to tonight?" I lean in until our shoulders touch and order a beer I plan on nursing.

She scans the room and frowns. "I don't know. I was think-ing about having a fire sale with my virginity. You know, get it over with so I can start mishandling the boys at Garrison." She gives me a quick wink.

I think we both know she's not that person—that she never really was. But maybe all she needs is one more push in the wrong direction to realize it. I just hope once she does—she also realizes she might have feelings for me. Because what I'm feeling is too wonderfully large, too fucking fantastic to ever be one-sided.

"Body shots." I pull my cheek back, no smile. "Lesson for the day is letting some slopped-up, drunk, virally hormone-induced frat boy lick your stomach clean." I try to hold back a laugh. If that doesn't send her running for the hills, I don't know what will.

"Body shots?" She looks around uneasily as she chews on her lips. God, how I'd like to chew on those full lips for her. "So you'd let some frat boy defile me that way, huh?" Her face deflates at the idea.

My heart gives an unnatural thump, alerting me that I should probably say no. That I should pony up right here, right now at the bar, and fill her in on a few pertinent details about how I really feel—how I'd hang any frat boy by his shoestrings who tried to get anywhere near her, including my ex-pal, Cal.

She swallows hard at my omission of words and bolts over to the viper pit, teeming with profusely tanked Greeks, at the other end of the room.

"Kenny, wait." I jump out of my seat just as the bartender sets down our drinks. Kenny hops up on the bar and sways her hips to the music like a seasoned stripper. Her jacket is miss-ing, and her shirt is unbuttoned all the way to the bottom with the ends tied just under her rack, and I know damn well that's country for *fuck me.*

"Shit," I say, trying to squeeze my way through the crowd. "Kenny," I shout up at her, but she's avoiding me all together. Way to piss her off on her birthday.

"Body shots!" she yells over the music with the enthusiasm of a cheerleader during a Hail Mary touchdown. She lies down on the bar, and I lose sight of her due to the insurmountable interest she's drawing from the boozers sporting their boners on their sleeves.

I try to wrestle my way through the crowd, catching a glimpse of her between drunken frat boys, only to find some idiot's face buried in her chest, rocking his head side to side.

"Shit."

Kenny sits up and tries to bat him away as I plow through the tangle of bodies. I lose any polite bone I may have ever had and blow through men and women alike before snatching the asshole by the back of his shirt and launching him across the room like a ballistic missile.

A pair of arms yanks me backward—a fist crashes square over my lips.

Shit. Idiots usually travel in packs, so the barrage of limbs firing in my direction doesn't surprise me. What does surprise me is the fact that I launch my own assault and land three of the morons on the ground in a heap.

"Kenny?" I turn back and catch her buttoning her blouse. She looks over at me with a naughty smile pulling at the corner of her lips. My insides explode in a ball of lust at the sight of her. Nothing like a bar fight to confirm that the girl you're going to spend your life with is staring you in the face.

My legs pull out from underneath me, and I land hard on my side, knocking the air from my lungs. A swift blow to the gut leaves me choking, followed by the more traditional kick to the nuts. Then, as a grand finale, a power blow to the head stops me cold from participating in the fine art of nursing my balls.

The world warbles in and out like a dream as the room fades to gray.

12

THE GIFT

Kendall

They killed Cruise.

I whimper as the bouncer drop-kicks him onto the snowy sidewalk like a rotten sack of potatoes.

"Cruise?" I rattle him by the shoulders, demanding he come to because I'll be damned if he dies on my birthday. "Cruise! Wake up!" I scream, slapping him gently over the face.

He pulls his knees in and winces. Maybe I should have left him unconscious for a little while longer. At least that way he could have staved off the pain of having his balls inverted.

"Shit." He gravels it out.

"I'm so sorry. It's all my fault." I help him to his feet and land his arm around my shoulders as we amble back to the truck.

"I'm okay," he says, dropping his head between his knees for a moment like he's totally not. He looks like he's about to hurl, but instead he draws in a deep breath and comes up fighting with a flicker of resolve, determined not to pass out again.

"I'm taking you to the hospital."

"What for?" He plucks the keys from his pocket, and the truck chirps to life.

"You're hurt." My voice cracks. Tears are pooling, turning the world into a watery illusion, and there's no way to stop them. I've turned into a monster and inadvertently may have cost Cruise any hope of carrying on his family name.

I catch a glimpse of my reflection in the window to confirm my beastly theory. There I am, completely disheveled. My lipstick is smeared, my shirt is buttoned wrong, and my mascara is a mudslick down my cheeks. Who's that girl, and what the hell am I doing to the people I love?

Did I say love?

"You're the one who's hurting, Kenny. I don't want you to hurt." He pulls me in and wraps his arms around my waist. His hug feels solid and strong. "I don't want you to do this anymore."

I lean back and take him in. His silver eyes illuminate in the night, causing my body to quiver at the sight of him.

"What don't you want me to do?" I say it low in the event that I won't like the answer.

"Pretend like you don't care." His dimples press in like twin shadows. The muscles in his jaw clench as he swallows hard. "You're not the kind of girl who runs around after guys for the thrill of it. You had some vendetta to prove your stepfather wrong, and in an effort to make a point, you came close to degrading yourself on a level that I'd never want for you in any lifetime." Cruise presses in like he's hedging for a kiss. There's a tenderness in his eyes that I've never seen before in him or anybody else. "You're special, Kenny. You deserve to be loved, wanted, and desired by someone who appreciates you for the treasure you are."

His words cover my wounds like a balm. All of the self-doubt, the self-incrimination, the pity parties rolled into one—Cruise is healing them with his mouth, his kind heart.

"You think I'm a treasure?" The words stream out like the plea of a child—an unpretentious question that has its hope pinned on only one answer.

"Yes." A smile blooms from his lips, and joy percolates to the surface. "I thought so right from the beginning. I never intended to throw you to the wolves." A rumble of laughter ripples through his chest, and my body moves in rhythm. "Kenny?" He tilts into me. His features grow altogether serious. "I don't want you to become the female version of me." His Adam's apple rises and falls. "I'm not so interested in being me anymore, either. When I saw you at the party that first night, you changed everything for the better. I think you're the best thing that's ever happened to me, Kendall Jordan." He takes in a breath as if he were bracing himself for a leap off the Empire State building. "And I love you."

Every cell in my body sighs with relief. It's as if Cruise had taken me under the shelter of his wing, covered me in the membrane of those powerful words, and for the first time in my entire life, I felt safe, secure in every way.

"You love me?" I whisper it breathlessly at the thought of being loved by someone as kind and gorgeous as Cruise. I'm not sure I've ever heard those words from anyone outside of my mother, and from her, they were borne with grief, as if she were apologizing for my existence on some level.

"Yes, I love you." His brows dip, amused—baffled that I could believe otherwise. "I love you, Kenny. I love everything about you."

Cruise sinks a kiss over my lips that emphasizes his newfound affection for me—far greater than words could ever hope to express. He's pouring an intoxicating elixir right down into my soul. This is ecstasy, rapture. Cruise is turning water into wine, and I am ready and willing to drink down the miracle.

The snow dances over us, soft like a blessing. Cruise rides his warm hands up my shirt, singeing me with his heat, and suddenly I want nothing more than his entire body covering mine.

I pull back. My eyes remain closed an inordinate amount of time. I'm dizzy with his words, drunk on his kisses, and I want so much more from Cruise tonight.

I blink. He's still here. He's real. All of this is real.

"I love you, too, Cruise. I've never felt like this about anybody. I've never wanted anyone like I want you." I press my lips against his, dragging them all the way to his ear. "Let's go home. I want to show you exactly how much I want you."

———

Cruise glides us over icy roads and lands us in the driveway at record speed, seemingly fine after having his body rearranged. It's as if our profession of love buoyed him past the pain and straight into nirvana. He whisks me into his arms and carries me over the threshold with his lips adhered to mine. Perhaps he's afraid I'll change my mind, and this is his way of keeping me quiet; but the love he declared just moments before resonates through my soul like a bell you hear high and clear long after it's stopped ringing.

I slide down his leg, playfully tugging him toward his bedroom.

He shakes his head and pulls me into my room instead.

"It's this bed I haven't defiled. I want everything we share to be special—pure." He dots my forehead with a heated kiss. "I want you to remember this."

My heart thumps in a series of wild convulsions. Cruise wants this to be special, memorable, and pure. I don't turn on the lights. I simply flick off my heels and pull him to the mattress.

Cruise lies on top of me as we exchange a kiss that pulls out for eternity—the hot bite of lust fresh on his tongue. The bulge in his jeans aches for me already. I try to memorize the husky moans emanating from his throat, the way his body presses into mine as if it desires nothing more than to melt over me—*into* me. But deep inside I don't want to simply remember this, I want to relive it night after night.

My hands spread over his chest in one sweeping move and pull off his coat as I fumble with his buttons. Cruise peels off my jacket. We're all hands and teeth as we discard our clothes in staccato jerks. Cruise reduces me to panties and a bra, while I manage to strip him clean in less than a minute.

I pull back and examine him as an anemic spray of moonlight dusts over his body—his broad chest, the curves of his well-hewn arms. I run my hands over his skin and appreciate the granitelike texture, nothing but skin over steel. A ragged breath escapes me as I reach down and run my fingers through the soft curls just below his hips. Cruise is hard, like he was this afternoon, and this time there's no metric distance between us, no audience to depreciate the moment, just the two of us, all night, nowhere to go.

I close my fingers around him, and he lets out a heated breath.

"Kenny." He buries the whisper directly in my ear. My fingers flex over him. He's smooth, like velvet covering marble—a ridge traces up the back toward the tip. I run my hand to the base and touch him underneath where the skin is soft and tender, so incredibly full. It takes both my hands just to hold him.

"I love you," he whispers, dotting my neck with kisses. His hands slide down the back of my underwear and stop high on my hips. My body arches into his, and every ounce of me cries out for him to remove them, to explore every intimate part of me with his touch, his mouth. Cruise runs his fingers along the elastic and gives a gentle tug.

His heart pounds erratically over mine, letting me know without a doubt, he craves this as much as I do.

He pulls off my underwear, unhinges my bra, and I'm quick to toss them to the side. Cruise pulls me in with erotically slow, barely there kisses.

This unbearable ache to have him is mounting to an all-out explosion.

Cruise hikes up on his elbow and washes over me with a peaceable smile. I glance down at my pale arms, my breasts that bloom like magnolias in the night, paper white and glowing.

His dimples flex as he takes me in. "I've never done this before." He whispers it like a secret buried in midnight, and for a moment, I wonder if all the male prowess was nothing but an act, but I doubt that.

"Done what?" I gently drag my nails across his chest like I'm painting a picture. "Had sex?" I tease. "Are you feeling like a virgin?" I meant for it come out soaked in sarcasm, but it sails from my lips as if I were presenting him with a menu—myself as the virgin. I'm too locked up in the beauty of the moment to leverage any of this with humor. I run my fingers through his hair and quiver for him.

"I've had sex plenty of times, but I've never made love." He says it with an earnestness that can only be born from the truth.

Cruise lies back on me with the curve of a naughty smile— and the sheets—the bed—the room ignites in an invisible blaze. He pours over me with a string of molten kisses, drags his lips to my breast, and my body electrifies with a charge of erotic bliss like I have never known. A staccato series of breaths choke out of me as his tongue lashes over my body. Cruise puts his mouth over my nipple and drinks me down, eliciting a groan from my throat as I tremble beneath him. My insides melt. A soft ache pinches my stomach as I writhe with fervor. Cruise enjoys each one in a wash of affection as if they were enough for the evening all on their own.

He slides down to the end of the bed and sinks a kiss just under my belly before gliding farther south as if he has in mind a far more intimate location to grace me with his lips.

"Whoa." I hike up on my elbows as a surge of panic rails through me. I try to reel him back by the wrist, but he rides his hands lower and presses my knees apart. Cruise buries the hot of his mouth over the most intimate part of my body before I can protest, and I let out a cry as his tongue rides over me.

A breath gets trapped in my lungs from the erotic shock. Cruise devours me at a quickened pace, and I dig my fingers in his hair as the room spins out of control. Cruise loses himself in me for a blissful eternity—hours, weeks, until a surge of pleasure rockets through me that redefines ecstasy on a completely new level. My back arches as my muscles spasm, leaving me to quake uncontrollably. Cruise sweeps soft kisses over my belly, and I cinch my legs together hard, still reeling from the oscillatory pitch of Cruise's love.

He gives a husky laugh as he swims back up and lands a kiss just shy of my ear.

"You came for me." He says it out of breath, brazenly covering my mouth with his, and I taste him, sweet and wet from his love for me.

I melt under the supervision of Cruise's affection, stunned into a honeyed surrender. Cruise was the sky, and I was his star. I want to shine for him, to radiate all of my glory. We were writing the lyrics to the most beautiful song with our bodies, and I want us to replay the chorus well into the future.

Diamonds and wedding bouquets spray out in my eyes. Something unimaginable has suddenly become my heart's desire.

I want nothing more than to drink down Cruise and all of his love—to tune our bodies to the same rhythm and never let this night end, never let this feeling dissolve like vapor. What Cruise and I have is going to last. I can feel it in my bones. Cruise has found a crack in the armor. It's only fair he stays.

I want him to.

I want Cruise Elton in my life forever.

Cruise

Kenny lies beneath me warm and wet as summer rain. I bury my face in her hair and take in her scent, linen and lilacs. My chest riots against hers as she grazes my ear with her teeth.

I slip my hands over her nipples and roll them between my fingers before sinking below her waist.

"You're so wet." I grin like an idiot with my lids half-closed, drugged from the pent-up tension my body is unforgivably trying to release. I reach over to the dresser, and she pulls me back by the neck.

"Where you think you're going?" It bubbles from her with a laugh. Kenny shines a killer smile up at me, her pale eyes flashing with lust.

"I need to get something. You know, keep us safe—protected."

She slips her hand around my dick and pulls me in like a leash.

"Hold that thought," I choke out the words.

"You don't need anything," she rasps it out, low and sultry. "I'm on the pill."

"You are?" I'm shocked. A girl like Kenny doesn't strike me as the type to voluntarily put her cherries on ice, especially when she's not utilizing the parts necessary to protect. I remember some girl telling me once she had been on the pill since the seventh grade to keep her periods in check. Maybe that's why. Either way, I don't plan on overanalyzing the situation.

I dive back down with a kiss, thrusting my tongue around her mouth as if we were waging battle. She wraps her legs around my waist and tries to guide me into her body, but I tease both her and my cock over the warm slick I've induced in her.

She lets out a whimper and pushes her hands into the small of my back, so I cave. Kenny wants this. She's pleading for it, and I plan on obliging her in every way possible, tonight and every night hereafter.

I interlace our fingers and raise her hands over the pillow. Kenny blinks up at me with a breath caught in her throat. The moon bleaches her out into pale perfection, hair as dark as midnight. She bites down on her lip, looking nervous as hell and far too beautiful to be gracing my bed. Kenny is the person I've waited for my entire life, and I didn't even know it.

I push in carefully, and her eyes blink back in ecstasy. A groan pulls from my gut as I bury myself deep inside her. I thrust in those last few inches, greedy for her to envelop me—warm and tight. Kenny lets out a gasp, and her eyes spring open. I run my tongue across her lips before collapsing my mouth over hers. I ease in and out of her body, methodically and slowly, drinking down the moans of pleasure that strangle from her throat.

"Am I hurting you?" I blow the words in her ear, trying to control my breathing. It's taking all of my strength not to drive in fast and furious like a racehorse, like I want to, the way my body demands.

She chokes out another moan. "No." She breaks the word into two equal parts, so I slow it down even further, pulling in and out lethargically as if I were back to teasing the both of us.

"Aw fuck, Kenny." I groan, losing all control. I bear down in an all-out assault and slam into her, unleashing my fury. "I'm going to come." I heave out the words, and my body trembles over her as I bury myself inside her, as deep as her body allows.

Kenny digs her nails into my back and holds me there with the strength of a lioness. She doesn't have to worry. I don't plan on moving. There isn't any other place on the planet I'd rather be. Kenny is a drug, and I've just had the best hit of my life. I'm not losing this addiction. I'm in, all the way, pledging my voluntarily servitude to the gateway of my desire. Kenny is the freedom I was longing for. Love and all this wild pent-up desire has proved to be the combination that set me free. But only Kenny had the power to unleash me. She scrubbed the impurity from my life and washed clean the world, so I can see it stark and clear for the very first time. Kenny has perfumed my existence with her regal charm, her sovereign splendor. Kenny is, in every way, sublime.

I glance down at our bodies locked together, her smooth legs relaxing over mine. It's as if the gates to paradise have opened, and I want to run and explore everything with her by my side. She washed the tragic coating off this last year and painted it new with her body. She brought music to where there was only noise—color to a black-and-white world.

"What are you thinking about?" Her voice hums low and secretive as she tries to catch her breath. Kenny runs her fingers through my hair like strumming a guitar.

"You," I confess. "About how incredible you are." I peel a kiss from her lips.

"Did I do okay?" she asks, unsure, and I drink down her wide-eyed innocence.

"You did better than okay. I'd say that's an A++ performance." I rumble a dry laugh over her as my body rouses from its temporary slumber. I'm growing again, this time inside of her. Kenny sucks in a breath and closes her eyes. "God, you're so beautiful. I love you so damn much it hurts."

"I love you, too." A smile glides up her cheek. "Don't let it hurt. Let it linger like a kiss that never ends."

"Like a kiss." I press my lips to hers. I never want anything I share with Kenny to end.

My hips grind over hers.

This time I try to make it last for the both of us.

13

AFTERGLOW

Kendall

In the morning, after our first incredible night together, Cruise sleeps silently next to me as I get up gingerly to use the bathroom. I watch his back rise and fall as the newborn sun adheres her pale light to the curve of his skin, jealous to have him.

I scoot off the bed and take a few careful steps.

Oh. My. God.

Shit, shit, shit!

FIRE!

There's a freaking *fire* in my vagina—as if somehow my soft, silky flesh were replaced with live coals, and I find it very fucking hard to convince my body to take the very next step.

I try not to whimper out loud as I scuttle to the bathroom.

"Oh my God, oh my God, oh my God!" I mouth the words as I close the bathroom door.

What the hell was that? Did he perform exploratory surgery while I was freaking sleeping?

I snatch my compact off the counter and slide the mirror to places where mirrors and, therefore, glass should never venture.

It looks normal enough. I mean, it doesn't look mutilated—I'm not bleeding or anything.

Crap. I must have done something wrong. There must have been some step I missed, like prepping my insides with barbed wire in the event that he decided to draw his unholy weapon. Obviously, other girls are privy to the tricks of the trade because if anyone else felt like this the morning after, all coital options would be swiftly taken off the table. The entire human race would have died out long ago if women blazed a forest fire each time they had sex.

For a second, I contemplate calling Lauren or Ally and confirming my theory because clearly I did not get the fucking memo on how exceptionally horrific intercourse could be. Surely, there's got to be some quick fix—emphasis on the quick. Obviously, Cruise is expecting more of the same and more than likely in just a few minutes.

I made the decision last night that I won't be going to math class later. It's my only class today, and it's so not worth ruining all this good mojo between Cruise and me. The "I love yous" alone warrant me to abort the entire spring semester.

I need to find a cure for said ring of fire before he decides he wants to dip back into cupid's cupboard and discovers an inhospitable environment.

Cupid's cupboard. More like Pandora's box of horrors.

Think, *think!* Maybe it's his inordinate size? Didn't Ally say he was built like a redwood?

I *so* should have let him use the rubber. I'm so stupid! I'm like some vaginal martyr. Maybe all condoms come equipped with some special lubricant that's supposed to quell the morning-after pain?

I start the shower, and my thighs shiver with terror.

"Fuck." It comes out frail. I spot a bottle of ibuprofen and don't hesitate in downing two with water straight from the sink. *Bathroom* water. Everyone knows it's equatable with human sewage.

I gag down the pills.

I can totally envision the live amoebae swimming their way into my intestines. I can just picture them waving back at me like some happy Sea Monkey family as they go on to terrorize my digestive system.

Perfect. I'm going to die of parasites because I don't know the first thing about maintaining sanity in my nether regions. Who knew sex would be the first class I'd flunk? They should seriously hold a seminar for dumbasses like me.

I hobble my way into the shower and let the blistering hot water needle over me in an effort to take my mind off the live grenade that went off in my pelvis while I was innocently sleeping. I try to focus on the curative properties of the molten lava that's spraying over my skin, subtle as a welder with a blowtorch. But instead of healing, it magnifies the fact that my vaginal walls have morphed into sandpaper. I start in on a shiver. Oddly, it feels as though I've just dipped myself into an ice bath because my poor body is so damn confused and wounded.

The curtain pulls back, and Cruise hops in quick as jackrabbit with a Cheshire cat grin plastered on his face.

My hand rises to my chest. "You scared me." I jump a little and my boobs bounce into him, apparently ready and willing to take on whatever he's going to dish. Traitors. They know damn well my bottom half has yet to recover from his double-edged sword.

"Come here." Cruise swims with lust. He picks me up by the thighs and secures my legs around his back—leaving me spread wide and vulnerable to the carnage he's capable of inflicting.

Honest to God, his penis should be classified as a weapon of vaginal destruction.

Cruise lets the water spray over us as he warms me with his resolute kisses.

"Jeez." He pulls back and reduces the heat. "Is that okay?" He smolders over me with a look of wondrous lust and my insides squeeze tight.

"Better." I dot his wet cheek with a kiss.

Cruise rides his hand toward my thigh and slips a finger deep inside me.

I close my eyes and bury a groan in his neck. It burns to have him there, but in a good way.

He repositions the nozzle, so the shower sprays against the tile.

Cruise presses me against the wall and the warm waterfall cascades over my shoulders—his mouth never leaving mine. He hoists me high over his hips and takes me just like that, pressing in achingly slow, so amazingly deep. He secures his chest to mine, digging his fingers into my thighs. Cruise glides in and out at a pressured pace, and soon the ravaging effects of last night's love making disappear, leaving the incredible feeling of his body throbbing inside mine. He pushes in hard, sliding his thumb over that delicate area where his mouth made me wild last night, and I jump. He rubs ever so gently until I'm clawing at his back—the breath pumping from my lungs—and the entire universe inside me explodes into a million beautiful pieces.

"God, Kenny." He pants as his body quakes over mine.

I press in and feel him tremble through me as if I had just electrocuted him in the most erotic way.

My lips flutter over his ear like the trembling wings of a butterfly.

Cruise drops a mouthwatering kiss over my lips and gently bites down on my tongue before releasing. "Let's get moving so you can get to class."

"I'm not going," I pant, giving an impish grin. "I'm far more interested in the things you're going to teach me today, right here at home."

"What do you mean you're not going?" He ticks his head back bewildered, as if I'd just declared I wasn't wearing clothes in public anymore—although, he probably wouldn't mind that one too much. And, really? I don't get why he minds my private ditch day, either.

"I mean"—I pause to swipe my lips over his—"I've got some research to do for Gender Relations, like what makes an innocent girl like me vulnerable to a bad boy like you." I run my tongue along his jaw and he groans, pushing himself deep inside me. I let out a cry in response to the lightning that shoots through my body.

"Whoa." He pulls out carefully and lifts my chin with his finger. "You're not okay, are you?"

"So, maybe I'm not going to class because I can't walk." I bite down hard on my lip with the admission.

"Well, then"—he presses out a dirty grin and turns off the water—"I guess you'll just have to be catered to all day long."

He flicks the towel off the rung until it topples over my stomach.

Cruise carries me straight back to bed and licks my wounds quite literally.

The next morning, Cruise asks if I'd drive to school with him even though he has a faculty meeting an hour before class. Of course, I say yes. I would rearrange my entire schedule to spend just a few extra minutes with him each day.

I make my way to the student café, where I'd planned to meet up with Lauren and Ally.

They wave me over to their table in the back, and I make a beeline to them without bothering to pick up some much-needed caffeine. Needless to say, I haven't done a whole lot of sleeping since Cruise decided to gift me with the best birthday present on the planet—himself.

"Morning, ladies," I say out of breath as I settle in between them. I rattle out a quick confession of the fornicating festivities that have ensued since the most memorable night of my life and the mind-boggling pain that glommed onto my privates there-after like, well, hellfire. "I considered faking a twisted ankle just so I could use those crutches he keeps in his hall closet. Crutches!" I hiss it out in a heated whisper.

Lauren and Ally explode in a fit of hysterics, and, swear to God, I think Ally just wiped a tear from her eye.

"What's so funny?" I ask. "It's not normal, is it? Knew it. Worse yet, what if I've got that viral form of the clap Aunt Jackie hexed him with at Christmas? What if the female version was launching an inferno in the 'field of dreams'?"

Ally screams through her laughter.

"You're funny." Lauren says it drily before gulping down the remainder of her coffee. "That happens to everyone."

"Crutches?" Ally chokes it out as they continue their descent into maddening titters on my behalf.

It is kind of funny when I think about it.

I suppose I'll never look at crutches the same way again—or a penis. Definitely not Cruise's extended appendage. God—it's the size of a golf club.

"So, is he huge?" Ally's eyes augment in size as if to answer the question herself.

"I don't really know." The urge to gossip about Cruise's unusual size and stature has suddenly left the building. He's my boyfriend for Pete's sake. Boyfriend.

I give a dreamy smile.

"What do you mean, you don't know?" Lauren dips into me, confused. "Didn't you see it?"

"Yes, I saw it. And so did everyone in my art class." I spill the little tidbit about our foray into exhibitionism. "He's sort of, you know . . . like an arm." There's that.

"Get the hell out." Ally shouts it so loudly people actually snap their necks in our direction, as if she'd just told me off. She's not telling me off, is she?

"No, it's more normal than that. Oh, I don't know." I try to shake it off and change the subject. A familiar blonde saunters past the window and grabs hold of the door as if she's about to step inside. "It's Blair from my art class." I wave, but she glosses over us and sits by herself a few tables away.

Lauren and Ally exchange looks, and the table grow increasingly quiet.

"Everything okay?" I ask because I so know it's not. I can totally read silence like a book.

"Everything's great." Lauren lifts her coffee, prompting Ally to do the same.

"To conquering Cruise," Lauren says it so loudly her voice practically echoes off the walls.

My face burns with heat at the proclamation, and suddenly I'm thankful he's not in the vicinity.

"To love," I counter.

Blair shoots me a look and darts out the door.

"*Aw*, to love," Lauren and Ally coo in unison before they drink to this beautiful oblivion that has enveloped my existence.

The truth is, Cruise conquered my soul, and now every part of me feels free in every way.

Free to love.

Free to drown in the bliss that is Cruise Elton.

Cruise

Class begins, and my favorite student is ten minutes late. I'm half tempted to tell the other students to bury their heads in a book, so I can go out and track her down. She probably fell in the snow trying to cool the sting. I feel like shit knowing I physically hurt her and, to top it off, repeated the offense on multiple occasions yesterday—once again this morning.

A familiar dark-haired beauty walks through the door and I breathe a sigh of relief. She offers a shy smile as she takes a seat up front.

"Almost forgot." I snatch the stack of papers off my desk. "Revised syllabus." I slip the special one I made for Kenny under the pile until I make my way over to her. Our fingers touch and an electrical charge moves from her to me.

Kenny has trimmed the days in silver—the nights in gold. This is too rich, too sweet—far too wonderful to fully comprehend.

I give a little wink as I move down the row.

The only thing I managed to revise on the actual syllabus was switching the dates on the first two essays. Not that I'll ding anyone if they get confused.

I sit back on the lip of my desk and watch as Kenny's mouth falls open. I can't wait to conduct a sexual tour of duty around campus—hell, around Carrington—with Kenny by my side. Not that it hasn't been done before, but without Kenny and me, it has yet to be done right.

She runs her tongue over the curve of her lip and tilts her head toward me.

"Erotic love," I say it aloud, never taking my eyes off Kenny. I could care less if the entire student body becomes aware of the special brand of affection I'm unleashing on her. Kenny is quickly becoming my star pupil in and out of the classroom. Something is galvanizing. Something strong is boiling between the two of us, and the whole world should bear witness to the spectacular event. She has hypnotized me, and now I'm drunk off the wine of her love. "Any thoughts?" I open the concept up to the entire class, but it's Kenny's musings I'm most interested in.

"Eros," Kenny rasps it out like an erotic whisper, and half the guys in class fix their eyes on her. I'm pretty damn sure she just gave every male in a ten-seat radius a boner.

"Eros," I repeat. "The Greek god of erotic love. It's also the term used to describe the impulses of man to satisfy basic, intrinsic needs that propagate the survival of the species."

"Or just plain sexual yearning." She says it slowly with a slight drawl that captivates me—makes me want to give her the entire Bible to read while I lie at her feet listening to her.

Cheryl raises her annoying little hand.

"Yes?" I take my gaze away from Kenny, slowly, like pulling lead weights.

"Conceptually, it can also be classified as a basic source of energy. A passion, a juice—a hunger for living." She smirks, satisfied by her textbook analogy.

"Juice and hunger." I drip the words from my mouth. That pretty damn well describes what I'm feeling for Kenny right about now. My boxers shift at the sight of her, and I'm quick to walk around the desk to take a seat.

"Today's journal topic is Eros love, thanks to Ms. Jordan." I glance up at the room as they get busy with the assignment. I'm pretty sure the entire class will be in response to Ms. Jordan in one way or another.

———

The students drain from class as if there were free beer available in the hall, but not Kenny. She walks up with smooth, easy strides. She cups her hand boldly over my crotch and melts a kiss over my lips, heated like a tropical sunset.

"You don't know the war you're starting," I murmur.

"War? Is that what that little sheet of paper you dropped on my desk was about? A strategy guide?"

"Did you like it?" I wrap my arms around her waist and pull her in so tight our hips are immovable.

"I don't know what to think. Let's see . . ." She rolls her head back, and I run a line of fire up her neck with my tongue. "Candles and a bath, that was a great one." She says it low, and my body responds to hers. "That may require months of practice before we get it right."

"Months," I confirm, dusting her lips with mine.

"Role-playing—police and thief?" She tilts her head to the side. "Let me guess, you'd like me to handcuff you?"

"No." I shake my head as a wicked grin twitches to life. "You're the thief. I'm the cop." I bite down gently over her lip. "A very bad, corrupt, tainted, unethical officer of the law."

"Why am I the thief?" Her eyes sparkle when she says it like maybe she knows.

"Because you stole something from me." I run my hands up the back of her sweater, and she groans.

"And that would be?"

"You stole my heart, Kenny."

"Cruise . . ." She says it sweetly as her skin flushes with color. "You just melted me." She reaches down and unbuttons my jeans. "I'm going to have to reward you."

"What's this? Bribing law enforcement with sexual favors?" I knew she'd make a damn good criminal.

She caresses her hand over the bulge in my jeans until there's an ache in my gut only Kenny and her unstoppable body can cure.

"I'd like to speak to the 'head' of police, please." She gives my crotch a gentle squeeze when she says it.

"Now?" I glance around at the empty room, inspecting it for signs of unwanted life. The slotted windows, on either door, afford a view of bodies milling in the hall.

Kenny pulls off her jeans with lightning speed, leaving her sweater hanging low in the back. I'm caught off guard by her overeagerness to please.

"I checked the schedule." She lowers her lids, already thirsting for more. "This room sits empty for the next four hours."

"Kenny . . ." I tick back a notch, wondering why the hell I'm even implying a protest. "You're still sore."

"I'm over it." She bites her lip until all color bleeds out then slowly releases.

"You're lying."

"Do you care?"

"A little." Okay, a lot, but she's ground down my defenses with that smoldering look in her eye. I want her badly and am willing to risk everything I've worked for at Garrison to have her right here in this classroom.

"Desk or chair?" Her breathing grows rapidly as she moves her hips in time with mine.

"Most definitely desk." I cup my hands over her bare bottom, and she takes in a quick breath.

Kenny slides onto the desk without ever taking her eyes from mine. She pulls me between her smooth silken legs, and I burst out of my boxers like a wound-up spring. She guides me into her body, tight and wet, and that alone evicts a groan from deep in my gut.

I've had sex at Garrison before. I'm not too proud of the time I spent in the many janitorial closets or the new wing of the music building while it stalled in construction, but this is Kenny opening her wings for me like a dove. I can't get inside her fast enough, deep enough. Just knowing it's Kenny I'm experiencing this with makes it the only time that matters.

I knead my hands into her hips, pull her forward, and indulge in a deep, strong plunge that makes me groan a little louder than intended. I try to ease in and out, glide my way to ecstasy, but I've crossed the line and it's impossible to slow down now. I sink my hand over her warm slick and rub until she's along for the ride. I want Kenny to remember the thrill of the moment, experience every good sensation right along with me. Every time she looks at this desk, I want her to blush ten shades of crimson.

I wait for her until she's almost there, but the tiny whimpers, the strangled moans that wrench from her are driving me insane. I push in and spasm over her, blowing a sharpened breath in her ear. She shivers beneath me and trembles while clutching at my shirt as if she were about to die.

I pull back and lock onto her lethargic eyes, clear as ice. She looks stoned, drugged out of her ever-loving mind for me.

"Let the record show I don't go easy on criminals," I pant.

"Let the record show"—she leans in and whispers—"I don't give a flying fuck about your badge." She bows into me with her words, and I fire up again like an engine.

I press a kiss against her ear. "Sentencing for your crimes will begin this evening. Be warned, I specialize in cruel and unusual punishments."

She looks up with a devilish grin. "Oh, I'm counting on it."

The bad boy in me perks to attention, and I give a little laugh. "I loved you the minute I saw you, Kenny. And now I know why."

She brands me with her lips, and I push into her all over again.

14

HAT TRICK

Kendall

Okay.

Don't panic.

I'm sure there's no real injury taking place in my baby-making station. It just feels as though I've managed to sterilize myself forever thanks to the self-inflicted ulcers.

I try to engage in even-keeled breathing as I walk into my final class of the day, where I secretly plan on drawing Cruise's body instead of the relic who is posing for this birthday-suit pictorial.

I'm hoping at some point technique will be integrated into the lessons, but I'm guessing that's not today since I spot Professor Webber near the back toking off a hookah. God, I hope there's something legal floating around in that oversized bong of hers.

I'm still hopped up on my exchange with Professor Elton. And that syllabus entailed quite a laundry list of public facilities—the library, the staff lounge, the tower.

Blair gives a friendly wave, and I head on over.

"Saw you this morning in the coffee shop," I say, dropping my book bag as a myriad of loose papers vomit out. *Gah!* Just the thought of bending over and dealing with it sets my nether regions on fire. Blair starts to scoop things up for me. "Don't worry, I'll get it in a second."

The two newest victims to be inaugurated in Webber's exclusive nudist-for-hire ring strut out of the makeshift closet, clutching at the signature purple robes, and, oh my God, they're ancient! A series of low-lying gasps erupt once they drop the robes, sort of like with Cruise, but, well, for entirely different reasons. Honest to God, there's a crypt keeper out there somewhere who is not doing his freaking job.

Their bodies are a strange hue of gray, and they have more folds of skin than a litter of shar-pei puppies. Their limbs have odd bruising on them, and their gnarled fingers are nothing but skin over bone, green and purple with blooms of yellow interspersed. It's safe to say they've taken decomposing and turned it into a performance piece.

"So what did you say you were studying again?" Blair scoots her bench into mine with a reserved sense of calm. I totally envision two empty caskets with the words "flight risk" slapped across the front. "I set out your papers for you." She points up at my easel.

"Thanks." Blair is such a nice person. I can totally see her hanging out with Lauren, Ally, and me. I can't believe how fantastic everything is in my life now. "I'm studying boys," I whisper. "One boy in particular."

"Oh?" Her dark eyes round out. "It's not Mr. Glad to See You, is it?" She gives a knowing laugh. "That was wild, by the way."

"That would be him—and, believe me, he's very, very wild." My body experiences a private summer as a Cruise-inspired heat wave takes over. "Especially in bed," I whisper that last part so low it's almost inaudible.

"I thought you said you were a virgin?" She snaps it out as if I'd misrepresented my citizenship in the land of Not-So-Wholesome Milk and Money, a.k.a. Garrison. "I mean, you implied it. It's a big virtue, so I thought it was pretty cool and stuff."

"Well, I was." I pinch a quick smile. "But I'm not anymore. He's a god, so how could I resist? You did see him, right?" It comes out more fact, less question.

"Oh, it was 'hard' to miss." She glances down and sweeps the floor with a look of irritation. "I tried to save it once, and it all went haywire."

"I'm sorry." I touch my chest, appalled by the fact that I'm inadvertently rubbing my perfect boyfriend in her face when it's obvious she's coming off some big emotional breakup. "I'm sure your Mr. Right will walk through the door any day now."

She glances up and her eyes widen; a villainous smile twitches on her lips. "So he will."

I follow her gaze and spot Cruise sharing a few brief words with Professor Webber. He looks visibly rattled as he speeds in my direction.

I bolt to his side, still out of breath from our erotic in-class encounter.

"What's going on?"

"My sister called." His face reduces to an ashen shade. "She says there's some kind of emergency back at the house. I need to take off."

"I'll come with," I say, happy to abandon an entire hour of geriatric studies.

I snatch up my book bag and run out the door with him.

———

The snow molds over the hills, smooth and sweet, like a Valentine. The world is lost in the blue and purple hues of late afternoon. But the closer we get to home, the more a caustic amber glow casts blinking shadows over the horizon, and my heart seizes. Everything was going so well and now there's danger. A siren goes off in the distance as it screams its way over. It's almost as if the cruel world's whispering that this fairy tale I embroiled myself in is too good to be true. And deep down inside, I sensed this all along. I can see the handwriting on the proverbial wall—in the snow banks as they clap in reds and blues; even the wind blows a little harder here as the evergreens scold me with their needlelike protrusions. They all say the same thing. Tragedies occur, even here. This place wasn't special—neither was I.

Face it, Cruise and I probably stand as much of a chance as my mother and her revolving-door relationships.

When we finally arrive at the bed-and-breakfast, we're horrified to find a small army of paramedics and fireman has overrun the property.

"Shit." Cruise dips into the windshield disbelieving. "Molly said it wasn't that big a deal."

I want to say, that's because she's got a forked tongue, but don't. I bite the inside of my cheek instead, as we take in the melee.

"Jeez," I say as they pull a stretcher out of the wide mouth of the ambulance.

Cruise and I speed over. I've never been to the bed-and-breakfast before. I've been behind the scenes, literally.

The Victorian-style building, with its sunny disposition, looms larger than life as we barrel past the litany of emergency crew workers.

Molly straggles outside, looking frightened out of her mind.

Cruise snatches her by the shoulders. "What happened? Where's Mom?"

"She's inside. She fell."

Cruise races past her, and we follow.

At the base of the entry, sits his poor mother, howling in pain as several EMTs struggle to land her on a gurney. She lets out a deafening bellow as they count to three and swing her just the way my brother used to maneuver me before throwing me in the pool.

"I'm okay." She clutches at Cruise, digging her freshly manicured nails in his flesh like she's totally not. "Fell from the top, lucky I didn't damn near kill myself. Just twisted an ankle, that's all."

"You could've broken your neck," Cruise says, glancing up at the uniformed technician to affirm his spine-snapping theory.

"You never know"—the EMT ratchets up the gurney, and Sam lets out a riotous cry—"X-rays might show exactly that."

———

Cruise, Molly, and I follow the ambulance to a hospital situated by the cape. We sit in a waiting room for hours as the doctors assess the damage.

Cruise sits on the couch hovering over his laptop while Molly flips through an old issue of *People*. But it's the view outside that captivates me, casts its spell over me, and makes me linger. From the large picture window, I can see the Atlantic seize against the icy shore. A blanket of fog penetrates the vicinity as the moon slices through its shallow curtain, but I can still make out the jagged shoreline as it's illuminated through the mist. The whitecaps glow as they release against the sand in a fit of sensual delirium.

I have lived all my life near the ocean and never witnessed such magic, such brazen prowess exhibited by the stormy sea. The anxious waves thrust their hips against the shore, roaring as they push deep into the pliable sand until it smooths into submission. The water trembles over her tawny expanse until it ejaculates all of its foaming affection, reducing itself to a whisper. The waves roll back into themselves in a bionic rush, just to repeat the effort. Cruise is the sea, insatiable and hungry, all whispers and roars.

Molly creeps up beside me while Cruise continues to work diligently on his thesis. I can't help but give a private smile. I feel like a leading character in a book he's writing.

"It's almost time." Molly sings it low and mean like a bully. "A week and a half and we're good to go." She pulls at one of her blonde curls and lets it spring back into shape.

"Good to go for what?" I feel a threat coming on like a cold.

"You know . . ." Her eyes bug out as if I should finish the sentence. She plucks at the pendant dangling from her necklace, inadvertently showing off her chipped black polish. Looks like Molly steers clear of the Not-So-Happy Hair and Nail Salon, and for good reason—skunk isn't exactly the latest hair craze.

"I don't know what you're talking about." I can hardly walk, let alone recall anything from our last encounter. God—how I'd like to forget our last encounter.

"The *pill*." She elongates the word as if it had special meaning, but I'm still not picking up the psychotic connection. Come to think of it, I'd much rather Molly go *skunk* than *skank*. Why did I ever drive her to the free clinic to begin with?

"I don't know what the hell you're talking about." I curl my *L* in the same manner. I wouldn't put it past little Ms. Manipulation to fake some conversation just to make me feel senile.

She draws back with horrified surprise, and her mouth squares out as if she were truly shocked by something. "Did you have sex with my brother?"

"Shh!" I give a little spastic dance on my tiptoes. The last thing I want Cruise to hear is Molly and me shooting the sexual breeze. It's all kinds of wrong for me to be talking to his little sister about s-e-x.

I dart a look over to Cruise, who sits blissfully unaware of the fact that I'm busy discussing pills and coital encounters, with, of all people, his bratty little sister.

"Sorry," I whisper, "that kind of classified information just might get me arrested." I'm totally alluding to the role-playing game Cruise initiated and give a private smile over to the sexy sheriff himself.

"You *did!*" She belts out the accusation, probing me with a hostile stare.

"Keep it down!" I grit it through my teeth.

"You know what that means?" She bares her fangs with a haughty little smile.

"No." I panic. "What does it mean?" It *so* doesn't mean anything. The only mean thing around here is Molly.

"It means we'll be right back here in less than nine months, dumbass." She jets out her leg in a defiant stance, awaiting my reaction to her oh-so-vague declaration. "Unless, of course, you were pulling double duty and making sure my poor sucker of a brother put a hat on it."

I take in a quick breath. Back here in nine months? *Hat?*

He didn't wear a hat!

He didn't wear a hat!

I fight the sudden urge to run in a spastic circle as all-out hysteria sets in, and I'm not entirely sure why.

"Weren't you listening during orientation?" She rocks back on her heels in disbelief. "Those stupid little pills are worthless."

Dear God! Why am I such a dumbass? A question, I'm sure, Cruise will be asking in the very near future.

"No, I wasn't listening during orientation. I was too floored over the fact you weren't getting a refill, remember?"

She scoffs at my gynecological misstep. "The pills are worthless until after the first solid month. You may as well be downing Tic Tacs. So, I guess I'm going to be an aunt." She shoots an angry look over at Cruise as if somehow his penis had just taken down all three of our lives.

"You are *not* going to be an aunt." I spit the words out, quiet as possible. "Cruise and I are responsible adults who understand the importance of basic protection. I also happen to know that seventeen is way too young to be experimenting with pills and penises. So, steer clear, missy, or I'm so going to sic your brother on that hypersexual boy toy of yours. And, trust me, there is nothing more embarrassing to bring to prom than one of your own relatives. Don't think for a minute Cruise would ever let you out of his sight again."

I try to bolt from her den of insanity, but she snatches me back by the elbow.

"You know what else he's not going to take so well?" She sets her pretty little face in a snarl. "The fact that his bimbo girlfriend let him put a bun in the oven because she doesn't understand the basic principles of procreation!"

I seize at the thought before yanking myself free from her evil little clutches. Technically, I totally understand the basic principles of procreation. I have the perfect letter grade in A.P. Biology to prove it. It's the basic principles of the birth control pill that seem to have eluded my good senses, and suddenly, I'm virally pissed at the entire pharmacological industry. I might just fire off an angry e-mail to the manufacturers, who may have unwittingly assisted in the conception of my first child, and suggest they outfit that pretty little compact they gave me with a fucking skull and crossbones. I'm a visual learner. And, after years of institutionalizing myself in all things scholastic, I've practically trained my brain to mentally check out during an orientation of any kind.

I stalk off to crash on the sofa.

She is *so* not going to be an aunt.

Is she?

———

Cruise's mother managed to break her leg in three different places—spiral fracture of the tibia and fibula and a clean break of the femur. The orthopedist took us to the back and showed us the X-rays. He even let us assist in wrapping the gauze before he set a cast over it. He was sort of an ass though, clamoring on and on about how he was itching to take his girlfriend to dinner and wasn't expecting an emergency. So I kept reassuring Sam she did nothing wrong.

And after pulling a shift at the hospital, I sort of feel like a doctor now myself.

Cruise starts a fire after we return home while I shower and change.

"You know you kill me in that T-shirt," he says as I saunter into the living room.

For most of my life, all I've ever slept in is a nice, long T-shirt, so if Cruise thinks I'm doing it for him, all the better.

"I'm so sorry about your mom," I say, circling his waist in front of the crackling flames. "They'll take good care of her at the clinic once they move her."

"She can't go." He swallows hard. "Insurance won't cover it, and it's thousands of dollars a day. We'd lose the bed-and-breakfast in a week."

"What are you going to do?"

"Set up a room for her downstairs. Molly will help, and I'll have to take over the business for a while."

"Can you handle all that with school?"

"I'll have to." Cruise closes his eyes a moment, looking completely fatigued.

"I can think of a few ways to help you relax." I wet my lips in case he needs a compass to direct him.

The idea of a laugh trembles from his chest as he pulls us down in front of the fire. Cruise rocks me gently in his arms as we sit mesmerized by the blue and purple tongues of the flames—the same colors that the snow offers in the shadows. The fire, the ice, it's all related on some level.

"I can't lose my mom." It comes out morose—as though he considered the options life had to offer and found this one unacceptable.

"Give her some time. She'll be okay." I tighten my grip around his waist. "Believe me, my brother has cataloged a ton of broken bones. She'll be back to her old self in a few weeks. I promise."

"I guess you're right."

"She's always been there for you, hasn't she?" I can feel his love for his mother, the only real family he has, outside of Molly.

"She's been a rock, and I let her down. I used to run the house while she took care of the salon. Last summer I more or less gave life the kiss-off, and part of the fallout was leaving the business square on her plate. She's had me working shoulder to shoulder with her since I was twelve, and I abandoned her. I guess a part of me wanted to forge out on my own, and all I managed to do was morph into a giant asshole."

"And that's how we met." I give a tiny laugh and brush my lips over his neck. "Cruise"—I glance up at him, his handsome features reflecting the hues from the flames—"what happened last summer?"

He pulls me in, burying his face in my neck and lets out a warm breath.

"I escaped a fire that I didn't even know I was in. Then I ran around feeling sorry for myself when what I really should've done was move on, hold onto who I was, and not turn my life into a testament to condoms."

My face ignites with heat when he says the word condom. God—what if there's a miniature person with us in this room right now, swimming laps inside my belly? Cruise is going to hate me for being so virally stupid.

"Anyway . . ." he says, slipping his hand up my shirt and landing it flat against my stomach. "I think we met our quota on drama for the night. We'll save the story for some other time. It was one of those backward life moves that could have really screwed with my future. I'm glad it's over, and I'm very glad you're here."

I shrink a little at the thought of unintentionally screwing with Cruise's future and assisting him in any more backward life moves. Those stupid pills probably work in reverse if you don't take them correctly, and I'll be prone to having one of those litter pregnancies with six or eight babies. God—we're going to be on the news.

"I'm especially glad things turned out the way they did with me and you." Cruise rides his oven-hot hand a little higher and cradles my breast, fully in his palm.

I take an unexpected breath as I relax into him.

He moans into me with a kiss. "I'm so glad you were at the party that night. I've been thanking God every day since I laid eyes on you." He seals the sentiment with a mouthwatering kiss that lingers. His tongue sears over mine, hotter than a live coal.

Cruise plucks off my T-shirt, and our lips hardly miss a beat. His hands smooth over my skin, covering every inch of my body with a few lusty swipes. He pulls back and inspects me, twitching his brows in a naughty manner.

"Going commando?"

"I thought I'd surprise you." I give a little wink. "Underwear is just a formality at bedtime."

"Best surprise since this afternoon. You really know how to brighten a person's day." He purrs like a motor.

Cruise unbuttons his dress shirt, and I peel it back revealing his chiseled chest that glows underneath. I run my lips over the wall of flesh, drag them up over the hard ridge of his neck until I meet with his mouth.

Cruise lies on me, nudging his body between my thighs, and the idea of him firing off his baby-making missiles sours my mood.

I spike up on my elbows. "I think we should change things up. You know—you should put a hat on it." I wince when I say it, should he be quick to do the irresponsible math.

"A hat?" He ticks back a notch, with a playful grin because I just don't think he gets it. "I got a hat right here." He plucks a baseball cap from under the coffee table and secures it to his head before diving over me with more of his delicious kisses.

"No"—I press a kiss in close to his ear—"not that kind of hat. I mean, you know, a condom."

"A what?" He pulls back clearly confused by my bizarre request. His brows pinch as though the entire concept were vexing in nature. "No thanks. This is the first time I've gone natural, and there's no way I'm ever going back."

"Oh, right." I close my eyes a moment as he hedges his way near my procreation station sans the appropriate Cruise missile shield. "But I can't truly appreciate it like you can." I say it weakly because it sounds stupid. "Don't you think I should try it both ways? You know, see how the other half lives."

"Other half lives?" He spikes up on his elbow and examines me—most likely for signs of head trauma.

"I probably just advanced too quickly," I add. "You know what they say . . . the grass is always greener and all that good stuff."

"It's not good stuff. It's bad stuff." He brushes a kiss just behind my ear. "The grass is definitely greener on this side. It's that fake indoor-outdoor crap on the other side of the fence. Trust me, you don't want to go there." He nestles his hips over mine, and I can feel his rather large protrusion pressing against my thigh like a reproductive menace. "Believe me—what you gave me was a gift, and I won't let you take it away." His lids are closed partway, but I can still see the flames reflecting in his eyes as his smile morphs into a seductive promise. Cruise is glazed over with his lust for me.

He swiftly moves us past the talking phase of the evening and well into the potential conceptional phase, where the lottery of life will eventually conduct itself in my uterus for a lucky sperm and ovum, if it hasn't already.

Think, *think*!

I grab hold of his overeager member, and a thought springs to mind. My lips trail a stream of volcanic kisses down his chest, his belly, and straight for the launcher that has the potential to rocket us both into parenthood.

"Kenny." He moans because he knows what's coming— him, most likely.

I brace myself as I slather him with kisses. Obviously, I should have paid extra attention that day in the coffee shop when Lauren was sexually mishandling a banana. I glance down at it a moment. Ally was right. It sort of does look like a storm trooper sans the arms, and legs, and assault rifle.

Cruise could be gargantuan in size compared to other men and I have no idea. Nevertheless, that's research I don't plan on conducting, ever. I lay my lips over him and try to mimic Lauren's motions, riding my tongue over the hard ridges. Cruise exhales so quickly his stomach cinches. I must be doing something right.

"No teeth." He says it so fast, it refutes my theory.

He lands his hand gently on the back of my neck and guides me for what emerges as a season of loving Cruise in a way I hadn't imagined until now.

"Hey." He tries to pull me off, and I keep at it like a good little sexual soldier. "*Kendall.*" My name chokes from him like a dull ache just as an explosion of warm, salty liquid fills my mouth. "*Kenny.*" He pants it out in a fit of ecstasy this time and less of a warning. I wait until his throbbing ceases before spitting it out onto my T-shirt.

"Sorry," I say, as I make my way back up to him. "That might be something I have to work up to." And even that seems doubtful at the moment.

"You didn't have to do that." Cruise grins through his erratic breathing and pulls me in. I try to give him a kiss, and he's quick to deflect my efforts.

"No fair," I whisper. "You kissed me after."

"That's because you're different."

I trace him with my finger, his rough stubble, the sharp M of his lips, his filament-like lashes.

Cruise peers over me while resting on his elbow. His sharp features catch the light and bless him with all of the adulation the flames have to offer. His skin washes out in bronze, and he looks like a statue that's miraculously animated to life.

"Turnabout's fair play." He dusts the curves of my body with his mouth and a beautiful ache erupts in the pit of my stomach. Cruise melts over me, pulling my thighs up over his shoulder. He buries a kiss in my most intimate part, and everything in me surrenders to Cruise.

Cruise

Friday morning, snow blankets the earth like manna from heaven while all of Garrison disappears in an arctic layer of fog. Our world is unreasonably beautiful, but just as cold, and I've got two hundred dollars cash waiting to turn into a winter coat and boots for Kenny. That'll have to wait until the day is through. If I manage to have anything left, I think I'll throw in dinner—hell, I'll throw in dinner anyway.

She spent all day yesterday helping my mother get settled. I gave Kenny a tour of the B and B and she loved every square inch. I've always known I'd inherit the place one day, and walking Kenny through those hallowed halls felt like I was giving us both a glimpse of the future.

"Professor I-Don't-Bang-Chicks-Anymore Elton!" A caustic male voice booms from behind.

I turn to find Cal following me into Hoffman Hall, where my newly minted office is located.

"What are you doing here?" I don't slow down my pace for him.

"Consulting. They asked me to help renovate the weight room."

His bald scalp is dusted with snow, and it gives him that dignified asshole look he'll achieve in about twenty years.

"I owe you something." A shit-eating grin hedges on my lips. I walk up, clock him in the jaw, and feel a satisfying pop beneath my knuckles.

"Shit," he barks, nursing his wound. "I think I lost a filling."

"That's because you're a pussy." I head upstairs, and he continues to tail me like the stray dog he is.

"What the hell was that for?"

"For being an ass. Why the hell did you hit on Kenny? And don't deny it," I say, stepping into the glorified closet which officially houses a plaque lucky enough to bear my moniker. "I saw you with her at Starbucks."

"That?" He falls in the seat across from me with a dumbfounded, albeit slightly injured, look on his face.

"Yes, that." I pluck out my laptop and fire it up. "Look, if you're going to cheat on Lauren, pick on someone else. Kenny is off-limits."

"For your information, *she* was hitting on *me*."

I give a little laugh at the thought.

"And what's this 'Kenny' business?" He balks. "As far as I know, the rest of the planet refers to her as Kendall. Don't go down the thorny trail of pet names, my friend. It only leads to more misgivings." His nostrils flare as he slides into the seat.

"Kenny fits her. It's cute, like *Kenny*. You're not allowed to call her that, by the way."

"Cute." He mocks. "You know what's not cute? The ex-great love of your life stalking me."

"I have no ex-great love of my life. Therefore, I know not of what you speak." I pluck a stack of papers from my briefcase and scan them.

"Blair, you moron. We're talking about Blair."

"You're talking about Blair. I wouldn't classify her as any great love. More like an unnecessary evil."

"Evil? A bit harsh, don't you think?" His brows peak as though suddenly her virtuous standing were a matter of personal interest.

"I stand by my statement. Although, I retract the word 'unnecessary.' She was very much a necessary evil on many levels. First and foremost to contrast what true happiness is. And that, my friend, is what I have with Kenny. Things are progressing."

He shakes his head. "Never mind Kenny. When are you going to have the big powwow with Blair? You know it's coming. Blair is like a piranha when she gets her mind set on something. And right now, that something is you. Besides, she assured me she just wants to be friends."

"I don't need any more friends."

"You guys have a history together. You lasted longer than my father's last three marriages. I don't know. I think you should at least have a sit down. It's going to be a long life, and Blair Lancaster just so happens to run in the same social circles."

"Then I'll find new social circles. Look, I'm not interested in any kind of relationship with her. I've moved on. I wish her happiness, success, and someone else's dick to occupy her time. My body is quite content with the woman I intend on spending the rest of my life with."

Cal jerks back like he's having a seizure. "You talking marriage?"

"I don't see why not. Kenny is beautiful and sane, so already she's two up on Blair."

"Low blow."

I consider it for a moment. "You know all those girls I rolled around the sheets with these past few months? I never once felt satisfied." A sigh escapes me. Countless hours, and fruitless pleasures I subjected myself to just trying to fill some hole. I wonder what it would have felt like with Kenny if I had waited for her—if I hung on until I met her that night at the party, and we shared everything together for the first time. My skin electrifies at the thought, and my dick ticks in my boxers like a bomb. "Anyway"—I blow out a breath as I scan through the stack of papers in front of me—"I have no intention of fucking things up with Kenny, so you can tell Blair to beat it."

"She'd love to beat *it*. Just listening to her blabber on about her bodily regrets is making me insane. Why don't you bend her over your desk and put her out of her misery already."

"*You* bend her over your desk," I fire back, not quantifying his diction with so much as a glance. "I'm over her. In fact, I'd go as far as saying I was never that into her compared to what I feel now."

A shadow sweeps across the door, and I peer out to find a familiar red coat dashing down the stairs.

"On second thought, you don't have to tell her," I say. "Looks like she heard, firsthand."

15

DINNER THEATER

Kendall

The Student Union café smells almost as heavenly as Starbucks, but misses the mark in coffee. It's nothing short of a bad knockoff, a near miss, something that I once accused love of being. I wonder if all those marriages my mother sunk under like weights were nothing short of knockoffs for something pure she was trying to emulate—something special like what Cruise and I have. I wish I could gift that to her. Wrap up all of these wonderful feelings and ship them off to her boxed with a shiny red bow. My mother deserves to have this. Everybody does.

I spot Lauren and Ally huddled near the window and head over. A vagrant hand snatches me by the wrist, and I trace the red peacoat up to find Blair staring back at me.

"Boy, you left in a hurry the other day." She reaches into her bag and pulls out a stack of loose papers. "I got your stuff."

"Thank you!" I take them from her. "My boyfriend had an emergency. His mom broke her leg."

"So, you two are pretty close, huh?" She sours at the thought. Couples like Cruise and I probably make her want to vomit, especially after coming off such a miserable breakup.

"Very close." I shrug almost apologetically. "He's amazing. I never thought I could have something like this with someone like Cruise. He's the nicest person on the planet." I can't seem to control my urge to gush.

"I don't know." She shakes her head. "Don't you think you're too young to settle? And guys like, Cruise, did you say? When you're that good-looking, you're always getting hit on. They say 'pretty boys' are ninety percent more likely to cheat than some average Joe." Cal walks by outside, and she points a finger in his direction. "Now take that guy for instance. He would make much better boyfriend material in the long run."

"That's not what his girlfriend says." I'm quick to correct. "Anyway, I'd better go. Hey! It's your special day," I tease. "You ready for the big reveal?" Blair is scheduled to collect two hundred bones after class today and most likely just as many boners while conducting the semi-indecent exposure. Blair is pretty. I'm sure any of the guys in art class, or Garrison in general, would love to get to know her better. But she's totally been burned, so I doubt they have a chance. Wounds like that need serious time to heal. When you hurt that deep, you're probably still emotionally clinging to the person who hurt you. It's that whole power exchange thing Cheryl hit on in class. Someone still very much holds all of Blair's power, and she needs to take it back before she could ever hope to move on with her life.

"The big reveal?" Her forehead wrinkles. "Oh, I've changed my mind." Blair slits me with a look that could cut my throat. "Unlike some people, I'd rather keep my dignity intact." She walks out the door with the verbal snipe still fresh on her lips.

Really? *Some people.*

I go over and take a seat next to Lauren and Ally.

"Morning!" I sing.

Lauren's face is bloated and patchy as if she'd been up crying all night.

"Everything okay?" Everything is not okay, but I'm pretty sure who-the-hell-shit-on-you isn't the best way to start a conversation.

"Lauren unearthed some serious incriminating evidence," Ally whispers, speaking in code. "Lace panties tucked in the couch." She makes a face. "That's the calling card of every tramp who wants to get discovered."

"Cal?" My mouth falls open as I gape at Lauren.

"Bright red, crotchless." She whimpers. "I found the matching bra under his bed."

"Sounds like a progressive dinner was enjoyed by all," Ally snipes.

"I'm so sorry." I reach over and lay my hand over hers. I genuinely feel bad for Lauren. And if it were the old me, I might have given her a spiel on how love doesn't exist, but I don't buy that anymore. A very real part of me wants to give her hope. "You'll find someone else. There's someone special out there just for you. Believe me, the last thing you want is someone who strays." I hate cheaters. This is the exact kind of bullshit my friends in high school had to deal with. It seemed like everyone's boyfriend was prone to dip his wick whenever the offer presented itself. It was part of the reason I wasn't so quick to jump into a relationship. Not that Cruise would ever do that. We have something special.

"I thought we had something special," she bleats.

I swallow hard. There's no way in hell Cruise and I could ever land in the deep end of the shitter like Lauren and Cal. What we have is forever.

"I thought we would be together forever." Her words meld with a cry.

"She hasn't called him out on it." Ally nods into Lauren as if coaxing the truth out of her.

"He has a lot of parties at his place." Lauren digs her pinkies into the corners of her eyes and is quick to recompose herself. "There's a good chance he's innocent. Besides, I think I should throw a pretty brunette at him one more time to solidify my theory." She hardens her gaze as if to insist I have no say in the boyfriend-trapping matter.

"He was totally resistant the last time we tried," I say, trying to break it to her gently. "Besides, it felt like I was assaulting him."

"That's because you were in public, and Ally works there. He knows I'm never that far from Ally. It extinguished his potential hard-on."

"No." I shake my head.

"One last time, I swear," she pleads.

I hate the thought of disappointing her, but something about it doesn't feel right.

"Look," I say, getting up to head to my English class, "I know a girl who has some unspoken vendetta against anyone with a spare appendage hanging between his legs. She'd probably be happy to do it. I need to run."

They offer anemic good-byes as I head out into the cold.

It seems like everyone has a boyfriend, or husband, who cheats. Maybe Mom's long line of ill-gotten suitors wasn't such a fluke after all.

Cruise is different. I can feel it.

I wonder if my mother ever said that about any of her ex-husbands.

Dear God, Cruise had better be different.

In the evening, under a sterile bloom of moonlight, Cruise drives us to an Italian restaurant called the Della Argento. We round the building and find a parking spot not too far from the entrance. It looks busy, but Cruise lets me know he made reservations. Strangely, the sheer mention of reservations makes me feel more adult than either living three thousand miles from my mother or copulating with him like a sexed-up bunny. Reservations require forethought and planning, a phone call— all of which my adolescent fast-food brain quantifies as a giant leap into adulthood.

A large gift-wrapped box sits wedged behind his seat. I pretended not to see it when I climbed in. For all I know, it could be a birthday gift for maniacal Molly.

"I have something for you." The sweet kiss of moonlight pours in through the windshield, caressing his features. Its clean glow highlights the fact that Cruise is born of God's own breath and beauty.

What Cruise Elton sees in me I will never know. He reaches back and pulls the gift up front. The slick red box takes up the entire space between us. "It's sort of a belated birthday gift." His dimples implode, sending an entire riot of pleasure spasming through me. Soon, all I'll have to do is look at Cruise, and I'll have a spontaneous orgasm. That should make for an interesting hour during Gender Relations.

"You already gave me the perfect gift for my birthday. It was you, remember?"

"No, I don't remember." His cheek digs in with a naughty half smile. "Maybe you can jog my memory."

I give a little laugh as I unwrap the shiny crimson package. A glossy white box lies beneath. Even that feels expensive, something far too opulent for me to ever own. I lift the lid and pull back layers of tissue, revealing a dark wool coat. I extract it with care as I feel its heft, its warmth already radiating over my fingers. It's so beautiful—charcoal gray with matte silver buttons, a svelte woolen sash attached at the hips.

"Cruise," I gasp as I pull it to my chest. "It's gorgeous. You didn't have to do this." I happen to know these are damn expensive.

"I wanted to." He rounds out his gaze over me with a quiet stillness.

Cruise bought me a gift. One he couldn't really afford. I don't think anyone has ever done anything so thoughtful for me before.

"Besides," he continues, "no matter how hot you look in that jean jacket of yours, it won't stave off pneumonia. And if you get sick, who am I going to do this with?" He leans over and indulges in a gentle kiss—the barely there flick of his tongue caressing mine. A soft moan squeezes out of his throat and drives me insane with pleasure. For a moment, I think of abandoning our dinner plans, but he went out of his way to call ahead, so I don't say anything.

Cruise comes around to my side, opens the truck door, and helps me put the jacket on. It stops just above my knees and warms me as proficiently as a heater. I cinch the belt around my waist, and he groans while embracing me.

"I didn't think you could get any hotter." He presses out a gorgeous smile and my insides cinch just like that first night we met. "But you are on fire, Kenny."

"Well, thank you." I give his lips a slow seductive lick in lieu of a kiss.

"And frisky." He slips an arm around my waist while adjusting the hard-on in his pants. "You don't even know what you're doing to me."

The Della Argento is dimly lit with a romantic ambience spon-sored mostly by an arsenal of candles strewn about. A lush red carpet rolls throughout the walkways, and replicas of oil paint-ings from the Renaissance period cover the walls. A false lattice stretches across the ceiling and rows of grapes hang overhead like a canopy. Bodies fill the tables as if they were giving away free booze while a moody instrumental hums throughout the speakers.

A gorgeous blonde greets us with a pair of menus. Her hair is curled down to her waist, and her eyes sparkle a clear shade of green. One eyebrow is arched higher than the other, giving her that perennial-vixen appeal.

"Well, hello, handsome." She gives Cruise the exclusive greet-ing as she lunges her cleavage at him. "Is it snowing outside?" She offers a conciliatory glance in my direction. Her teeth shine like glass, so white against her perfect red lips. Just the sight of her turns my stomach. I'm not sure I like the idea of her smil-ing so widely at my boyfriend, let alone calling him handsome, even if he is.

"Nope. Perfect night." He glances over at me, and his dimples go off like sirens.

She motions for us to follow her, but she keeps pace with Cruise, eyeing him every now and again even though he's openly holding my hand.

"I think I know you." She bites her finger playfully while inspecting him. "That's right, you were in Osborne's class with me last year. I didn't fare so well." She stops shy of the table and lays our menus down. "I could really use someone who knows what he's doing. You know, like a tutor." She brushes her hip against his in a not-so-accidental manner, and my heart sinks like a brick.

Cruise steps out of the way like a perfect gentleman.

"Good luck with that." He pulls me in and kisses the side of my cheek. I can feel the heat from his body envelop me like a cloud born of desire. I hope the bleached bimbo is physically and emotionally crushed from his outright disregard for her. But she's beautiful—far more in his league than I can ever be.

She disappears, and we take our seats. I'm sick over how blatantly she flirted with him. I'll probably arrange for her to take a terrible fall at some point this evening because my immature and bitchy nature demands it. I never said I was above stretching my legs at an opportune moment.

"Sorry about that." He picks up my hand and kisses it.

"Don't apologize." I take him in under the flicker of candlelight. I wouldn't blame every woman in the vicinity for wanting to get on her knees for him, begging him to tutor her—*hell*, I did. "I guess it's an occupational hazard."

He shakes his head. That budding lewd grin widens as he affixes his gaze over mine.

"Kenny"—his eyes glaze over the way they do just before he pours out all of his lust for me—"you're the only woman I see. I used to wonder if love existed. I thought I knew, but I had no idea. Before, I simply stepped off the ground, but with you— I'm in the stratosphere. You leave me breathless." He needles me with a smoldering gaze, and I take off my coat, slowly and seductively. I lean in and my chest bulges from the low-cut dress I specifically chose to entertain him with this evening.

We place our orders, and Cruise never once looks up at the menu-wielding menace. She crimps her lips with disappointment and stalks off while he openly molests me with those sky-born eyes.

"Come on." He jumps to his feet and takes my hand.

"Are we going to steal kisses?" I pant, trying to keep up as he moves us toward the back in haste.

"No. I'm going to fuck you."

Cruise

The blackened hall of the Della Argento stretches out seamlessly like a tunnel void of reality, nothing but a dark arid space. I pull Kenny into a private alcove laden with spare tables rolled onto their sides, the entry partially covered with curtains.

"You're so damn beautiful," I say before plunging my tongue down her throat, my hands running wild over her satin dress. The minute I set eyes on her tonight, she got me going. There was a second, back in the truck, when I thought of taking off, hell—ripping off her clothes right then and there.

I pull down the top of her dress and close my mouth over her nipple, flicking my tongue around it gently until it's nice and hard.

Kenny gasps and scratches at the back of my neck just enough to let me know it's driving her insane.

My hand slides up her dress and between her thighs.

A dark laugh rumbles from me.

"You're not wearing underwear," I whisper, already out of breath.

Kenny doesn't say a word. She simply unzips my pants, dips her hand into my boxers, and my dick extends like it's ready for a handshake, more than happy to greet her.

Kenny's teeth shine in the dark. "Number seven on the revised syllabus clearly stipulates a carnal act in a public establishment is required to pass your class." She offers a sarcastic sigh before lifting her dress and slipping me into her, hot and wet. A groan gets buried in my chest. "And I do plan on passing your class, Professor Elton." Kenny hikes her legs around my waist, and I catch her by the thighs.

Kenny runs her fingers through my hair, and I push in deep until she gives a small cry. She digs her nails into my back as I plunge in over and over with a primal ferocity.

There's a transgender language reverberating between the two of us—one that resonates in a palace as easily as a zoo—and apparently the corridor of a hundred-dollar-a-plate restaurant as well.

We're drinking down the juice of our lust, satisfying the hunger of our flesh as we engage in the power exchange of a lifetime. But I'd give it all to Kenny willingly, kiss the ground she walks on just to be in her presence.

Her head dips back, and the arch of her neck rises and falls in front of me. I watch captivated as she glows, riding high, crashing over me like a wave. Our movements hit a fevered pitch. I bury a kiss in her cleavage and tremble into her as I detonate with all of my love. Her legs begin to slip, and I hoist her over my hips with a husky laugh.

Kenny bites down a smile, her eyes clouded over with lust. I slip my fingers in the beautiful warm slick between her thighs, pleasuring Kenny until her breathing becomes labored—until her face ignites with ecstasy. Kenny writhes in my arms, and I welcome it—running my lips over the landscape of her features.

"Cruise . . ." She pants into my neck. "You didn't wear a hat," she whimpers.

I give a little laugh and peel a heated kiss off her lips. "You're so fucking cute."

———

Over the weekend, Kenny doesn't get out of bed. Instead, she spends some serious time retching, and I entertain the fact that maybe the waitress I shut down poisoned her food.

Molly said she'd handle things with Mom after I told her Kenny wasn't feeling well. It's kind of nice having both Mom and Molly know who Kenny is—to have seen her. All those girls that comprised my life before—it was as if they were phantoms—an entire invisible parade of entities that evaporated like smoke once I was through with them. It's horrific knowing there were so many, and the fact that I don't remember most of them doesn't sit well with me, either. Some nights there was enough alcohol in my system to ensure I forgot who I was in the process. And right now, I wish they wouldn't remember me. I wish every one of them would forget me and every intimate act I may have carried out with their bodies. That waitress had me rattled. For a split second, I wondered if I had her, if she were simply trying to come back for more. That's the unwanted gift I've accidently given Kenny. Every girl she sees will be a possibility—someone who had slept with her husband.

Husband.

I keep trying it on for size.

I'm going to ask Kenny to marry me. She'll probably want a long engagement—that is, if she says yes. Maybe after she graduates we'll make it official. But I'm okay with right now if she wanted. I'd crawl down the aisle on all fours if she asked just to have her next to me until I'm no longer breathing.

Kenny bolts from the bathroom and flops on the bed. I slide up next to her, wrapping an arm around her waist. Her hair is tangled, and the sharp smell of mouthwash plumes in the air.

"That's the third time you threw up today." I run my fingers through her hair, softly so as not to hurt her.

"You keeping score?" She burrows her face in the pillow and moans like an injured dove.

"Yes, I'm keeping score. Three strikes—you're out. Come on." I pull her up and throw her coat over her shoulders. "I'm taking you to see a doctor."

The only financial perk of being a student at Garrison is the fact that they make sure your ass is covered with a solid-gold insurance policy.

The medical facility is stark in nature. A few people sit in the waiting area, each a good couple feet away from one another in an effort to avoid brewing a microcosm of germs in the un-aired room.

I help Kenny fill out a mountain of forms, then let her lie on me with her hair splayed out over my chest in long, dark ribbons.

"Cruise?" She looks up at me with those watery baby blues, and I wish with my entire being I could make this misery go away for her. "Do you think you could ever hate me?"

"Hate you?" I give a small laugh into her delirium, and she rides up and down my chest with the effort. "Nope. Not happening."

"Just in case—don't freak out or anything." She nestles into me and sniffles. "I'm not the brightest bulb, you know.

I'm human." She says human like it's an unfortunate condition. "I'm prone to making huge mistakes—like really big ones." She sniffles again, and this time I'm pretty sure she's crying.

My insides turn to stone when she says the words huge mistake. Am I the huge mistake? Maybe I'm the one who's making her sick.

The nurse calls us back and I help Kenny into the small room.

"You don't have to stay." Kenny shakes her head a little too aggressively as her cheeks fill with color.

"Relax. I'm not going anywhere. And you don't have to feel embarrassed. I've participated in more public hurling sessions than I'd like to remember." I stroke the hair away from her face and give a weak smile. "You're family, Kenny. You couldn't get rid of me if you tried."

"Family?" Her hand covers her lips. Her eyes explode in crimson tracks at the mention of such an intimate bond.

A light knock erupts at the door followed by a giant beast of a man with a neck the size of a tree trunk.

"Shit," I mutter. His tag reads Dr. Gaines.

"I didn't know they let the wrestling team play dress up." I say it lightly, but damn, I mean it.

"I *am* a wrestler." He gives a slight bow.

Kenny straightens. Her eyes widen at the sight of him. She's probably scared to death he's going to pin her to the ground. I bet she's really glad I decided to stick around.

"So, what's going on?" He looks over the chart briefly before inspecting her.

"She's been sick, throwing up all weekend," I offer.

"Diarrhea?" he asks.

Kenny averts her eyes and shakes her head. Not sure she would cop to it with me in the room. Maybe I shouldn't be here.

"Noro's not going around," he muses.

"We ate the same thing for dinner the other night and I didn't get sick." I pull a bleak smile. "Maybe you could run some tests, and see if she ate something she's allergic to—or something poisonous." I had to go there. I was thinking it, for God's sake.

He lets out a graveled laugh. "Let's start with a few more obvious suspects. We want to capture all the horses before we start chasing zebras. I'll have the nurse run a blood panel—probably just the flu. Kendall—is there anything you suspect might be making you ill?" He gives a plain smile, his eyes dull out awaiting her response.

"Yes," she rasps. "And I'd like a pregnancy test to prove it."

16

BABY, BE MINE

Kendall

All of the color bleeds from Cruise's face. He staggers a moment until Dr. Beefcake shoves some smelling salts under his nose and perks him back to startled attention.

"You'd better take a seat, buddy." Dr. Gaines tries shoving Cruise into a chair, but he resists the effort.

"I'm fine, really."

The doctor nods and leaves the room, sealing the door behind him.

A rail of panic rips through me, and suddenly I want to be anywhere but in this overbright room with, of all people, the unsuspecting father of my surprise pregnancy.

"Pregnant?" His brows dip into a sharp V, and it makes him look undeniably provocative. Although, I'm pretty sure now's not a good time to drool over his astonishing good looks, especially since committing a felony or two against me is clearly still on the table.

"You're going think this is funny." I open my mouth to tell him all about my egregious oversight at the free clinic then remember his seventeen-year-old sister is tangled in that web as well. Speaking of which, I'm thrilled Dr. Muscles didn't remember me from his rotation at said free clinic.

"I'm going to think what's funny?" He tilts his head because he so knows it's not.

"Oh, um . . . you see . . ." Fuck. Fuckity fuck fuck fuck. This isn't going to end well. Cruise is going to explode when he finds out I couldn't figure out how to use a simple birth control pill. "I . . ." Words dam up in my throat, and I hesitate in spewing out a sea of lies.

"Kenny . . ." His forehead wrinkles. Cruise pulls me in. He wraps his arms around my waist with a strong, hearty embrace. "Is this what you thought I would hate you for?" He huffs a laugh. "I could never hate you. And something like this—you didn't do anything wrong." He pulls back, and his lips twist as he considers this. "Besides, you can't be pregnant. You're on the pill." His face swells with relief. "All that puking messed with your brain. You must have forgotten."

My mouth opens to correct him, and nothing but air comes out.

"You're not on the pill?" He says it pressured, his face flooding with panic.

God, he's going to think I'm a liar—that I'm one of *those* girls who feels the need to fill a void in her life by planning a pregnancy. Right about now he's probably thinking that whole virgin thing was a ruse, too.

"Kenny? What's going on? Talk to me." He's got a frightened look on his face that suggests he just realized he's been drilling without hardware.

The nurse comes in and instructs me to follow her—so I do.

When I finally make my way back to the tiny, white room, Cruise has long since defected. I bet he's clearing all my crap out of his house right this minute—ransacking his wallet for the receipt on that coat he bought.

I should have known it would be my own stupidity that would ruin things between the two of us and not some fictitious inclination in him to cheat. If anything, that night at the restaurant proved Cruise doesn't give a rat's ass about other girls. That waitress could have qualified as a bona fide supermodel on seven different planets. You could see the invitation she was giving him, plain as the boob job wedging out of her blouse. But it was me Cruise hauled to the back. It was me he thrust all of his affection into until I thought my spine would snap from the pressure—me he pleasured until I gave a heated scream. Now, the only one screaming will be Cruise as he runs the other way when he sees me coming.

Face it. We're over. And now we're going to have a baby, of all things, to remind us both for the next eighteen years what a complete idiot I am.

My brother, Morgan, was an accident. My dad hung out just long enough to produce me then made a beeline for the state line before I hit preschool. That would paint a rosy picture for Cruise and me. I would give anything to have him love me with that body just one more time.

The nurse walks in and jolts me back to reality.

"Kendall Jordan?" She gives a knowing smile. "I have your results."

After the nurse breaks the news, I speed out of the bowels of the medical facility and through the waiting room, hoping to chase down Cruise's truck, but it's still safely parked in the lot sans its drop-dead gorgeous owner.

I spin around, and there he is with that sexy, devilish grin. He wraps his arms around my waist and plants a full kiss on my lips that neither feels like a felony in the making nor angry in the least.

"So tell me"—his breath evokes a plume of fog, round as a halo—"am I going to be a father?" He expels it with such peace, such wonder and beauty, that for a fleeting moment I wish it were true.

"Not this time." I give a wry smile. "But you just might get the flu."

"The flu?" He touches his forehead to mine as he breathes a sigh of relief. "I was sort of rooting for the baby."

I let out a laugh, and for the first time in twenty-four hours, I don't feel like I'm going to hurl a lung.

"You're off the hook," I say, slipping my hands into his sweatshirt to keep from shivering.

"I can deal with that for now, but one day we're going to have an entire tribe of gorgeous dark-haired children."

"A tribe?" I take in a breath at the thought.

"With those genes? You owe it to humanity."

Cruise and I get into the truck, and he runs the heater while I tell him about my misunderstanding with the little magic pill. Turns out, putting a hat on it was simply a precautionary measure for the first cycle.

"That, and it helps prevent STDs." He nods into his knowledge of all things prophylactic.

Oh shit!

I didn't even think of STDs. *Gah!*

Having sex with Cruise means I've technically had sex with hundreds of girls—wait, that doesn't sound right, but I think it totally is.

His eyes round out in horror at my silent, yet terrified, reaction.

"I swear to you"—Cruise gently picks up my hand—"I'm clean. I just had a physical before school let out for winter break. I'm free and clear, and I've never had a single thing."

"Oh, um . . ." Forget about me. I need to warn Molly before she becomes infected with all sorts of warts and blisters no thanks to Brayden I-Sleep-With-Sluts Holmes. "Actually no, I wasn't thinking about STDs." Because apparently, I'm an idiot.

Turns out, I was more worried about babies than I was rabies.

"You went on the pill just for me?" He looks humbled by the idea.

I don't answer right away. Instead, I press his hand against my lips.

"And you thought we were going to have a baby." He reaches over and covers me with his arms, tightening his grip around me as if I might drift away. "Kenny"—he bounces a kiss off my temple—"if something like that happened, you don't have to hide it from me or think I'm going to hate you. I swear, I'm not going anywhere. I'm in this for the long haul. You couldn't get rid of me if you tried."

"Then I guess you're stuck with me." I take him in against the backdrop of a deep navy night.

"And I guess you're stuck with me." He cradles my face in his hands and examines me as if he's peeled back all the layers and is seeing something new, something far more defined than before. "I love you, Kendall Jordan." He offers the softest kiss under a bed of burgeoning stars that peer in through the windshield.

I pull back and soak in all of his perfection both inside and out.

"I love you, too, Cruise Elton."

Cruise

In the next few weeks, the north winds scour the sky clean. They scrub the details out of the fir-lined hillsides and draw the oils from the eucalyptus like perfume straight from the throne of God.

Kenny and I file through the syllabus of my own making as if it were some sexual bucket list that begged to race to completion.

On a Tuesday, at five thirty in the morning, I convince Kenny to join me in watching the sunrise from Barrels' cliffside. Barrels lies tucked at the far end of a thicket, a good thirty minutes away. Juniper and myrtles gnarl their branches together, locked in a perennial swordfight as I drive the truck down the congested dirt road.

I happen to know firsthand Barrels affords the best damn view of the sunrise.

"My dad took me here once," I confess. "We went camping when I was a kid."

I may only have a handful of memories when it comes to my father, but that camping trip we took when I was seven burns in my mind, alive and fluid. For some unknowable reason, I'm able to crawl back into the moment and live it over and over again. It was the last time I did anything of quality with the man who would grow to be Pennington's father, not mine. Maybe that's why I held on so strongly. It was the eulogy of the father-son relationship that would never progress beyond that point.

"Really? Did Pen go with you? I bet you beat him up a lot." She bites the air, teasing.

Kenny rolls her head back, slowly and easily. Her neck peaks as if calling my lips to bless it. Her sleepy eyes send a silent invitation to drown in her kisses. Kenny is the heroin and the wine—the choice opiate of the gods, and I want nothing more than to lap her up by the bowlful.

"Nope, not Pen—just my dad and me. It was the last time he ever made the effort. I keep thinking about how beautiful this place is. In my mind, it's become this living postcard."

"Is that why you wanted me to see it?" She says it softly, uncertain of what my real intentions might be.

"No." I park as deep inside the overgrowth as possible before killing the engine. "I was sort of hoping to stomp out all those old memories and make some new ones today—with you." I reach back and grab the fleece-lined sleeping bag I keep for emergencies. It weighs ten pounds, but you can survive a sub-arctic winter nestled inside it if you had to.

We get out and make our way to the edge. The cliff is blocked off by wood fencing that's cracked in two places like a car might have tried to plow through, and I know for a fact a couple of them did.

A tangerine glow surprises the darkness far in the east and sprays the new day with promise.

"Come here." Kenny pulls me in and lays her cushioned lips over mine. "Let's hop in the back of the truck and start building that memory." She dips her iced hand into my sweats, and I take a quick breath.

"Sounds like you mean business. Let's give the sun another thirty seconds to show." I help her to the hood of the truck then spread the sleeping bag over the roof.

"Have I mentioned I'm afraid of heights?" she asks as we climb to the roof. "You make me feel safe."

"You make me feel safe." I echo the sentiment.

Kenny purrs as she washes those pale-stone eyes over me. "Hey . . . anybody can do the back of the truck." She whispers it smooth like a promise. "But the roof at sunrise . . . how would you like to build that memory?"

"The roof," I muse. "You, my love, are frightfully brilliant."

"And eager to please." She peels off her shirt in one lithe move.

I pull the sleeping bag over us, slip off both my sweats and Kenny's as though they were one. Kenny closes her hand over me and guides me toward my newfound nirvana. I cup her breast and give a gentle squeeze.

"This is my new favorite way to start the day." I inhale sharply as she pushes me deep inside her warm body.

My hands ride over her smooth skin, and I pull her knees up high to afford maximum entry. I secure her by the shoulders and push in with soft easy waves, trying not to launch either of us off the truck in the process.

When Kenny walked into my life, she blew away all of my bad luck like dust. Kenny is the anti-Blair, the one I could love forever and then that wouldn't be enough. Together we are ushering in a new day with all of our explosive passion; the frigid mountain air can't cool the fire brewing between the two of us. Kenny has peeled away the old memories, the ones born of pain and yearning. She fills in the crevices of my thirsty soul better than my father could have, far better than any of those one-night stands could ever hope to do. This is a new dawn in our lives, the beginning of the best season—the very first bite of sweet, delicious fruit that could satisfy for a lifetime.

We ride the waves of our affection, and I hold out until she's panting, just about to detonate. Then I release, and we shake uncontrollably for a few of the most blissful moments that love has to offer.

I always want to remember Kenny like this—the kiss of a new day, glowing over her skin.

"Good or great?" I heave the words in her ear through a ragged breath.

"Neither." She plants a wet kiss over my lips. "It was perfect."

Her hair encircles her marble features like a charcoal-colored wreath. Her eyes reflect the virginal morning light, clear as cellophane.

"I think we're perfect, Kenny." I collapse over her just as the sun pierces us with its luminescent joy.

We birthed a new memory at sunrise. We made it happen.

With Kenny, all things are possible.

Weeks sweep by, and the bed-and-breakfast, much like my mother, is hobbling on its last leg. Thank God for Molly, crutches, and home nurses who are willing to pop in every now and again. But, mostly, thank God for Kenny, who not only brings Mom and Molly hot meals, but is helping at the salon when needed.

Mom and I sit in her bedroom, which she sacrificially ventured up to on my behalf.

She takes a breath after espousing the woes of the B and B. "I've got one couple next weekend, but after that, it's dead," she laments while digging through the top drawer of her antique dresser.

The furniture has been in the family for generations—sage and cream oak, inlaid with carvings that decorate the edges. Mom took the smallest room in the house to make sure the guests would have a great view of the stream out back and the sun as it sets over the hillside. Molly has a room downstairs behind the kitchen, and now that Mom is gimpy, she's bunking in my old room next door to Molly. But today, she hobbled up a flight of stairs to gift me with what's going to be one of the most treasured memories I have ever known.

"You didn't give this to Blair," she says, cradling my grandmother's ring in the cup of her hand.

"Nope. Went store-bought, three months of imaginary wages down the drain, but I'm not too broken up over it."

"That's because I let you sell my vintage Beetle for the damn thing." Her marionette lines depress as she holds back a laugh. "Honey, you sure you're ready for this?" Her voice shakes as she hands me the round platinum band. It holds a simple diamond in the center and winks in the light as if my grandmother herself approved of the situation.

"I'm more than sure."

"You could take your time—sow your wild oats. If she's really the one, things will work out in the end."

"Sowing my oats wasn't all it was cracked up to be."

"I figured those bad-boy shoes never really fit you." She runs her fingers through my hair and lifts my chin in her direction.

My mother has aged decades these last few years. She used to believe in love, had men in her life, and brimmed with excitement each day. Then the last one took off, and she never recovered.

"How about you?" I toss the ring in the air and catch it. "Are you writing off that chapter in your life, or are the books still open to finding that perfect someone?"

"There's always room for someone to love, Cruise. It's just about finding that special person. It's all about time and place."

"I thought it was about destiny and soul mates," I say, half-teasing.

"It's mostly that." She winks. "A little magic now and again doesn't hurt, either."

That's the exact ingredient I'm looking for to make this next moment with Kenny most memorable—magic.

<hr />

On Valentine's Day, I drive Kenny up north to the Alexander estate on a crystalline afternoon that makes the snow on the ground glitter like fallen stars.

"Is Pennington somehow involved in this surprise?" She makes a face as she notes his sports car parked in the circular drive.

"God, I hope not," I mutter under my breath, driving down another quarter mile to the barn where Jackie houses her prized thoroughbreds. Kenny's face lights up as she spots the horses roaming in the corral. They're all regal in their own right, but it's the Appaloosa that's my favorite—white with black spots like a snow leopard. Kenny is going to look like an angel riding him through the fields.

"Horses?" Her face smooths out in wonder as we park by the stalls.

I head around to her side and take up her hand.

The sun starts to dip in the west, washing the landscape in gold.

"We'd better hurry before we lose light," I say as we make our way toward the overgrown barn.

"What are we doing? Are we going to ride?" Her dark hair whips around her face until she shakes it out and makes the wind sweep it back into perfect compliance. It doesn't surprise me that Kenny can get the elements to do her bidding.

"Nope, no riding," I tease. "Just cleaning up around here. I've been working for Jackie since I was fifteen. She pays me fifty bucks to scour the stalls clean once a month. I thought I'd bring along a helping hand." I give her shoulder a little squeeze.

"No way. We're shoveling Jackie's horse crap for a lousy fifty bucks?" She gives a wry smile before dotting me with a kiss. "Okay. I'm in."

A gentle laugh rolls through me. "Actually, that was yesterday—and the fifty bucks comes in handy now and again. But for now, I have something a little better planned." At least I hope she thinks it's a little better. The truth is, I'm shaking like a virgin on prom night. My palms won't stop sweating. I keep wiping them down on my jeans, trying to get a grip as each moment passes.

"I have a gift for you." I bring her hand to my lips and press in a kiss.

Kenny keeps her arm strapped around my waist as I lead her to the back. We bypass stall after stall, the scent of lemon oil clotting up the air from the wash I gave the walnut doors a month ago. Our shoes scuff through the hay, creating a hushed whisper as I walk her over to a large box with a bow on it. It's light as a feather, and I gingerly hand it to her.

I decided to ditch the wrapping in the event that one of Jackie's prized equine possessions decided to fill its stomach with parchment. She'd undoubtedly sue my ass the second they shit tinfoil.

"Cruise! You didn't have to do this."

"I wanted to." I press in a quick kiss and nod for her to open it.

Kenny pulls back the ribbon. She lifts the lid, and her eyes round out in wonder. "Boots!" Her lips quiver.

"They're lined with fleece, so they'll keep you warm."

Kenny holds up the sable-colored leather boots and admires them.

"They come with a stacked heel, so you can propagate your vixen-like ways." My heart thumps as she continues to examine them. I almost opted for the homelier ones that cost twice as much just to keep Kenny from looking so damn hot on campus, but Kenny's beauty is a fire I can never put out—wouldn't even want to try.

"Thank you." Her eyes glitter with tears as she buries her arms in the warmth of the boots. She looks up at me from under her lashes and sighs. "I love you."

"I love you, too." I land my lips over hers and linger before pulling away. "Let's check them out." I help her put them on, trading her high tops for something that might actually ward off frostbite.

"I think I've died and gone to heaven." She moans as her feet sink into the plush reserve.

"That good, huh?"

She gives an impish grin. Her mascara is smudged in the corners from the fresh dab of tears.

"It's because you're in my life." She warms my mouth with an exploratory kiss. For a second, I think maybe we should lie down right here in the hay, but I've got a ring burning a hole in my pocket and the sun is working against me.

"Let's do this." I pull the horse named Lady Luck Tonight out of the stall and saddle her up. I help Kenny mount, and she gives a solid yank to the reins.

"Whoa." I jump off the stall, landing on the horse behind her. Kenny hands me the leather straps, and I teach her how to use them as we make our way out of the barn.

"We're going to kill this poor thing," she whimpers with her body pressed against mine. Our hips move in time, slow and circular.

"She can handle it." I bury a kiss in Kenny's hair, close my eyes, and soak in the glory of the moment. "She's sturdy and stout. She's got the endurance of a Mack truck. Plus, we're heading out less than a mile."

We make our way past the corral, and the chaparrals press themselves against the sky like felt. Kenny scoots to the back of the saddle as far as she can, and I wrap my arms around her. I pepper her with kisses as we disappear down the bridle trail laden with bare maples. The evergreens loom, large and daunting, like nefarious shadows that refuse to give their secrets.

"I've never done anything like this." Kenny touches her fingers to my cheek, and I kiss them. "You really know how to pull the magic from the air."

And there it is. Magic. Kenny feels it, and so do I.

Lady Luck pulls in just shy of the meadow by the frozen pond. A spray of dappled light filters through the centurion oak. Plumes of ethereal sunshine rise in vapors, transforming the snow-covered landscape into something just this side of a fairy tale.

I hop down and help Kenny slip into my arms before leading us over to the boulders that skirt the area.

Kenny pulls me in gently by the neck and loves me with her lingering kisses.

God, I want her right here in the frozen tundra of the Alexander estate. I envision us laid out like silhouette cutouts, her hair sprayed out like ebony wings.

I drop to my knees, and she follows me down.

I pinch my lips at the oversight. "You weren't supposed to do that." I can't hide the smile anymore. Joy has bubbled to the surface like hope unstoppable.

"Was I supposed to do this?" She unbuttons my jeans and looks up at me with a dare.

I pull the ring from my pocket before we have my hard-on splitting the difference between us as a lasting matrimonial memory.

"I love you, Kenny." I draw in a ragged breath. "You saved me. You taught me to breathe and showed me how to appreciate the beauty in every single moment. I never want to be without you." I lick my lips, and the glacial breeze bites over them. "Kenny, I beg of you from the bottom of my heart—please, be my wife." I hold out the ring like an offering. My cheek slides up on the side, and I hold my breath as her eyes widen with disbelief. I give an apprehensive smile. "Marry me—yes, or no?"

17

PERFECT LOVE

Kendall

"Cruise!" I can't stop staring at the beautiful ring he holds between us as we kneel in this frozen version of heaven. Everything in me surges. An explosion of brand-new feelings goes off inside me like fireworks, so potent and viral they put excitement and wonder to shame.

Through the eye of this ring is a portal, a bright shiny path to a future with Cruise. It comes with a promise, backed by love, and everything in me sighs with relief because the very thing I decried as a fallacy has materialized in the only person I have ever wanted. And now, he holds something tangible for me to have and to hold, from this day on.

"Yes!" It drills from my lungs, loudly and capriciously—crisp as the air that sings it back to me in an echo.

"Yes?" He looks unsure, as if maybe he'd dreamed it.

"Yes! Yes, yes, *yes*!" I lunge into him with a swarm of wild kisses salted with tears. I have never felt so whole, so happy, and so overwhelmed all at the same time.

"Yes." Cruise closes his eyes a moment. He picks up my left hand and slips the ring on my finger. It glows against my skin. The diamond shimmers in the reserve of light like a star encased in a seam of moonlight. "It was my grandmother's ring. I hope you don't mind."

"God, no. It's beautiful. I'm touched it belonged to her." I shiver into him. "And it fits. That's a miracle."

"You could trade it in, or we could get you something different for the wedding. I just thought it'd look gorgeous on you, and I was right." His gaze never dips from mine.

"I don't want anything different. This is perfect. You're perfect."

Cruise melts a kiss over my lips and runs his hands up the back of my sweater, warm and strong. The same arms that will love me tomorrow and the day after that until eternity unravels like a spool.

My coat acts like a blanket as I pull Cruise down to the snow. His face is alarmingly attractive against the backdrop of a sodden sky, and my stomach melts at the sight of him—at the thought of knowing he'll always be mine. He kneads his hands over my body as if he were a sculptor, working my jeans down, anxious to have me. He dusts his fingers over my belly, slips his hand between my thighs. His dimples dig in like twin shadows. Cruise watches from above as I writhe from his touch—he supervises with a heated intensity as he sets me on fire from the inside. This erotic bliss, this inflamed burst of ecstasy is the threshold to a new era in our lives. He relaxes over me and pushes in with his hips, slow and sweet, meeting me right there in my fevered delirium.

Cruise makes love to me on a bed of snow with those tender groans that wrench from him with an aching passion. He blesses me with a kiss, soft and careful as his tongue strokes over mine. Cruise satiates me from the inside out with a pull of dizzying affection. I memorize his touch, take in his scent, fill my ears with every errant sound that emanates from his throat. Everything

ADDISON MOORE

about Cruise makes me greedy for more. He covers me with his body and buries himself inside me in the most intimate way.

This is all I want.

Forever.

———

The next week, after Gender Relations, Cruise says there is someplace special he wants to take me.

Cruise holds my hand as we walk boldly through campus. I'm still hopped up on our newly engaged status. We've spent every night tangled in one another's arms, locked in the bliss of what the future holds for us.

A parade of bicycles clutters the walkways. They speed by as if this were a busy New York sidewalk—the Tour de France taking place right here at Garrison.

He pauses just shy of a tall, brick building. His gaze rides to the top, then to me. There's a mischievous look in his eye that suggests the architectural erection standing in front of us has something to do with his special locale.

"If this involves rappelling, you can count me out." No use placating him with false hope. I'd just as soon leap from a building as I would eat a bowl of greasy worms.

"No rappelling. I promise." Cruise brings my hand to his lips and presses in a kiss that warms me down to my toes.

My mouth opens to say something, but a blonde in a red coat catches my eye off in the distance. It's Blair from Art, which reminds me, I meant to ask her if she'd be open to trapping Cal. Lauren has been after me every chance she gets, even though I've assured her I won't be hitting on another guy anytime soon. Not when I have Cruise.

He reels me in and we duck into a narrow door through the back. It's dark inside. The stench of mildew and rust lights up my senses.

"Welcome to the tower, Kenny," he says, nodding over to a stairwell that leads dozens of stories to the top of Garrison's most prized phallic symbol.

"This will take hours," I'm quick to point out. Plus, this is one vertigo-inspired workout I'm not looking forward to.

He pushes a button behind me, and an elevator door silently opens.

"Clever," I say, more than slightly relieved. "My feet appreciate the reprieve."

We climb in and ride to the top at gravity-defying speeds. Cruise makes himself at home, nibbling on my earlobe with his hot, hungry mouth.

The doors open to an icy bite of wind, and that revised syllabus comes flooding back to me. Number ten, the grand finale—the tower.

"Oh God." It comes out frail.

"I got you," he whispers with a devious smile.

Cruise leads us outside to the giant globe that floats over campus like an insignia. The graphite sky looms above. Burnt-gray clouds bow so close you could touch them. I half expect the finger of God to reach out like a fresco come to life.

I catch a glimpse down at the tiny people shuffling around campus. The landscape zooms in and out as I sway on my feet.

"Don't be afraid," he says, steadying me. He pulls me gently into the metal frame of the sphere with the utmost care. Cruise wants this. This is the pièce de résistance of his orgasmic outline, the one he drew up for my eyes only.

I give a naughty grin as I drop to my knees and peel open his jeans. He clasps his hand over mine and kneels beside me.

"Kenny, you're a work of beauty. You know that?"

"No, I don't know that," I whisper as the color rises to my cheeks. "But I'm damn glad you think so."

Cruise scoops my face into his palms, kissing me full on the lips with the fire from his mouth.

The wind slices through the gap between our bodies as if it were trying to keep us apart, push us over the edge—trade in our love for tragedy. But Cruise lays me down, holding me steady with the weight of his affection. He hovers over me with a wicked grin, taking me in, soaking up the experience as if this were the sum total of all he ever wanted. He runs his hands inside my sweater and frees me from my bra with the dexterity of a magician. He bows into my neck with steamed kisses before creating a trail down my chest, slow and steady as if the world and everything in it were ours. We have a million years to love one another, wherever we please—whenever.

Cruise maneuvers me free from my jeans, pulls down his boxers, and his love for me dives into the open. His warm body rides over mine, teasing me with barely there kisses. He kneads his hands into my hips, rolling me into him until I'm panting for what he's about to offer. I reach down and guide him in, soft and easy, until my body arches to meet his, and I take in a breath. Cruise pulsates in and out as we create a soothing rhythm. He lands his lips over mine; they drift to my ear, my neck, quick as lightning. Cruise bites and licks, moans and calls my name until we're lost in that beautiful oblivion built just for the two of us. My lids flutter. The clouds rotate dressed in navy and black while the wind sears us with its wrath. With Cruise, I no longer fear the heights the world has to offer. Now I would crave them.

With Cruise, I no longer wonder what it would be like to be loved. Now I'll know forever.

"*God, Kenny.*" He boils the words into my ear as his body launches into a series of convulsions. Cruise lets out a guttural roar and arches his neck back, his eyes closed to heaven. I want to remember him this way—nothing but Cruise and sky—the pinnacle of lust with a backdrop of cinder.

My insides sail me past passion and reason, and I flex into him hard and fast. Cruise doesn't let up. He thrusts in deeper until all of the breath leaves my body. I clutch onto his back, pulling him in with violent intention.

A dark laugh rumbles from him as his skin blisters against mine.

"I love you, Kenny." His heart knocks against my chest as if demanding to come inside.

"I love you, too, Cruise." I pull a wet kiss off his lips, trying to catch my breath.

Cruise always leaves me breathless.

I tried to convince Cruise we should go home and continue the prequel to our honeymoon, but he insists I go to my afternoon classes, poor hygiene and all.

In Art, Ally, of all people, surprises the hell out of me by being the next student hungry for two hundred solid. She lends her body to the class as a landscape with a smile, and every guy in the class is perked to attention. The male model never showed, so she's a one-woman show. I can tell she's uncomfortable because she keeps trying to cover her girl parts by crossing her arms and legs, and Professor Webber keeps barking at her to knock it off.

A little warning would have been nice on Ally's part, but, then again, she probably doesn't know I'm in this class.

I trace her out in charcoal—thin and wispy, making her limbs look as though they've been run through a pasta machine. I want to make her face as beautiful as possible because I know she's going to want to see this. Anyway, Ally is gorgeous, so I don't have to worry about trying to make her look good—more like trying to make her look human. Needless to say, my aptitude for sketching people leaves a lot to be desired. Speaking of Ally—that totally reminds me of Lauren's ludicrous plan to sick a faux tramp on her boyfriend. That's so twisted I don't even know how to classify it.

"Say, Blair?" I take her in as she wistfully sketches Ally, giving her ballooning hips fit for birthing an elephant. "Would you mind trying to seduce someone's boyfriend to prove he's not a cheat?"

Her tiny mouth opens. Blair looks at me with wonder as if a backhanded miracle had just taken place.

"You want me to seduce your boyfriend?" she stammers, flustered at the idea of hitting on Cruise, and suddenly I'm sorry I ever brought it up.

"No, not my boyfriend. He would never cheat. It's for a friend."

"Nope, wouldn't do it." She whips her pencil across the oversized sheet of paper. Funny how her enthusiasm waned once *my* boyfriend disappeared from the scene.

"Is that a ring on your finger?" Blair's eyes magnify and retract at the sight of the shiny band of platinum.

"His grandmother's." I hold it out for her to inspect and her face turns a strange ashen shade. "Are you okay?"

"I'm fine." Her lips pinch tight. "So how'd he do it? It's the boy with the penis, right?"

I don't like her reducing Cruise to such indelicate body parts, but I let it slide since she's bitter. Nothing like a broken heart to turn you off to men forever, or so my mother says. Although with Mom, forever is the span of time between her divorce finalizing and her next visit to the local bar.

"He took me out on horseback," I whisper. "It was this place that looked like heaven on earth, and he dropped to his knees— made love to me in the snow after, right there in the field like we were the only two people in world," I say it low, mostly to myself as I relive the memory. A thread of heat rises through me, and suddenly it's too warm inside the jacket, inside the boots he bought for me with his careful attention to my needs. "He's perfect."

She huffs into my admission. "I bet his last fiancée thought so, too." She shrugs as if I should already know this. "Does he ever talk about her?"

The ground beneath me sways for a moment. I knew Cruise had a girlfriend, but he's never brought her up. For sure he never mentioned an engagement.

"No, he doesn't say much."

"Funny." She smirks, continuing on with the distorted picture in front of her. Blair's pencil glides across the page in a series of spastic strokes as she disfigures Ally's forehead to make it look twice its natural size. "For a couple that's supposedly so in love, you don't seem to know a lot about him. Then again, he probably doesn't want you to find out why they broke it off."

Why they broke it off? "Do you know why they broke it off?"

"*Oh* . . ." She grunts with marked aggression. "I do know. They crashed and burned." She says it with an exaggerated sadness as if there were an irony in there somewhere. "He cheated. He's prone to wander. But you know that. He's slept with at least five hundred girls. He's got pig's blood coursing through his veins just like his daddy."

A breath gets caught in my throat. She so did not go there.

"What the hell are you talking about?" The words edge out as if each one were taking me one step closer to stepping off a cliff. "Take it back. Cruise isn't like that, and I don't appreciate you reducing him or his father to farm animals." My blood boils right down to the marrow to hear her talk about Cruise like that.

She gives a solid laugh. "It's true. But you're one of those girls who needs to find things out the hard way, I can tell."

The sudden urge to slap her rails through me, and the only thing stopping me is the fact that a bitch like Blair would most likely file assault charges.

"Boy"—a frustrated laugh gyrates through me—"someone really screwed you over, didn't he?" This is the last conversation I'm ever having with this psycho. I'm sorry I ever sat on this side of the room.

She needles me with those dark, brooding eyes. Her face is hard as flint with all of the sweetness drained right out of her.

"You're right. Someone really screwed me over. Or maybe I did it to myself." Her arm glides over the page in front of her, violent and spastic. She creates large black X's through her meticulous sketch until the pencil knifes through layers of onion paper. She stops cold and looks right at me with a fire in her eyes that looks downright caustic. "He still loves her. You know that, right? That's the reason he never brings her up—because it hurts so bad. He'll always love the girl he was going to marry. You don't really want to be second place in his heart, do you?"

I pack my things and turn to go, but she catches me by the elbow.

"Look"—she closes her eyes briefly—"I'm only trying to do you a favor. I never want you to feel as bad as I do. There's someone special out there for you, Kendall. It's just not him. His heart still belongs to me."

My stomach lurches. I scoot the hell back, knocking down easels like dominos and half the room erupts from the chaos.

This is *her*?

She never once said so, and yet she listened as I told her the intimate details of our relationship.

I run out of the building.

I plan on never going back.

Cruise

The text from Kenny reads, **Caught a ride home with Lauren. xoxo.**

Ride with Lauren? Huh. Maybe she's not feeling well.

I would have left early if she wanted. I'm all done with classes— just logging the last few minutes of office hours.

Strange. It's usually me waiting for her. We've been driving together the past few weeks to save on gas. It won't be the same leaving without her next to me. I actually miss her.

I let out a little laugh. It looks like Ms. Jordan has me whipped after all. My, how the mighty have fallen.

A shadow darkens the doorway, and for a fleeting moment I'm convinced it's Kenny. She's probably going to tie me to the chair and make good use of this paper penitentiary.

"Cruise?" A female voice scratches the air.

My blood runs cold before I turn around.

I recognize that sharp tone, that curt inflection. Blair. She never did say my name with an ounce of respect.

My shoes dig in as I spin in my seat. I knew this was coming. Deep down inside, I never wanted to see her again, but her persistence, her stalker-like abilities ensured otherwise.

"Can I help you?" I look right at her. Her bright-red coat glares at me like some damn alarm that I wish I would have run from all those years ago—her lying lips, those deceptive eyes. Now that I see her again in this new light called reality, she's plain compared to Kenny—downright skeletal in contrast to my future bride's well-placed curves. For sure she's hideous on the inside where it counts.

"What the hell do you want?" I say it low, to not stir the professors in their microcosms around me.

"You're to the point." She slinks in and closes the door behind her. She thinks she's caged me in, but I'm not above leaving.

"Heard you put a ring on it." She pulls her shoulders to her ears before taking a seat on the desk right next to me.

It feels uncomfortable being this close to her, smelling that familiar perfume that unloads a truck full of bad memories.

"Listen"—she pulls her head back—"I'm just here as a friend. I don't know how it happened, but I sit next to her in Art, call it kismet, fate, whatever the hell you want, but she tells me these wild things about other guys and I thought you should know."

"Really." I used to buy whatever Blair sold by the gallon, but I stopped scooping her shit down my throat like ice cream once I discovered she was spoon-feeding me lies.

"Yeah, really. She said she's in training to be the town whore and that she's 'playing the player.' Trying to get him to believe he's actually falling in love."

My stomach bottoms out.

"I don't know what you're talking about, and I don't want to. Why don't you go back to Dartmouth, or did they not want you there either?" I didn't need to say it. I could have picked up my briefcase and bolted for the door, but a part of me wanted to push in the dig. Although, in the end, I'm glad it happened. I don't know what I would have done if Kenny walked into my life, and I was still serving time with Blair.

"I've come back to you." Her eyes widen like cesspools filled with malice and loathing. "I came back for *us*. We spent four years as a couple."

"Four years I'll never get back." I shut my laptop and slip it into my briefcase.

"We had good times, Cruise. It doesn't have to end like this. We could forget all about that guy and all about this silly girl. We could be Cruise and Blair again and spend the rest of our lives together. I won't ever bring her up, I swear."

Blair spins her fantasies like a witch trying to cast an impotent spell, and a laugh gets caught in my throat. "You won't bring up my fiancée because you won't be around to do it. Kenny and I belong together, not you and me." I stand, towering above her. "Sorry things didn't work out for you and that, who was it? Basketball player?" I head to the door and turn around. "Heard you cheated on him just like you cheated on me. Looks like we both get what we deserve. I get true love, and you get screwed." I head out of the building so fast my heart tries to detonate out of my chest.

That felt good.

Damn good.

18

CHAIN REACTION

Kendall

Lauren was kind enough to pick up a pizza for Cruise and me, so we don't need to worry about dinner. She thought it was awful what Blair did. She went so far as saying she was going to lay into her the next time she saw her. Of course I protested for like a second, but if Lauren is determined to kick some white-trash ass, then who am I to stop her?

After a quick shower, I wrap myself in my fuzzy Hello Kitty robe then reapply the mascara I cried off at the thought of Cruise ever wanting to marry someone as vindictive as Blair. At least he had the good sense to break it off with her. It doesn't take a rocket scientist to figure out she's driving the entire fucking crazy train.

I try to hide the red patches all over my face with foundation in the event that Cruise asks what's wrong. That run-in with his ex is the last thing I want to talk about. I'm just not ready to go there. I'm too afraid that Cruise is keeping her under the cuff because maybe deep down inside he still has feelings for her. Anyway, Cruise isn't a cheat. I can tell by the way he loves me.

By the time I make my way back to the kitchen, the pizza is cold, so I heat up a slice. My foot snags on something under the microwave stand, and I pull out the human leash I spotted the first morning I was here.

A dull laugh rattles through me at the sight of the kinky cord.

I pluck the dust bunnies off and examine it. Long red and purple straps are interwoven throughout the chain. It looks strong enough to walk an elephant.

Lavender feathers and spikes decorate the three cuffs that dangle from it. The steel collar flexes in my hand as if daring me to try it on for size.

I look at my reflection in the black glass of the window and snap it over my neck until it clicks in the back.

I guess it looks sexy, even if it does have bondage and discipline written all over it. I pluck at the collar to take it off, and the latch jams. I head over to a mirror and twist it around, and the buckle doesn't seem to have release mechanism.

"Crap," I whimper. Surely there's a key for this satanic contraption. I'm not going to wander through life with a leash dangling from my person. Am I? I'll get wire cutters if I have to. People get jewelry sawed off their bodies all the time. Although, this is one solid sheet of steel, and it sort of looks impervious to getting hacked off without taking my head along as a casualty.

My phone vibrates, and I pick it up. It's a text from Mom.

At the airport. Andrew is picking me up. Will head straight to the B&B. See you in a little while. Can't wait!

My mother? I give the collar a hard yank, and it doesn't loosen. In fact—it just cinched a little tighter, and now it's getting difficult to breathe.

Oh my God, I'm going to asphyxiate myself. Cruise will find my body, wearing nothing but this stupid contraption and my

Hello Kitty robe. Then, of course, my mother will show up to see that I've strangled myself with a sex toy. Just perfect.

A pair of familiar headlights floods the living room.

Cruise!

Reflexively, I jump on the couch and pull his grandmother's afghan clear up to my nose. I'm pretty sure she didn't anticipate her grandson's incompetent girlfriend needing it to hide sexual accessories.

God—Cruise is going to think I'm such an idiot. He'll probably trade me in for Blair by midnight.

"Hey, beautiful." He bursts through the door with his right hand cleverly hidden behind his back and bolts on over. An icy tail of wind follows him through the opened door. "Surprise." He reveals a giant bouquet of long-stemmed roses. They bring the entire room to life with their gorgeous tongues of crimson fire.

"Oh—I love them!" I beam with the blanket still snug to my ears. "They're perfect. Really, you shouldn't have." And I'm betting in less than a minute he'll more than agree.

He cocks his head to the side and examines me in this impractical semifetal position. Cruise looks resplendent in his dark coat, his pale-blue shirt glowing from beneath.

"You feeling okay?" His dimples depress with concern. He looks amazingly tall from this vantage point and impossibly gorgeous, per usual.

"I feel great." And lying to Cruise makes me feel like shit. "Well, not really great." I hate this part because I'm totally going to have to do the big leash-thingy reveal.

He backtracks and shuts the door.

Cruise makes his way back, smoldering at me with a sexy as hell, rather stern expression. His chin dips. He's hedging a maniacal smile like he suspects something is up, so I play along and pull down the blanket with a false air of confidence.

"Holy shit, you started without me." His eyes grow in amazement at my sexual misadventure. And, strangely, I think I've managed to arouse him in ways I've never imagined.

"That's right." I swing the butter-soft leather like I meant it all along. "Just waiting for you to catch up."

Cruise grabs hold of the chain and gently lifts me off the couch. He reels me in and growls a laugh that echoes right down to my belly. "You do realize I have no idea where the key is." His stomach vibrates against mine as he says it.

"No idea?" I swallow hard at the thought of spending the rest of my days embellished with purple feathers.

He dips his gaze. "I see you're wearing a robe. How perceptive of you. Otherwise I'd have to cut your shirt off to undress you."

"No cutting." It speeds from me in a flurry.

Cruise licks his lips. He peels off my ode to Sanrio, leaving me naked and vulnerable, and suddenly all too aware of those cruel watts of electricity glaring down from the kitchen.

Cruise leads me across the room with the leash—slowly— never taking his magnetic gaze off me. He brazenly washes over my body with his eyes as though he were a cartographer mapping out the lay of the land.

Heat rises to my face as he gives the hint of a smile. His eyes burn like gas flames, blue as the ocean. Cruise reels me in and turns me around. His warm fingers press into my waist like he were the potter and I were the clay—the perfect medium for him to indulge in, create whatever he liked out of me.

With my luck my mother will magically burst through the door. I'm sure finding her only daughter naked, in a strange man's living room, with a chain dangling from her neck is not what she's expecting. She'll most likely think I'm being held as a sex slave and call the police. The feds will haul Cruise out to a prison for the criminally insane. More like, insanely gorgeous. Regardless, I don't want to think about my mother, nor do I want to think about bitchy ex-girlfriends. Right now, Cruise Elton is doing an incredible job of arousing the hell out of me without so much as laying a finger on my flesh.

He takes up my wrists behind my back and binds them with one of the stray leather straps. I guess he's forgoing the cuffs since we're one key away from confining me to permanent restraints.

"You like this, Kenny, don't you?" It comes out low, almost chastising, and my insides throb at the sound of his voice.

He double wraps the leash around his hand before giving a swift tug.

Cruise leads me to the bedroom, and I don't resist.

It's exhilarating like this, following my scorching-hot boyfriend through the dimly lit hall, my hands tethered behind my back while at his complete sexual mercy.

Cruise flips on the lights to the bedroom with a demonic grin blooming on his face.

"No lights." I have a feeling it could never be dark enough for what Cruise is about to do to me—and with my wrists bound together, I can only hope he'll listen.

"Lights." He kisses the nape of my neck, and my body trembles for more.

"Is it your birthday?" I slather on the sarcasm. "Because unless it's your birthday, or a red-letter holiday, I'm pretty sure I'm not entertaining you with my pale ass." There, I said it.

He pushes a gentle laugh into the back of my neck. "You have the body of a goddess. I want to look at you." He leans in close to my ear, and I can feel his erratic breathing as it creates a fire line down my back. "You're the one being dominated, Kenny. You don't have a choice." He cinches the leashes until my hands are drawn tight and walks me to the bed. I try to take a seat, but he's quick to lift me to my feet.

Cruise gives a wicked grin with a smoldering look of seduction. His brows dip in a *V*, revealing the sinister intent brewing behind those blue-topaz lenses.

Every intimate part of me is quivering, cheering on my newfound carnal revolution, and now here I am, standing in front of the god of Garrison in the exact amount of clothing I was born in.

"Down," he instructs.

I get on my knees, and he pulls my head back. Instinctively, I know this is going to hurt, and I want it to. I want to feel everything Cruise has to offer—all that he's willing to thrust my way.

He steps into me and unbuttons his jeans. He flicks at his zipper and gives the impression of a wicked grin.

"With your teeth," he commands.

And I do.

Cruise launches toward me, smooth and hard. I take him up in my mouth and feel a groan echo throughout his body. My lips move over his heated skin with my tongue pulling long strokes in obedience to his movements. He takes in a ragged breath, his body bowed back with pleasure. His fingers rake through my hair. His hips beg to sway with ecstasy, but I've bound him just like he's bound me.

Cruise and I are awakening in each other a new dimension of vulnerability—of trust. This dark corner of fantasy still holds the underpinnings of our affection, the lust inside us detonating on a cellular level. Cruise brings the gunpowder and I bring the matches. We're varnishing a new layer of intimacy in our relationship as the room burns around us. This invisible fire rages through us—exhilarating, as if we harnessed a chariot and are riding through the sun.

Cruise carefully pulls me up to him long before he trembles to completion.

"Bend over." He rasps it out as a simple demand, and I relax into him, already lost in a sensual haze. "Bend *over*." He says it curt this time, a nefarious smile hedging on his lips. It comes out a strict order that might have consequences attached if I don't comply, so I lie over the bed and feel the cool of the comforter glide against my chest; my stomach retracts from its touch.

Cruise gently kicks out my feet until my legs are amply parted, and suddenly I'm regretting ever laying eyes on these demented chains. I imagine what I must look like with my body splayed out like this, him hovering from above with an eagle-eye view, and I feel vulnerable—far more so than simply being naked.

Cruise slides his heated hands over my back, down my bare bottom, and between my thighs. He glides a finger in and out of my body as I writhe over the bed, leaving me uncontrollably aroused.

"I'm going to make you come, Kenny." He says it plainly, as a fact. "What do you think about that?" He runs his thumb over the delicate folds and enlivens my pleasure points until my throat constricts.

He leans in with his searing-hot skin raking up against my thigh. He runs the pad of his fingers softly over me before plunging in again with dynamic force.

"Do you want more?" His voice rumbles through me. It echoes through my bones as my body waits for that very thing.

I let out a breath, unable to answer.

Cruise spins out delicious circles over me until my breathing grows erratic. With every writhing movement, he tightens the reins just enough until I let out a cry, and my body spasms uncontrollably. I spiral into a beautiful delirium that I never want to end. I try to cinch my legs, but he blocks me with his knees. Cruise guides his body into mine with a violent force that sends me choking for air. My mouth rakes against the bed from the brilliant shock of pleasure. He thrusts inside me, over and over, pulling me back by the chain until my back arches into him. He slides his hand down over me again, and I explode, this time with Cruise—the two of us lost in ecstasy, perfectly in sync. He collapses over me, shaking and trembling, pressing himself in deeper until his breathing is restored.

Cruise rolls next to me. His eyes shine like glass as he pulls me in.

"You're a little vixen, you know that?" He seals the sentiment with a careful kiss that dissolves any doubt Blair may have tried to plant.

A loud knock explodes over the front door, and a familiar female voice calls out my name.

"Who the hell is that?" Cruise glances in the direction of the chaos with a slight look of alarm.

"I believe *that* is my mother."

Cruise

"Your mother?" I glance down at Kenny, locked in chains, looking more sex slave than angelic daughter. I send a 911 text to Molly to retrieve Kenny's mom and walk her over to the big house while I try to unleash her daughter from her self-imposed stocks and chains.

We make our way to the kitchen table as I work at freeing her from the device.

"Nice," I say, unhinging the last of the leashes from around the collar with a set of needle-nose pliers. "And that's all I can do."

"What am I supposed to tell my mom?" She clasps at the metal necklace still latched around her neck. Kenny looks pretty hot with a heavy, metal choker, but I'm sure now's not the time to point that out.

"Tell her it's a fad." I give a bleak smile. "Or wear a turtle-neck. I have one you can borrow."

Kenny is wrapped in a towel and barefoot. She's got a row of spikes encircling her neck, and my cock is ticking back to life at the sight of her. If it weren't for the unexpected company, I wouldn't resist the effort.

"I'll look ridiculous in a turtleneck." She chews on her lip. "Besides, she'll grow suspicious if I try to hide it. I need to work it." She speeds off to the bedroom to presumably pull off the miracle of working it, and I make use of myself by putting the flowers I bought in a vase.

I take a breather as I wait for the water to fill. Outside the kitchen window, a three-quarter moon spreads its light over the snowy world. I think back to the fairy tales I used to read to Molly. Kenny is the princess in my fairy tale. Although, it's a slightly sadomasochistic fairy tale at the moment. And fairy tales always have a happy ending—not even Blair can ruin that. They also come complete with a witch, and I think I've just discovered Blair's new role in my life. Let's hope that bucket of truth I doused her with evaporates her to nothing.

Kenny steps back in the room wearing a low-cut sweater, jeans, and the boots I gifted her with. Her dark hair frames her face, and the spiked cuff around her neck looks a lot more costume jewelry and a lot less obscene paraphernalia.

"Well done." I wrap my arms around her, still amped from that heated exchange. "Does your mom know about us?"

"Not yet." She pulls her lips to the side. "I'll let her know we're dating, but maybe I should ease her into the engagement. I'd hate to kill her on her first night here."

"Fair enough." I narrow into her with a devilish grin. "Whips and chains—good or great?"

Kenny bites down a smile and pulls me in. "Spectacular."

———

Kenny and I walk through the dark night and into the bed-and-breakfast at the top of the property. Mom is already settled at the dining room table with a woman who I presume is Kenny's mother, and my eyes have to readjust a moment as I spot my father seated beside her.

"Dad?" I'm dazed seeing him here in my childhood home without my mother shouting at him at the top of her lungs for child support.

Molly enters the room with a pot roast and potatoes as if she were about to break out an entire Thanksgiving dinner.

"Dad?" Kenny's mother touches her hand to her chest. "Oh my God, is this Pennington?" She leaps to her feet and engulfs both Kenny and me in an all-encompassing hug. She has the same dark hair as Kenny, although short, and her eyes are a honeyed brown.

"Nope—not Pen," I say, pulling back. "Cruise Elton." I offer her a hand, and she gives a light shake, unsure of what to make of me.

"This is my oldest," Dad pipes up, and something warms in me. I'm not sure I've ever been introduced as his offspring before. "Kendall, nice to see you again." He offers her an embrace and slaps me on the back for good measure.

"Oh my goodness!" Her mouth rounds out with surprise. "Little Cruisy! I'm so sorry I didn't put two and two together. I'm Karen. So nice to meet you." She looks to Mom and closes her eyes a moment. "And you're Samantha! What a small world."

"Just Sam." Mom winks as everyone finds a seat.

"Kendall?" Her mother makes a face that suggests she should explain a few things.

"Oh . . ." Kenny swallows hard before taking a seat next to me. "Cruise and I are . . . um just friends."

Friends? I'm not sure I was expecting my demotion to sink so low.

"Now, now—don't be shy," Mom sings like a canary. "These two are indivisible with injustice for all." She gives a hoot into her wine. Just the thought of what might come next makes me want to crawl under the table and bring Kenny with me. "You can practically see the steam rising out of the guest house the way they parade around."

Nice touch.

I glance over at Kenny with an apology written across my face.

Her cheeks have entered tomato territory, but it's her lusciously swollen lips, the perfect curves hedging out of her sweater that make me want to whisk her away from here in the event that my mother has another live grenade stashed in her arsenal. Who knew Kenny would need protecting from my mother, of all people.

"Parade around?" Karen shoots a look to Kenny. She looks more amused than angry, although to be fair, I don't know her. She could be on the cusp of a full-on rage for all I know.

"Come clean, Kenny." Molly joins in on the fun as she turns her attention to Kenny's mother. "She told me a few weeks back I'm gonna be an aunt."

A collective gasp circles the table—Kenny's being the most dramatic.

Fuck. Leave it to Mom and Molly to tag team Kenny in front of her poor, unsuspecting mother. I wouldn't be surprised if they hopped the next plane to LA after this fiasco.

"So not true." Kenny spits it out with venom aimed right at Mol. "Nobody is going to be an aunt." She gives a nervous laugh to her mother.

How the hell does Molly know about that?

Mom clears her throat. "Excuse my daughter. She's prone to exaggeration. They are not having a baby. Isn't that right?" She looks to the two of us, and we deny the bullshit Molly decided to confetti the table with. "They're simply engaged."

"Kendall!" Karen's face lights up like a flare.

Shit.

It looks like my mother and sister have managed to inflict both Jordan women with third-degree facial burns. Although, according to Kenny, her mother has long since bypassed the Jordan phase of her life.

I look to Kenny, urging her to deny it if she wants to. She certainly has the opportunity. In the least she could backpedal and say we're dating, but she doesn't. Instead, she sits there with indistinguishable choking sounds emitting from her throat, reminiscent of earlier this evening. A severe flashback of Kenny writhing over the bed sears through my mind. Not even the fact that both our mothers are in the room has the power to kill that fantasy-come-to-life from replaying itself in real time.

I doubt I'll be fessing up to having used that leash before. That it was a gift from Cal, of all people. He gave it to me as a gag gift on my birthday the week before Kenny arrived. He's been living vicariously through my sexual renaissance from the beginning. It was his way of outfitting me to live out every one of his warped fantasies. Although, in hindsight, this one wasn't all that warped. It was fan-fucking-tastic, and for damn sure I won't be sharing any of those details with Cal.

"So it's true?" Her mother looks from me to her.

"Looks like congratulations are in order." Dad puts on his bartending hat and pours us each a much-needed glass of wine, Molly included, and she guzzles it down before any kind of toast has a chance to commence. "To young love." Dad raises his glass while looking directly at Kenny's poor unsuspecting mother. "May we never forget the bittersweet fruit of its vine."

We? Bittersweet?

Karen raises her glass, and they exchange sad smiles with the pretense of joy. I get the feeling Dad was a player long before I ever walked onto the field.

Dinner goes off mostly without a hitch, other than the fact that Molly's cooking leaves something to be desired. The food is cold and flavorless, much like the relationship I've had with my father these past twenty-four years. I'm open to seeing that change, though. Kenny scraped clean all of the sludge that once lingered inside me.

"So, have you thought about a wedding?" Mom asks, stoking the flames.

"I'm sure they're not at that stage yet." Karen shoots a look to Kenny that suggests we'd better not be. She moves her attention to me, cold and steely. "Cruise? How do you plan on supporting my daughter?"

"Supporting?" Kenny scoffs. "I'm sorry this isn't 1955. Cruise doesn't have to support me at all."

Kenny shoots me an apologetic look, most likely because I have been supporting her, and I really don't mind. Soon I'll make her my wife and the mind-blowing sex won't feel like such a trade-off for room and board.

"I'm a graduate student," I interject. "I'll be working on my doctorate in the fall. I've been granted a fellowship and am currently in the middle of a teaching internship." Why does it feel like I've just spewed out an interview for some tame boardroom position? More like bedroom, and being with Kenny is anything but tame as evidenced by the shiny metal choker cuffed around her neck.

Dad places his hand over my shoulder and gives a slight jostle. "A fellowship? That's fantastic. I'm so proud of you, son."

Son? He's going for the gold tonight.

"So the wedding . . ." Karen drives us back to the subject at hand, and surprisingly she turns to my father. "We'll finally be family." She looks up at him with a startled smile as if she had always wanted to be family with my father. I'm feeling rather lucky this matrimonial mix-up didn't happen years ago because I would awkwardly, yet willingly, be fucking my stepsister.

I give a sly grin at the idea.

"We've always been family," he counters. "Would you like to take a walk?"

"I would love to." Karen rises hypnotically, and they head toward the entry.

"What the hell was that about?" Molly snipes. She's not one to be dragged off into the arena of the awkward. Her eyelashes are crusted over with mascara, and she's got on way too much war paint in general. I would like to know what the hell *that* is about.

"They had this thing." Mom swipes the air like it's no big deal.

"What thing?" Kenny's eyes and breasts both manage to provide a 3-D spectacle. Not that I mind.

"They dated," Mom whispers. "It was long after he and I disconnected. They were hot and heavy for a good long while, and then all of a sudden she took off to California, and he was with Jackie."

"Bet he cheated on her." Molly huffs. "Guys are assholes."

"Mind your p's and q's." Mom swats her on the arm. "And what's this wine-guzzling business?" She swipes the glass out of her reach. Not that it matters. It's long since been drained.

"Cruise isn't a cheat." Kenny picks up my hand and holds it to her chest as if I were a life raft.

"Cruise is an open cheat," Molly corrects. "He sleeps around because his dick suffers from the need to be strangled nightly."

"Molly," I bark at her. All that talk about her needing a father figure filters through my mind, and I'm moved to bolt her into her bedroom for the next four solid years as a tribute to good parenting.

"You think you're so perfect," she shouts back. "You and that little ho you're shacking up with, when just a year ago you were peddling the fine art of abstinence and taking me shopping for purity rings. Boy, you sure stomped out that bag of 'chastity' shit like it was on fire."

"You can go now." I say it low because if I raise my voice I might lose it and flip the damn table over.

"I will go." She rises. "Just know I happen to respect your new girlfriend more than you because at least she's honest and cool. Instead of trying to buy me a wedding ring for Jesus, she took me to the free clinic and got me on the pill." She tosses down her napkin and bolts from the room.

"What!" Mom snatches at her crutches before hobbling after my apparently sexually promiscuous sister.

"I'm so sorry." Kenny reaches over and lays her hand on my arm to soothe me.

"Don't be. Molly has spun her last fucking lie—"

"I can explain everything." Kenny blurts it out before I can finish.

I freeze a moment. Kenny wouldn't take Molly to any free clinic and put her on the pill.

Kenny's eyes elongate. She sucks her cheeks in as if alluding otherwise.

Oh shit.

"Does this have something to do with her thinking she was going to be an aunt?" I ask, but she doesn't say anything. "Kenny?"

"Um . . ." She touches her hand to her chest just the way her mother did when she was nervous. "It was sort of an accident. She's a lying little. . ." Her fingers fly to her lips. "I mean, I'm sure she's a nice person once you get to know her. It's just that I haven't really seen that side of her yet."

I start in on a slow, sober laugh.

My father has a very obvious hard-on for Kenny's mother, my sister is having sex with prepubescent boys, and it was Kenny, of all people, she manipulated into helping her get on the pill. Shit.

I stand and pull Kenny into my arms.

"My family is completely insane." A smile breaks loose on my lips as I take in the inordinate amount of beauty God saw fit to gift Kenny with both inside and out. I lean in and crush my lips against hers until my body stirs to have her in all four corners of this oversized house.

A soft bubble of laughter gets caught in her throat. "Sounds like we might be related."

"Maybe sooner than you think," I say. "Last fall, Jackie and my dad filed for divorce. They're just buying time under the same roof."

She sucks in a breath. "That's terrible!"

I nod in agreement. "So there's nothing else you want to tell me? Any baby news? Any more rides to the free clinic?"

Her mouth opens then quickly closes.

"I'm not keeping a single thing from you," she whispers as her face lights up like a Christmas tree.

And deep inside, I wonder if she is.

⌒

On Saturday night, Tri Delta is having a party. Kenny asked me to join her, but I assured her I'd be okay at home, working on my thesis. Besides, she mentioned Lauren asked her to do her a favor, and I didn't want to get in the way of a girls' night out. But as soon as she left, I felt the vacuum in the room. Kenny takes the air, the life all with her. I can't stop thinking about those amped up frat boys attacking her like a group of hormone-happy bears; so here I am, ready to cross the threshold into debauchery.

Tri Delta brims with mostly female bodies. Back in my scrotum-slinging days, this would have been an estrogen-laced paradise. For sure this is a much bigger venue and far more popular than the party Pen threw at Sigma Phi the night Kenny arrived. This time, all of Garrison decided to show. Although, in Pen's defense, it was Christmas break, and most people had flown home for the holiday. I'm glad things worked in reverse for Kenny—those Christmas kisses were the best gift ever.

A bevy of scantily clad coeds fills the room, each displaying a unique level of undress. Bra straps seem to be the order of the day, skinny jeans so tight they look like they might need to be peeled off—complete with G-strings spiking out the back, showing off whale tails of various shapes and sizes.

A bubbly coed dips her hand into the back of my jeans, and I take a giant step forward, only to have a brunette press her pillowy chest against mine. Her lips come into my face at Mach 5 and I'm quick to step away.

"Whoa, ladies." I hold up my hands and make a break for the nearest wall, otherwise known as the observation zone.

I pan the room for Kenny. As soon as I spot her, I plan on making a beeline over. I have every intention of hitting on the most beautiful girl in the room. And if I'm lucky, maybe she'll let me haul her upstairs and offer her another private lesson.

I'm sure she's been swallowed alive in a sea of testosterone by now.

Off to my right, a group of guys play beer pong. I hike a leg against the wall and watch as they toss a plastic ball at a mass of red Solo cups.

The object of coming to one of these events is to get laid. If guys have any inclination to unzip their pants, for reasons other than urination, then isolating themselves is going about it the wrong way. At least invite some girls to play. Amateurs.

"Hey, handsome." Blair springs up like an apparition. Her hair is pulled back so tight she looks ghastly. "Tall, dark, and lonely tonight?"

"Just looking for Kenny."

She makes a face. "Oh, I bet right about now she's hooking up with some poor, unfortunate soul—ready and willing to bless 'em with that body."

"In your dreams." I try to make my escape, but she yanks me back by the shirt.

"So why the big mystery?" Her dark eyes slit to nothing. "I would assume if you're so close to Kenny, you'd at least mention that you had an ex-fiancée. Or maybe it's not me you're hiding from her. Maybe you're just embarrassed by who you used to be."

I look right at her, and it feels like I'm seeing her for the very first time. The way her jowls protrude; her red lips are drawn in like a slash as if someone had lanced her face.

"Embarrassed?" I balk. "About what? The fact we met in youth group and decided to save ourselves for that magical someday, until you decided to feed the masses with your body? Guess what, Blair? I finally figured it out. You did me a favor. Without your insatiable desire to cram so many dicks inside you, I would've never met someone amazing who I actually fell in love with and who treats me with a level of respect I never knew possible."

Blair's features harden. Her eyes gloss over with tears, red as Tabasco.

"She's upstairs, probably screwing some guy—or girl," she hisses. "She doesn't seem too picky. Hope you have a fantastic unhappily ever after." Blair hits the door and disappears like a phantom.

Upstairs? Probably just some device to land me near a mattress. I take the stairs two by two and open and shut doors at random.

I make my way farther down the hall until the noise from the party is quickly replaced with deafening silence. Voices murmur from behind the walls of an adjacent room—a guy and a girl. The door is cracked open, so I peer inside.

A familiar mane of dark hair stands before a tall, very bald douchebag.

There they are, Kenny and Cal.

"It could just be this one time," she purrs, running her hand down his shirt. Her fingers work on unbuttoning his jeans, and my chest constricts at the sight. Kenny just threw a brick at my heart. "I won't tell if you won't," she coos.

I lean up against the wall and try to catch my breath. Kenny giggles from the other side, and her voice drills through me.

The sound of her laughter chisels down a toxic brand of misery right through to my bones, and I get the hell out of Dodge.

Late the next morning, I make breakfast for Kenny while she's still sleeping—eggs and bacon, toast with strawberry jam—her favorite—and I'm heavy with agony every step of the way.

I glance out the kitchen window at the gray, corrosive sky—all rust and iron locked in hurt and disbelief much like my heart.

Fresh air seems mandatory to clear my head out of this gutter of despair I've landed in. I grab a pen, and my hand trembles as I leave her a note.

"Going for a walk, be right back." I scrawl it on a napkin as quickly as possible—afraid if I stall, my true feelings might bleed out.

It's almost afternoon, and she's still knocked out. She didn't get in until three. I kept hoping she'd come to my room and ask why I was in my own bed, but she didn't. Not sure what I would have said if she did. I just laid there all night, wide awake, wondering how the hell my heart wound up crushed under the sole of her pretty little foot.

I guess Blair was right—Blair who was the first to gouge my heart out, or so I thought. The misery Blair caused was nothing in comparison to the utter desolation that set in after hearing—*seeing* Kenny in action with my own freaking eyes.

But I know she loves me. You can't fake emotion like that. Can you?

I head outside and a crisp breeze knifes through my clothes in cold, steely jags.

The late February sky holds a stainless shade of gray as if someone were about to place a lid over Carrington, cover us up for good, and a part me wishes he would. The pines still manage to cast detailed shadows over the snow in blues and lavenders, deep navy, dark as night. The strong-scented evergreens light up the air, fresh and cleansing.

My phone goes off just as I arrive at the stream. It's a number I don't recognize, but I stop to take the call before I hit a dead zone.

"Hello?"

"*Cruise?* I'm so sorry to bother you. It's Rayann, Blair's mother."

Every muscle in my body tenses as my bloodstream fills with concrete. What if Blair hurled herself off a cliff? Or what if she swallowed a bottle of pills? I'm sure there would be hell to pay, and undoubtedly it would start and end with me.

"Nice to hear from you." I manage to fake the kind sentiment. "What's going on?"

"It's Blair." She wails when she says her name. "She's been such a mess. She doesn't eat anymore. All she does is mope about how she ruined things between the two of you. Is there any way you could talk to her? Maybe you could take her to dinner and get this whole thing straightened out." Her voice rises with hope. "You do know that Stan and I think of you like a son. People make mistakes, Cruise—big ones. I really pray you'll find it in your heart to forgive her."

I blow out a hard breath.

Is that where this is headed? Can anyone really expect me to walk away from something so fantastic with Kenny and step back into a dead relationship with Blair again?

"I'm sorry she's having a tough time." I do mean that. Blair and I weren't always riding on the crap wagon. "I really hope the best for her, but I'm pretty sure what we had is long over."

We exchange niceties before hanging up, and I mute the damn phone.

Dad waves from the porch before making his way over—so much for time to think. On second thought, it's probably best I don't.

"Morning," he says with an ear-to-ear grin, and I'm almost afraid to ask why he's so ungodly jubilant. It looks like one of us got lucky with a Jordan woman last night and it sure as hell wasn't me. "Mind if I join you?"

I look up at my father in this new light, the older gentleman with graying hair, the newly minted playboy—the friend.

"Not at all." I lead us to a bench overlooking the stream that braids itself through the property, quiet as a yawn. My grandfather used to tell me stories of catching trout here, but I haven't seen a fish longer than my thumb since I was thirteen. The runoff from a nearby hillside keeps it flowing straight through winter. I used to come out here after the Blair debacle, then Kenny brought me a moment of peace, and here I am again.

"You have an upsetting call?" He points to the phone still cradled in my hand. He's wearing a pair of jeans, which is unusual for him, and a baseball cap of mine that Mom must have lent him. We resemble each other enough for me to know what I'll look like in about twenty years—that is if I eat like hell and forget the directions to the gym.

"Blair's mother." I rattle the phone before diving it into my pocket. "She's trying to play matchmaker. I'm sure Blair put her up to it."

"You ever think of getting back together?" He winces when he says it. The flesh on his face looks thicker than I remember as a child. A smile is permanently embedded in the lines beneath his eyes. "It's never too late to make things right."

"*Never* is the operative word. Let's just say I've been given a reprieve. A dying man doesn't run back to the guillotine."

He lets out a warm laugh straight from his belly, and it feels good to be out here with him, sharing a moment, even if it is a pretty crappy moment for me. Not that I plan on highlighting the heartache I'm having with Kenny anytime soon.

"I had a relationship once that I let go of too soon," he starts. "Never forgot her. Thought about her every day of my life after I let her walk out that door." His gaze softens over mine.

I have a feeling I know exactly who he let walk out that door, and I'll be damned if I'm going to follow in his footsteps.

I'm going to fight for Kenny.

I just hope there's something to fight for in her eyes.

19

HEART OF GLASS, HEART OF STONE

Kendall

A glimmer of light pours through the curtains and rouses me just enough to let me know that I've got one hell of a power headache pumping through my skull.

I let Ally talk me into hanging out with her at the party last night, well after Lauren disappeared with Cal. Turns out, no matter how hard I tried to bring Cal to his so-called cheating knees, he held onto his resolve and, apparently, his relationship. Lauren burst out of the closet and the rest was make-up sex history.

Of course, I'll have to confess everything to Cruise since it's his friend from the gym, or things are bound to get really weird the next time Cal's around.

I pull my hair into a ponytail and head to the kitchen. There's a plate on the table loaded with eggs and bacon and two slices of my favorite kind of toast, and my heart melts. The way Cruise loves me is indescribable. It feels like heaven to be cared for like this.

There's a note set to the side.

"Going for a walk, be right back."

I don't hesitate slipping on my boots and coat before heading out the door. I need to collect my morning kiss. It's practically a necessary vitamin to kick-start the day.

The air outside is crisp. The wind picks up and wraps itself around my bare neck like a scarf made of icicles. If it weren't for Cruise, I'd literally be freezing to death and homeless. I guess I should be thankful Pennington didn't have the foresight to get me keyed in with the Housing Department—thankful for his beer-bong emergency that cropped up at the last minute. It's so strange how it all worked out. It's as if destiny stepped in and arranged every coincidence to work in our favor.

If ever there were a couple that was meant to be, it's Cruise and me.

Voices buzz through the shrubbery, and I follow the sound over to a dirt trail.

"But I don't love her anymore." Cruise's voice resonates loud and clear through the thicket; it reverberates through my skull like some horrible gong. Who doesn't he love?

I lean into the fat trunk of a pine—my heart already blistering from his words. Surely, they weren't meant for me. I peer over at him, seated next to his father.

"I regret every last thing," he continues. "Honestly, I don't know what I ever saw in her. I don't even think she's pretty." His voice escalates as if he'd just woken up from a long hibernation and wasn't satisfied with what he found lying in his bed. "She's totally screwed up on the inside. I'm sure she'll blame it on daddy issues, and now she's got her mother all over my back. If I regret one thing, it's ever asking her to marry me."

My heart pulsates through me like a series of grenades. It thumps through my ears until the world warps to the deafening sound of a jungle drum.

I stagger backward and trip over a root. The ground jolts, the entire universe spins on its axis as I gather what strength I have left and head back to the house.

———

Tears pour like rain for the first twenty minutes, as an entire cyclone of emotion rips through me. I hadn't seen the storm on the horizon. There was no time to batten down the hatches. Cruise doesn't love me anymore, and now he's sorry he ever put this ring on my finger.

I'm numb inside, a shell of who I was just an hour ago. I segue into the hiccupping, slap-cheek red phase of the ugly cry, but I need to pull it together.

I send a text to Ally. She says I could crash with her for a while. There's no way I'm staying in the bed-and-breakfast with his family, even if Mom herself has already taken up residency there. I'll fill her in on my trauma some other day. Besides, I don't think I could get the words to vomit from my throat, not with this boulder of pain Cruise lodged in it.

The door jiggles, and everything in me freezes. I wipe down my face with my T-shirt and brace myself for what I have to do next.

Cruise walks in and beams a sad smile while taking off his jacket. He looks resplendent, divine. How I ever thought someone as godlike as Cruise Elton could love me, want me, just shows how hard I've fallen.

"Look who's up." If I didn't know better, I'd think he was hurt, but it seems like I'm the only one hurting in this equation. He does a double take at my suitcase, packed and ready to roll by my side. "What's going on?" His features transform with genuine surprise, and I'm almost sold on the fact that he's aching to see me stay, but I know better.

"Just heading to Ally's." I shrug, running my fingers through the back of my hair as if he hadn't cut my heart out with the knife of his tongue and unwittingly served it to me for breakfast. "You know, just getting out of your way. Rumor has it your ex is interested in patching things up."

"That's what I hear." He rides his eyes up my body, slow, suspicious.

"So, I guess that means you're still into her." My heart sinks—you could tie it to my neck and throw me into the sea with the millstone it has become in such a short time.

His brows dip as if to protest the idea. "Are you into other guys, Kenny?" His strangled gaze remains unmovable.

I take a breath and hold it.

What's happening? This is Cruise. A few short hours ago, I would have bet my life that we were Garrison's next power couple, and now here we are, frying each other on the skillet, searing our hatred over one another for the hell of it.

Those hurtful words I overheard this morning waft through my mind like the stench from a rotting corpse.

"Maybe I am into other guys." I say it low. "That's how this whole mess started, remember?"

His chest lurches as if he were going to laugh—cry, but he aborts the effort. "I guess I trained you well."

"Guess you did." I glance down at his grandmother's ring still gracing my finger and gently pluck it off. He doesn't stop me or beg me not to do it with some impassioned plea, which only solidifies what I heard him say.

This right here—this stabbing rejection is real. Cruise and all his love for me was just another illusion. I jumped into love believing it was a battleship that would withstand the test of time when all it turned out to be was a paper boat that dissolved to nothing beneath my feet.

"I suppose this was just a test," I say, holding up the platinum band a moment before placing it on the table. "I guess I failed because a player never commits."

Cruise closes his eyes an inordinate amount of time and takes a breath that goes on for miles. "Look, I get it. You're not ready. You're in college—you're young. You want to see what's out there."

His lips tremble, and for a minute I think he's going to tell me this is all some joke, that he still loves me, that I should put that ring back on right this fucking minute, but he doesn't. Cruise is somehow trying to pass all this off on me because he's too chickenshit to admit the fact that he's over us—that he never thought I was pretty—that I'm prone to blame everything on my screwed-up, fatherless childhood.

"Maybe in the future." He takes a step forward, and I retract. "Maybe we can see where things lead."

My heart implodes. This is it. The big kiss-off. Cruise Elton has the balls to look me straight in the eye and offer me someday while hacking down any fantasy I might have had about forever.

"Fuck off, Cruise." I wheel my luggage past him at breakneck speed and open the door to the icy world waiting to comfort me with its barbed-wire embrace.

Tears bubble to the surface, and I refuse to do him the honor of letting them fall.

"Kenny, wait," he pleads.

My feet somehow find the strength to carry me over the threshold one last time. I glance back at him—his gorgeous frame stains itself like a bookmark in my mind. I never want to forget how bad falling in love can hurt—how quick the jagged granite comes up after you dive from the cliff.

"My name is Kendall," I stammer. "But don't worry. You won't have to use it. I won't be hanging around too much longer."

I toss my shit in the car and speed the hell away from the Elton House Bed and Breakfast where hearts are stolen and returned, mutilated, on a whim.

I drive down several miles until I come upon a sign that reads Now leaving Carrington. Please visit us again!

Carrington was beautiful, but its lessons were harsh. It watched with eager anticipation as its prized son cut out my heart with a rusted razor for the hell of it. The world tried to warn me, but I wouldn't listen. I wanted the fairy tale, the fantasy of it all. I wanted to be the princess that Cruise told me I was. I bought the lie, and my heart was thrown back in my face. I came to Carrington with a heart of glass, and Cruise crushed it under his heel. But today, as I leave Cruise and Carrington behind for good, I trade that heart of glass for a heart of stone.

No one will ever hurt me again.

I'll make damn sure of it.

I pull off behind a row of junipers and sob my eyes out for the next several hours.

My maxim comes back like a haunting refrain: Love never works out in the end.

I hate that I was right.

Cruise

What the fuck just happened?

I stagger over to the door and stare at the empty space where her car sat a moment ago. A plume of dust rises over the hill from the direction she sped off in. I step back into the house, panting—my heart threatening to evict itself from my chest. I should have fought for her. I should have laid down my pride and dropped to my knees, begged her to have me—hell, pencil me in on Tuesdays if she wanted.

Who was that imposter? It couldn't have been Kenny. Maybe she's got a twin, and she's punking me.

Then I see it. Neatly laid out over the sofa is the wool coat I gave her. Her boots sit on the hearth as if she were suggesting I use them for fuel.

A hard roll of nausea cycles through me. How could I have let this happen? Then again, how could I not? I'm Catastrophe Cruise, and fucking up relationships seems to be my specialty. Although it wasn't me who cheated on Blair, and it wasn't me who cheated on Kenny. But I would tolerate just about anything Kenny dished out just to be a part of her life. I'd take the leftovers of her love on every day that ends in Y if she let me. That's how far I've drifted from the person who built his life around ideals, when high standards and morals were the order of the day.

The baseball bat I keep in the corner catches my eye. I speed over and choke the shit out of it like my life depended on it— hell, my sanity. I blow out every fucking window in this psychotic love shack of ours—shatter them to millions of pieces just like Kenny shattered my heart.

———

True to her word, Kenny doesn't show for class that week or the following week after that. She doesn't return my calls, and her mother manages to give me to the cold shoulder each time I bump into her.

I've been holing up in the bowels of the bed-and-breakfast, going over the books, as if I weren't depressed enough already. Just as I suspected, Mom has let a few bills go unpaid, and now the creditors are breathing down our necks. I assured her I'd take over. There's no point in delaying the inevitable. The only question is, how am I going to handle school and run a full-time business?

On Wednesday there's a note on my desk, and for a moment my adrenaline skyrockets.

"Mandatory meeting. My office. 3:30. Dr. Barney."

For sure not the note I was hoping for. I was looking forward to something a little more erotic in nature with a big fat heart and a giant *K* gracing the bottom of the page. I've been fantasizing all week that she'd sneak into my room—that this had all been some great ploy to initiate the world's greatest make-up sex.

At 3:30 on the button, I stroll into Dr. Barney's office and try to forget about the constant ache gnawing at me ever since Kenny rolled her suitcase out of my life. I press out a manufactured smile and nod at the tired-looking man who holds my fellowship in his hands. I must be early because the rest of the seats are suspiciously empty. Either that or this is a private powwow. He probably wants to tell me how proud he is of me, handling Bradshaw's class with one hand tied behind my scholastic back.

"Mr. Elton." Dr. Barney raises his chin and expertly peers down his nose at me. He's plumped up a bit, and his age spots have spread evenly over his face giving him a tanned complexion. "I'm most devastated by some news that's recently come to my attention."

"Shit." I hiss it out low. "Is Bradshaw all right?" What the hell am I saying? Obviously, Bradshaw is not all right.

"Professor Bradshaw is in remission." He pulls back his lips, and his double chin quivers with anger. "Cruise, this news involves you, and, unfortunately, not you alone."

He slides an enlarged photo across the table and my blood runs cold with just one look.

It's Kenny and me that day back in my classroom. Her sweater dips past her bottom, her legs curve around my back, perfectly pale. My face is buried in her neck, and I can still feel the pleasure coursing through my veins as if I were reliving it.

He slides another shot my way. The tower stares back at me with its long, erect neck, the bony structure of the globe. Then a zoomed shot. You can't see Kenny, just my coat as I help her into the center of the steel-caged world.

"And this." He slips me another picture of the tower, this time a close-up of my face lost in ecstasy—Kenny's long mane whipping over my neck. "Well? What do you have to say for yourself?"

I stare down at them—Kenny and I in these compromising positions—her beautiful hair, her feathered skin, those lips I'd die to cover with mine just one last time.

What I'd really like to say is, can I have these? I'd like to spread them over my bed—lie over them naked, frame them, replicate them, and wallpaper my new crappy room with a dizzying pattern of who we once were—all of our adventures surrounding me like an erotic kaleidoscope.

"Now that I've rendered you speechless"—he rasps his knuckles over his desk—"I've one other thing to show you."

This time it's a simple sheet of paper he slides over—the revised syllabus I made just for her.

Fuck.

"How did you get this?"

"A young lady dropped them by, early this afternoon."

Kenny? But how would she take the pictures? Most likely Blair. I wouldn't put it past her to riffle through Kenny's things and steal what she needed. I hold up the syllabus as exhibit A.

"Cruise, I'm sorry to have to do this, but your brief teaching career has come to a rather ignoble demise. Not only that, but I've had to report my findings to the board. We've unanimously agreed—your fellowship has been revoked. You've been expelled from Garrison."

His words come to me in snatches. The room warps in and out, and I'm ready to bang my head over the table in the most literal fucking sense because all of my bad luck has managed to come crashing around me at once. The funny thing is, none of this bullshit matters.

"I'm sorry I've disappointed you, Dr. Barney." I rise to my feet and take a breath.

"You don't seem too broken up about it."

"I'm not." I press it out in a fit of honesty. "I lost the most important thing in my life last week—this is just a superficial wound in comparison." The brevity of truth gives me pause. "I'm sorry if I've insulted you."

"She asked me to give you this." He hands me a small folded note.

I unravel it to find the words "Consider yourself played."

———

Friday afternoon, I manage to crawl out from under my mother's watchful eye and head to the gym with the intention of tormenting every muscle in my body. I let her know I'm taking back the bed-and-breakfast. I'm ratcheting up the marketing to a whole new level and even suggested she air out those rooms because she can damn well expect more than a few guests. I plan on getting the financial cogs moving again. Maybe if I had more monetary stability in my life. Maybe then . . .

I wish I could I say I was over Kenny, but she branded herself over my heart, my mind. She haunts my dreams, my waking hours. Kenny is the ghost, the one that got away. I have a feeling I'll be wanting her, yearning for her long into my golden years until I take that eternal nap, and even then, I won't be put out of my misery.

I get a text from Pen as I stroll into the gym.

It's on like Donkey Kong. Alpha Sigma Phi tonight. See U there.

My stomach does a revolution.

Alpha Sigma Phi. That's where it all started for Kenny and me.

Cal spots me as I walk into the weight room and heads over with a spring in his step. I bet he's got a blow-job story I'm not going to believe.

"Long time no see," he chirps.

"It's on my calendar to beat the shit out of you," I say, taking a seat on the Frankensteinian workout equipment. I'm not really in the mood to confront him about what I saw that night at Delta.

"What the hell for?" He pops a foot up on the wheel and begins tying his shoe—his fucking shoe, like it's no big deal. It makes me feel like shoving mine right up his ass. "So, I got some news—Lauren says I passed the test." He hikes his brows like this should mean something.

"What test?" I down my water bottle to keep from socking him in the nuts.

He ticks his head as though this were big news. "The ambush hookup, the lover's limbo—how low can you go?" He holds his hands out like he's about to fly away, and I wish he would. "You know, relationship test."

"What the hell are you talking about?" Not that I care. It's not like I'm passing any relationship test anytime soon.

"Lauren. She sicced that hot girlfriend of yours on me, then watched me sweat it out. I turned her down flat, and Lauren jumped out of the fucking closet like a psychotic PI. But it was cute. It means she loves me."

My insides pinch to life. My face fills with heat as a surge of excitement races through my veins.

"Kenny said Lauren asked her to do her a favor," I say it mostly to myself. "You think that was it?" My entire body feels light as a feather, and my heart detonates in me like a rapid-fire assault weapon.

"Probably." He bobs his head like this were just another conversation—as if my entire existence didn't just point right back to Kendall Jordan, the great love of my life. "So, it looks like I'll be joining you on that unfortunate walk down the aisle, buddy." He slaps me over the back, solid and secure, without any notion that there was something amiss with our relationship this past week. "I nearly fell off the mattress when she asked, but who the hell am I to let a good thing go to waste?"

I look up at him startled.

"Congratulations." I smile for the first time since Kenny left, and my heart soars from the effort. I bet she didn't write that note either. "I gotta run." I spike to my feet. "Do me a favor—ask Lauren to bring Kenny to Sigma Phi tonight. And whatever you do, don't tell Kenny I'll be there." My feet fly to the door. I'm walking on air.

"Where you going?" Cal shouts with a wild look on his face.

"I've got to call someone about getting some windows fixed."

20

FOREVER

Kendall

The night sky washes an unnatural shade of lavender in what I'll always remember as the color of this spectacular heartbreak. The stars spray out their glory in number as if all the starry hosts were marshaled right over Alpha Sigma Phi. The evergreens shimmer a luminescent sage as if vying for my attention. It seems all of nature is peacocking—showing off its prowess, its inherent beauty that surrounds us like a song set to the tune of eternity. How anything could go so disastrously wrong in a world so beautiful astounds me. But it has. And now, I'm experiencing the horrific impact from the death plunge I unknowingly took. Cruise pushed our love off the sheer cliff of ecstasy and left me crashing through the flames, cracking my skull open on the rocky shore each time I thought of him.

I don't know why I expected anything different. I slid my heart across the table like it was a loaded gun, and Cruise blew a hole right through me with my own weapon. I've only my sheer stupidity to blame. I was so naive to think it could have ever worked, that we conquered something so spectacular, that it existed at all.

I run my fingers over my neck. It's still sore from picking at the collar. I'd finally managed to take it off by repeatedly stabbing the keyhole with a bobby pin.

"There's a beer inside with your name on it." Ally links an arm with mine as we enter the frat party that started it all. I suppose it's fitting that it'll be my last one here at Garrison. I missed classes all week and hung out at Ally's dorm in Russell Hall. Not a soul there was a loser. According to Mom, Aunt Jackie is the loser for cheating on her poor husband. It turns out they've been in splitsville for almost a year.

Mom wanted to know why Cruise was at the bed-and-breakfast and I was at Ally's. I guess he told her his windows were in desperate need of repair and that I was staying with friends, but she knew. Mom is an expert when it comes to crash-landing a relationship. And when she boards that plane for California, I plan on being right there with her. This entire semester was a waste. I got an education I never bargained for—never wanted.

Bodies cram into the boxy fraternity, overwrought with blaring music and bimbos. Alpha Sigma Phi holds the slight scent of used socks and beer much like Pennington himself. And speak of the devil . . .

His hair glints in the light, shorn a little too close to his head, but he's still safely tucked into his polo with the collar upturned, and a white sweater lies tied over his shoulders, ensuring no one will mistake him for a gangbanger anytime soon.

"I hear my dad has this thing for your mom." He nods as if it were every day that people staggered into new relationships like drunken sailors.

"I wouldn't know. How's *your* mom?"

"Busy"—he looks as though he could puke on demand—"with the pool boy."

"Ouch. Sorry."

"It's all right. I'm sure it'll be the box boy next week. She likes 'em young. Divorce is final in less than a month. So I guess there'll be a celebration. You down for that?"

"Celebrating the end of a relationship? Sounds horrible."

"You're right." Pen bows his head for a moment, and I reach over and hug him. I hold Pen a lot longer than anticipated until his chest heaves beneath me. "I better take off. I see a skirt with my name on it," he whispers, drifting into the crowd.

It's only then I notice Ally's gone, too.

I glance up, and a familiar-looking Adonis lights up the room from across the way.

He's here. He's coming in this direction, and everything in me wants to run, but my body solidifies. The room warps, the music drags, and I feel light-headed, as if I might pass out, right on the spot.

I spin around and look for someone to talk to, anybody . . . and there she is—Blair. I'd like to talk to her all right, with the working end of a sawed-off shotgun. On second thought, she wasn't too far off the mark. In fact, she hit the bull's-eye dead-on—Cruise was never that into me.

I take off into the crowd.

A swarm of girls coo as he fast approaches, and an entire demonic chant breaks out offering homage to Professor Elton.

"He's got a rash on his balls the size of Wyoming," I say, moving swiftly past their circle.

"Kenny," he shouts over the music, but I pretend not to hear. Stupidly, I land myself in a corner near the refreshment table laden with an emphasis on booze and hard liquor. Something tells me I'll need all the liquor I can get my hands on to wash this entire night—semester—out of my memory, at least temporarily.

Ally was wrong. This stupid party is the last place I need to be.

I spin toward the door and bump into a brick wall of a chest.

He's wearing a white T-shirt and jeans, my all-time favorite combo. He's got a baseball cap pulled low over his head, and his dimples invert into twin black pools.

"Coke or Pepsi?" Cruise gives a playful smile, but there's sorrow layered just beneath.

"I believe what you really want to ask is, in or out." I peg him with a hard look because he's never getting *in* again. "We both know damn well your only goal in life is getting laid. I'm sure you'll have no problem finding an entire herd of girls willing to give it up for you."

Cruise softens. A marked sadness takes over his features as his chest pumps with an increased volume.

"I don't want a herd of girls." He swallows hard. "I only want you, Kenny."

"Bullshit." I race to get past him, but he catches me by the wrist. "Let go."

"Not until we talk." His eyes glow in this dim light and afford him an animalistic quality, too divinely exotic to ever be human. Just bearing witness to his flawless brand of beauty hurts me even deeper. I was just a joke to him, nothing but a notch on his bedpost.

"I'm not above biting, so kindly let the fuck go." I belt the words out so loud, ten different heads turn in our direction.

Cruise holds his hands in the air like it's a stickup.

"I'm done talking and listening." I meant to scream it, but in truth, I'm losing steam. I see how handsome he is, that sweetness buried beneath the surface percolating, and I can't believe we were nothing but a lie.

From over his shoulder I catch Blair gleam a wicked smile. She wraps herself in my misery like a fur-lined coat, a lush experience at my expense, supple to the touch.

"Kenny, we can work through this." He says it so calm and solid it almost makes me believe him.

"There's nothing to work through because I happen to know for a fact that you think I'm repulsive and have 'daddy issues.' Oh wait—and that you wish you never asked me to marry you."

Cruise dips in. "What are you talking about?"

"I heard you!" It roars from the deepest part of me. Cruise opened the Pandora's box of grief I sealed off all my pain in, and now I've unleashed it like a missile right at the person I thought I loved—who I thought loved me.

"I would never say those things, let alone think them." His features blink back with surprise, and his mouth rounds out as if he were reliving a memory. I caught him red-handed, and he knew it. "Are you talking about a conversation I had with my dad?" His head ticks back a notch.

"Yes. I was going to surprise you. I was coming to collect my morning kiss." My voice breaks. "I heard you say—you said, you never loved me." And there it is, the wound reopened, the acid poured in because the admission came from my own lips this time.

"Kenny . . ." His face contorts in pain. "I wasn't talking about you. I was talking about my ex-girlfriend, Blair." His dimples blink like sirens trying to alert me to the severity of the situation. "Her mom called and wanted me to give it another try. I was just venting to my dad about it."

I glance past him and pick up on the hurt on Blair's face—the incredible heartbreak we were passing like a baton. But she relished in my misery. She wanted Cruise back and tried to drive herself between us. She pitted me against him, and I was too quick to jump to conclusions.

"Blair and I were together for years." He steps into me, and I want to surrender to him. The sweet scent of his cologne begs for me to do it. "We dated. She never wanted to touch me. She said she wanted to save herself for marriage, and I respected that. I held out." He says it low, almost reluctant to admit it. "She cheated on me, apparently with a number of guys, and last summer I found out about it. Kenny—when I asked Blair to marry me, she never said yes. And I only asked because I thought that was the next logical step in our relationship. After that, I ended up hitting on everything that moved. It wasn't until I met you that I realized two things." He steps into me and picks up my hands. "One—that breaking it off with Blair was a very good thing. I never really loved her. And two, I wish I could have held out a little longer and saved it all for you. I love you, Kendall. I'll love you forever."

My heart thumps wild in my chest at the prospect of Cruise wishing he had waited for me—loving me forever.

"I have a confession. There *is* one thing I was keeping from you." I take a step in until we're a breath away. "When my stepfather told me those lies about myself all those years ago, I wasn't necessarily shutting out guys because I was afraid of turning into some prophesied slut." I glance down at the floor, then sweep my eyes over him slowly until our eyes lock. "Deep inside I knew there would be someone special out there, and I only wanted him to have me. When I met you, Cruise—I knew you were that person. I knew it that first night. Remember when you asked if I believed in love at first sight? Deep down, I loved you right then. So, I guess I do believe in love at first sight after all."

"That makes two of us." He warms me with a smile that widens without end. "As soon as I laid eyes on you, my thesis went out the window."

"What exactly is your thesis?"

"The fallacy of love at first sight. Turns out, the only fallacy was my thesis itself. But I won't be needing it anymore." Cruise wraps his arms around my waist and pierces me with those eyes that shower me with affection in so many special ways. "Kendall Jordan, will you marry me?"

I can feel the words vibrate through his chest, the deep register of his voice sirens through me like a tuning fork.

"It's *Kenny* to you." I give the curve of a smile. "And yes, I would be honored to spend my life by your side." I jump up on his hips, and he catches me beneath my knees as our lips crash into one another. Cruise lays his kisses over me with a soulful intensity. This is holy and right and something destined to happen right from the beginning. His tongue sweeps over mine, soft and aching. Cruise cleanses me with the fire from his mouth. This kiss begs forgiveness and thanks me for the start of something new all at the same time. I can feel his desire growing for me, impaling my right thigh through his jeans, and a moan escapes my throat.

Cruise pulls back and cinches a forlorn smile. "I have something else to tell you." A sigh depresses from him. It brushes over my neck with a hint of heartache. "I was expelled from Garrison."

"What?" I let go and nearly fall to the floor, but Cruise catches me, dots a kiss on my forehead, easy as breathing.

"A certain journalism major"—he nods in Blair's direction—"made sure what I chose to do in private was well documented."

My hand flies over my mouth at the horror of it. "It was with me, wasn't it?"

His brows rise. "She had a copy of the revised syllabus. How did she get it?" He sounds honestly perplexed.

"*The* syllabus?" I take in a sharp breath. "That day in class." I blink into the epiphany. "I dropped my book bag, then ran out the door with you. It was the day your mom broke her leg. She gave me the papers the next time I saw her, and I bet that was one of them. Sorry."

"Don't apologize." He sinks a kiss over my lips. "I don't mind running the bed-and-breakfast for now. I'll happily accept it as my destiny, but only if it includes you."

"For sure it includes me." I tip into him and bite down on a smile. "I can warm the beds at night with my body."

"Just my bed." A naughty grin blooms across his gorgeous face. "You do realize that I'm going to have to arrest you for taking off with my heart again."

"Sounds like an incarceration is in the works." I gravel it out low and full of wanting. "Rumor has it you have the capability to induce a triple play of pleasure, all in the same night. True or not true?"

He ticks back his head, withholding a laugh. "I think you'd better find out for yourself. Why don't we get out of here and put some rumors to rest." He takes me in, and his smile softens. "Engagement—long or short?"

"Very, very short."

Cruise secures me over his waist and walks us out of Alpha Sigma Phi while kissing me with a tender affection. Bodies part like the Red Sea as we land outside under a bed of crystalline stars.

"Move back into the house with me, Kenny"—he closes his eyes a brief moment as if to stave off pain—"and please don't ever leave."

I brush my fingers over his cheek.

When you get right down to it, Cruise Elton was never a player. He has the face and heart of an angel, and he's all mine, forever.

I wrap my arms around his neck and whisper, "Take me home."

We press in a kiss under the magical lavender sky.

Forever begins tonight.

ACKNOWLEDGMENTS

To my husband, you rock my world. No more falling from rooftops, please.

It would be hard to have an acknowledgments section and not thank the wonderful Amy Eye for inspiring me to venture into this project. You save me from impending doom and disaster time and time again. You are an angel of the highest order. And thank you for including Kenny and Cruise in *Christmas Lites II*. You are a doll.

Of course, I want to *profusely* thank Sarah Joy Freese, who truly deserves a superhero cape. Thank you so much for all you do! Be warned, if we ever meet up, there will be a hug fest.

To Heather Smiddie Robbins, thank you for your ninja proofreading skillz. There just aren't enough letters in the alphabet to express how amazing you are. You really are a "Supa Gurl."

To my wonderful readers, you bless me every day. Thank you from the bottom of my heart for all of your kindness and support. I love you like family.

To Him who holds the world in the palm of His hands—to your name be the glory, and power, and honor, forever. Your word is manna for my hungry soul. I owe you everything.

ABOUT THE AUTHOR

Addison Moore is a *New York Times*, *USA Today*, and *Wall Street Journal* best-selling author who writes contemporary and paranormal romance. She worked as a therapist on a locked psychiatric unit for nearly a decade. She resides with her husband, four wonderful children, and two dogs on the West Coast, where she eats too much chocolate and stays up way too late. When she's not writing, she's reading. Addison's Celestra Series has been optioned for film by 20th Century Fox.

Feel free to visit her blog at:
http://addisonmoorewrites.blogspot.com

Facebook: https://www.facebook.com/pages/
Addison-Moore/140192649382294

Twitter: https://twitter.com/AddisonMoore